THE SHADOW LIST

ALSO BY TODD MOSS

FICTION

The Golden Hour

Minute Zero

Ghosts of Havana

NONFICTION

*Oil to Cash: Fighting the Resource Curse
through Cash Transfers*

*The Governor's Solution: How Alaska's Oil Dividend
Could Work in Iraq and Other Oil-Rich Countries*

*African Development:
Making Sense of the Issues and Actors*

*Adventure Capitalism: Globalization and
the Political Economy of Stock Markets in Africa*

THE SHADOW LIST

TODD MOSS

G. P. PUTNAM'S SONS | NEW YORK

G. P. PUTNAM'S SONS
Publishers Since 1838
An imprint of Penguin Random House LLC
375 Hudson Street
New York, New York 10014

Library of Congress Cataloging-in-Publication Data

Names: Moss, Todd, author.
Title: The shadow list / Todd Moss.
Description: New York : G. P. Putnam's Sons, [2017] | Series: A Judd Ryker novel ; 4
Identifiers: LCCN 2017004688 (print) | LCCN 2017011055 (ebook) | ISBN
9780399175947 (hardcover) | ISBN 9780698406414 (EPub)
Subjects: LCSH: Government investigators—Fiction. | Conspiracies—Fiction. |
Political fiction. | BISAC: FICTION / Suspense. | FICTION / Political. |
FICTION / Espionage. | GSAFD: Suspense fiction. | Mystery fiction.
Classification: LCC PS3613.O785 S53 2017 (print) | LCC PS3613.O785 (ebook) |
DDC 813/.6—dc23
LC record available at https://lccn.loc.gov/2017004688

Printed in the United States of America
1   3   5   7   9   10   8   6   4   2

Book design by Gretchen Achilles

The secret of life is honesty and fair dealing.
If you can fake that, you've got it made.

—GROUCHO MARX

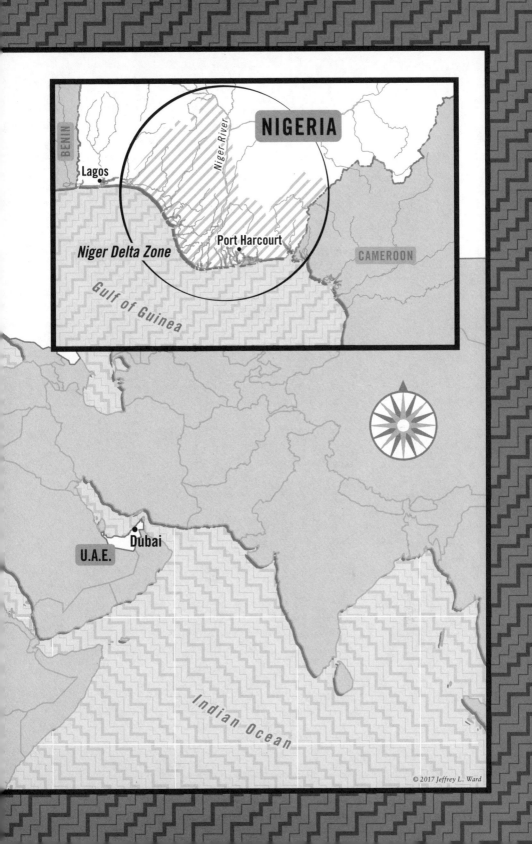

NIGERIA

BENIN

Lagos

Niger River

Niger Delta Zone

Port Harcourt

CAMEROON

Gulf of Guinea

U.A.E.

Dubai

Indian Ocean

© 2017 Jeffrey L. Ward

1

Free money.

The American had been taught there was no such thing. Yet, looking up at fifty floors of glass and steel in the heart of London's modern new financial district, that thought seemed ridiculous.

Back at NYU, one of his professors had told the old joke: Two economists are walking down the street when one spots a dollar bill on the ground. As he bends over, the other stops him. "Don't bother," he scolds. "If that money was real, someone would have already picked it up."

Of course there was free money, the young man thought. He was surrounded by it. His friends in Manhattan were practically drowning in it. Hedge fund arbitrage was all about grabbing that opportunity, being the first one to seize it, never hesitating. It was about bending over and snatching up that cash, sometimes from a filthy sidewalk.

That bill waiting to be grabbed was not only real, it wasn't a dollar. It was millions of them. It was big, fat *fuck-you money*. Hamptons-beach-house, G5-airplane, buy-your-own-private-island, hire-Jay-Z-to-play-your-birthday-party money. The only question on his mind: Would he finally have the balls?

The young man reached into the inside jacket pocket of his best navy-blue pin-striped banker's suit and extracted a letter. The paper was a quality stock, thick and weighty. The letter exuded wealth and confidence. So, too, did the red-and-black crest in the upper corner above Global Allied Financial, One Canada Square, London E14 5AB, United Kingdom. He rubbed a finger across the embossed crest and then reread the letter, for the third time that day.

Mr. Jason Saunders, Esq.

Holden Harriman Quinn

419 Park Avenue

New York, NY 10154

Sir,

Our firm has been designated by the Bank of England as probate agent for recovered funds from the Special Court for International Assets. In cases where the Court has identified

unclaimed and improperly earned funds with no national
jurisdiction, the Bank allocates said funds to an international
consortium for management on behalf of the Court. Global
Allied Financial has been allocated US$1,985,900,000
discovered in a Swiss branch of a British-registered bank that
authorities have determined originate with the ruling family of
the Republic of Syria.

At this point, the first time through, he'd nearly put the
letter in the shredder. The long-lost bank account of a foreign
dictator? Obviously a scam. How many of these had he gotten in the email and deleted without even opening? But he'd
been a little desperate that morning. Still was. So he had kept
reading.

As per Banking Regulation 34.7A, until the legal
proceedings are concluded, these funds must be held on
behalf of the Court by firms from at least two different
sovereign jurisdictions. Global Allied Financial is the designee
from the United Kingdom. We seek an urgent appointment to
discuss whether Holden Harriman Quinn might apply as the
designee from the United States of America. We are
approaching you on the basis of your past experience with
sensitive asset management, notably your record with Turkish
treasury bills.

That was the phrase that had grabbed him. How had anyone known about the Turkish bond trades? That was a com-

plete secret. On the other hand, it meant that someone really *had* written this letter specifically to him, not to a laundry list of random people. And what came next really caught his attention.

> If selected by the Court, HHQ would share in the
> management fees and the up-front legal costs. Please note
> that, as per Banking Regulation 34.7B, no individual firm's
> management fees may exceed 4.00% per year.

The American squinted at the digits on the paper and did the mental calculation again. Four percent of two billion equaled *eighty million dollars.* Every year. That was one colossal dollar bill just sitting there on the sidewalk. But was it possibly real?

Who ever heard of a four percent management fee? He didn't know of anyone even getting the old hedge fund 2/20 model of two percent plus a performance bonus of one-fifth of profits. Most clients had squeezed commissions down to a fraction of one percent. But four percent? To manage funds on behalf of an international court? Fat fees and no actual client to complain? It was highway robbery. If it was real. And he desperately needed it to be real.

The letter had been waiting for Jason on his desk back in Manhattan one week earlier. He had just returned from forty-eight sleepless hours in Atlantic City that had cost him a small fortune: a $1,500 bar tab, $3,000 for a Kate Middleton look-alike hooker, and $85,000 at the blackjack table. Those losses were nothing, however, compared to his bad bets at the firm. He had doubled down on Italian treasury bills, and the red ink was now running above $25 million.

Instead of telling Harvey Holden or any of the other senior partners about his mistake, he had hired a limo to AC. Jason had told himself what he really needed was to let loose, clear his head, and come back to work with fresh ideas. The only way to save his skin was to generate some quick profits to cover up the Italian bond debacle. A weekend of drunken debauchery was just what he needed to change his luck.

Jason had already earned himself unusual autonomy within the firm after his first Turkish bond trade. Three months earlier, Harvey Holden had come to him late one night, a tumbler of forty-year-old single malt scotch in his hand, with a tip to short Turkish treasury bills. Holden had also given him access to the firm's internal black accounts. So Jason had followed orders and placed a huge bet against the future of Turkey. The very next day the chief of police in the capital, Ankara, and the CEO of one of the country's major industrial conglomerates had been gunned down in a drive-by shooting. Bondholders had panicked, prices tanked, and HHQ made an absolute killing off of Jason's trade.

The young associate received a promotion, a modest bonus, and extended authorization to keep trading on HHQ's own accounts. He'd made several more successful wagers—quick profits on Ukrainian debt, oil futures, and Indonesian currency swaps—each time after receiving quiet instructions from Harvey Holden. But when Jason had on his own initiative bet big-time on Italian bonds, the gods of finance had conspired against him.

That's when he'd fled to the casinos of Atlantic City to figure out a way to make the money back before anyone noticed. But Jason Saunders had returned to Manhattan with only a pounding headache, an empty wallet, and no plan for salvation.

And then there was the letter—like a death row pardon from the governor—waiting for him on his desk.

Enclosed is a confirmation letter from the Bank of England.
Please contact me at your earliest convenience.

Yours
faithfully,
A.W. Windsor

Even through the haze of an epic hangover, though, Jason had been wary. He'd googled Bank of England, Syria recovery, Special Court for International Assets, Global Allied Financial, A.W. Windsor—and it had all seemed to check out. The British financial authorities were indeed hunting for stolen Syrian assets that had been stashed in banks across the world. Global Allied Financial had a simple but elegant website, a prestigious London address, and a Mr. A.W. Windsor (MA Cantab) listed as its managing director.

And if this Windsor knew about his Turkish bond trades,

then he must have done his homework. Or he was exceedingly well connected. Either way, Jason decided it was worth calling in sick and making a quick trip to London. If the offer was real, he'd be the hero. If not, then there was no need for anyone at HHQ ever to know anything about it. And that's what had brought him to Canary Wharf on an uncommonly sunny Friday morning.

Jason Saunders refolded the letter and tucked it back into his inside jacket pocket. He brushed both shoulders and adjusted his tie in the reflection of the front glass doors at One Canada Square. His heart rate jumped as he entered the lobby, a blend of adrenaline and subconscious anxiety. As instructed, Jason announced his arrival at the security desk, above which hung logos for the Bank of New York, HSBC, JPMorgan Chase, the Financial Services Authority. The officer made a quick phone call, then handed the American a pass for the 48th floor.

As the elevator rocketed skyward, Jason's mind returned to New York and to his first classroom at business school. He thought of NYU's motto: *Perstare et Praestare*. Persevere and Excel. Never give up. Go get what you want. That was exactly what he was doing. In the face of adversity, he had to persist. He'd made a mistake with the Italian bond bets. But the only way to thrive was to learn from his errors and press ahead. It wasn't the time for self-doubt. It was time to *double down*. That's what powerful, successful people did.

The elevator dinged on arrival. Jason Saunders, twenty-six

years old, aggressively single, a rising star at one of New York's most profitable hedge funds, who had already bought a coal-black top-end Range Rover for six figures and had his eye on a three-bedroom loft in Chelsea that might run eight figures, strode with confidence toward the front door of Global Allied Financial. Yes, he would size up this British twit A.W. Windsor, whoever he was. He would sell HHQ, hook Windsor like he had that twelve-foot marlin in the Florida Keys last spring. And then haul the cash in. He would make rich profits for HHQ and a huge bonus for himself. *Big fat fuck-you money.* No one would ever remember a few lost Italian bonds.

As the elevator door opened, Jason straightened his jacket and adjusted his testicles. He yanked open the door, feeling a cold blast of air. A man with a square jaw at the reception desk looked up without surprise. "May I help you, sir?"

Jason scanned the lobby. It was basic décor, a slight disappointment from the gaudy imperial Victorian motif he'd expected. This was Canary Wharf, after all, not the City of London, he reminded himself. He shrugged as the thought of *free money* flooded back into his brain.

"I'm Jason Saunders," he announced. "I have an appointment with Mr.—"

The room erupted. The receptionist ducked behind the desk as silhouettes, men dressed in all black and their faces covered with black balaclavas, stormed in from all sides and rushed at Jason. Before he could even think, he was forced to his knees, his hands quickly and silently bound. Duct tape was slapped across his mouth and the end of a pistol was shoved into his cheek. He whipped his neck trying to see his attackers, just as a hood was slipped over his head. At that moment, everything in Jason Saunders' world went completely dark.

THREE DAYS LATER

MONDAY

2

Judd Ryker glared at the image his assistant Serena had just delivered.

"This just arrived from Mr. Parker's office," she said. "Came in overnight from across the river." She nodded toward the Potomac, where the Central Intelligence Agency headquarters lay on the other side, about eight miles up.

Serena was dressed in her usual intense jet-black business suit that matched her personality. Even early on a rainy spring Monday morning, she was ready for battle. "What else can I get you, Dr. Ryker?"

"Nothing yet," Judd said, his eyes glued to the picture. He

stroked his chin and its two days' worth of stubble. "Maybe more coffee?"

The high-resolution satellite photograph showed a tiny island, green water surrounding beige sand in the shape of a letter G. It reminded Judd of the barrier islands in the middle of the Stratego board, one of his favorite games as a kid. He had spent hours during the long Vermont winters devising the best configurations for the flag, the bombs, scouts, and all the different warriors of varying strength and special skills. And, of course, the most valuable and cunning piece: *the spy.* To an opponent, the spy in Stratego looked like every other piece. It could be anything. The spy destroyed everything it attacked, so long as it struck first. The spy was always beaten if caught by surprise. Every move was kill-or-be-killed. The spy was the perfect mix of strength and vulnerability.

Judd had always preferred the challenge of arranging the Stratego pieces to playing the game itself. Finding the right balance between attack, defense, and especially deception before the fighting began. Even as a nine-year-old boy, Judd Ryker knew the game was usually won or lost before the first move. *Pregame was everything.*

What immediately struck Judd as odd about the island in the satellite photo were the unnaturally straight lines. The world was rarely straight. The long side of the G shape showed an airstrip, the lower curl an ideally placed seawall creating a safe harbor for naval ships in the protected center. The island was a perfectly efficient military outpost by no accident. The bottom corner of the photo was stamped with yesterday's date, 07:25:05, and Rogue Reef-14, the latest in a series of man-made islands the Chinese government was constructing in the heart of the South China Sea.

The United States government was closely monitoring events in this part of the world. The South China Sea was surrounded by China, Vietnam, Malaysia, and the Philippines. Each and every boundary was under territorial dispute. More than half of all global oil tanker shipments passed though these sea-lanes, making it five times busier than the Panama Canal. Half a billion people crammed along the coasts of the sea and its rich fishing grounds. If that weren't enough trouble in one place, seismic data hinted at massive deposits of oil and gas in the seabed.

Adding to this combustible mix of people, wealth, and supertankers—each carrying two million barrels of oil through a narrow space—was the heavy presence of naval warships. Each of the bordering nations had deployed dozens of vessels, as had Japan, Australia, and Russia. The U.S. Navy's Pacific Fleet also patrolled the region by air and by sea. And of course the U.S. government monitored it all from space. This dangerous cocktail had turned the South China Sea into the most crowded, strategic, and contested pressure cooker on the globe.

And Judd Ryker was supposed to come up with a plan in case it all blew up.

———

He was excited by the opportunity. It was true that the Crisis Reaction Unit, his special office known inside the building as S/CRU, had been created to spur the State Department to respond more quickly to international emergencies. But he was more than a little surprised that the South China Sea assignment had fallen to him. He wasn't exactly the most popular person in the State Department.

It had all started nearly two years earlier when Judd was just a professor at Amherst College trying to use data to figure out what caused political conflict around the world. Landon Parker, the Secretary of State's chief of staff and the man who ran the U.S. diplomatic machine from behind the scenes, had invited Judd to the State Department to present his "golden hour" theory that timing was decisive in ending war or political unrest. The conclusion was unmistakable: The United States needed to respond faster to events around the world. Parker was sold. He launched the Crisis Reaction Unit and hired Judd as its first director.

Unfortunately, like an organ transplant rejected by the host body, State Department insiders wanted no part of Judd Ryker and his S/CRU. To many of the old guard, Judd was just a pointy-headed professor with ivory tower ideas. They whispered that S/CRU was some crazy pet project of the chief of staff's and would eventually go away. The message was twofold: S/CRU could be ignored. And Judd Ryker was Landon Parker's pet.

Senior policymakers and diplomats never openly voiced their opposition to Judd's ideas. No one ever complained directly to Parker. They just quietly maneuvered to keep S/CRU out of their business and schemed to push Ryker as far from their turf as possible.

Judd had fallen into his first major mission by accident. A confluence of circumstances had given Judd an unplanned opportunity to fly to the West African nation of Mali to restore an ally who had been deposed in a coup—and the bureaucracy had never forgiven him for it.

After his success in Mali, Judd had been handed special projects by Landon Parker to rescue an election in Zimbabwe and later to secretly recover American hostages in Cuba. Judd had won these battles but was still fighting a longer war inside the building.

Word about his exploits in Africa and the Caribbean had gotten around the State Department hallways enough that ambitious young staffers were starting to make quiet inquiries about joining S/CRU. Among a certain segment of the Foreign Service—the thrill seekers and idealistic risk takers who still wanted to change the world come hell or high water—S/CRU was starting to look attractive. Judd Ryker's unit was becoming, to a very few officers in the know, even a little bit . . . *sexy*.

Yet Judd knew that, even as he racked up wins and quietly gained fans, he was still seen by the old guard as an interloper. And Judd's power and influence was still as beholden as ever to Landon Parker.

Part of Judd's strategy had been to accept, no matter how much it pained him, that the really big foreign policy hot spots—Iran, Egypt, Russia, China—were probably off-limits to S/CRU. They were too big. There were too many power players. The State Department's internal antibodies were just too strong. Judd was relegated to the minor leagues. Until Parker handed him the South China Sea.

Judd's mandate was to anticipate national security situations so the United States could spring into action in time to shape events. And there was no bigger potential national security situation than the South China Sea. So it made perfect sense that Parker asked Judd to analyze the risks and come up with new ideas for how the State Department could exert greater influence in that part of Asia.

What didn't make much sense was the total secrecy. The State Department's Bureau of East Asian and Pacific Affairs, the part of the bureaucracy that was officially responsible for the South China Sea, wasn't supposed to know anything about Judd's project. Neither was the Pentagon, the CIA, nor the White House. Landon Parker insisted that all intelligence requests were to come strictly through his office. Judd was instructed to figure out a plan in total isolation from the rest of the government. Judd Ryker was a one-man diplomatic Red Cell.

J udd eyed the photo of the artificial island, Beijing's latest audacious move to change the strategic calculus of the

South China Sea, and thought again of Stratego. What the Chinese were doing—asserting their growing power and daring the United States to react—was obvious. How the U.S. should countermove without igniting World War III was still a puzzle.

Judd tacked the island photo onto a map identifying all the disputed international lines and contested islands. He stood back and studied his whiteboard wall. He had scribbled headings for disputed borders, military facilities, sea-lanes, energy, fishing, finance, regional alliances, and USG assets. As Serena brought him the most important information from Landon Parker's office, he sorted each item and either discarded it or placed it beneath one of the headings. This triage was the first step in Judd's process, a path to the big picture of the major issues.

Next, Judd would crunch the numbers. As he had done with an Egypt assessment that had accurately predicted political upheaval—which, sadly, had been buried in departmental clearances and never saw the light of day—Judd would throw all the data he could collect on economic and political factors into an algorithm he had written to identify any irregularities. His program could find numbers—troop movements, construction of a port, a spike in social unrest—that were out of the ordinary, that didn't fit the normal pattern. Judd would then correlate these anomalies with the current U.S. intelligence coverage to identify gaps. That's exactly where he would know to hunt for the unexpected: *where no one else was looking.*

Judd was fired up. Maybe it was the complexity of the task ahead. Maybe he felt on a roll and ready for a bigger challenge. Maybe it just felt good to work on something more consequential than a few hostages or a small country far off America's national security radar. Something potentially historic. Or where failure could be catastrophic.

"Serena," Judd punched his intercom. "I'm ready for the sea-lanes intelligence."

"Yes, sir," Serena replied. "I'm bringing in the cart."

Cart? Judd thought as Serena backed into his office pulling a dolly with four large cardboard file crates.

"Here's the first batch, Dr. Ryker. Where do you want it?"

"There's more?"

"Christmas in April," she said without a smile. "I've got six more boxes in the lobby. Everything from Taiwan to the Malacca Straits. And this is just the shipping lanes. Wait until you see the oil files." Serena hoisted one of the boxes and dropped it with a heavy thud onto Judd's desk. "You need a bigger office."

"I have to narrow the intel request. This is a fire hose. Call up to Landon Parker's office and—"

"Hello, Ryker," Landon Parker interrupted, his face suddenly appearing in Judd's doorway.

"Sir, I wasn't expecting you," Judd said, startled.

"I came down to see how you're making out," Parker said. He pushed his wire-rimmed spectacles up on his nose and scanned Judd's whiteboard. "You getting everything you need from my people?"

"Yes. Serena and I were just discussing the intelligence requests. I think we're going—"

"I'm sorry, Ryker," he interrupted. "I came to talk to you about something else. It's sensitive. Can we have the room?"

"I'll be at my desk if you need anything, gentlemen," Serena said, and slinked out, closing the door behind her.

"I'm making progress on the South China Sea project. It's great to be working on something meaty. S/CRU won't disappoint you," Judd said.

"Yeah, I'm going to need you to stand down on that."

Judd's heart sank.

"I don't understand. You asked me—"

"The South China Sea will still be a powder keg next week. It's not going anywhere. I need you for something urgent, Ryker."

"Okay. . . ."

"I'm going to need your utmost discretion." Parker removed his glasses and cleaned them with his tie.

"Always, sir."

Parker replaced his glasses. "I got a call this morning from Shep Truman."

"Shepard Truman, the Congressman from New York?"

"That's right. Shep called in a tizzy because an employee of one of his bigwig constituents has gone missing in London. Who knows what this kid was into or what the hell he was doing there. He could be some punk on vacation who forgot to call his parents. Or he could be dead, for all we know. But Truman promised his man that he'd look into it."

"And now Truman wants State to look into it," Judd said.

"Bingo, Ryker."

"And that's why you're here?"

"You got it."

"Isn't missing persons a job for Embassy London?"

"It is. But I spoke with the Consul General. She says they'll add the kid to their list, but they're overwhelmed. She says they've got six Penn State students locked up after they stripped naked, covered themselves in navy-blue body paint, and mounted the lions in Trafalgar Square." Parker chuckled to himself, then became serious. "The point is this, Ryker: Truman is up my ass and I can't tell him that the embassy is too busy saving drunken frat boys."

"So you need me."

Parker pointed a finger gun at Judd and clicked his tongue.

"Who's the missing kid?" Judd asked.

"Name is Saunders, Jason Saunders. I'll send you all the details I have from Truman, and whatever else we have on him. It's not much. But it's a start."

"Mr. Parker, as you can see, I'm already neck-deep in the South China Sea project. Is chasing a lost tourist really the best use of S/CRU?"

"Nope. But Truman is on the National Security Oversight Subcommittee, next in line for chairman, and seems convinced that the State Department doesn't do its job, which means it's very much *our* job to keep him happy. Plus, Ryker, it's an open secret that he's gunning for the Senate. We definitely don't need Truman making trouble right now. We need him to love us. That's why I want you."

"But why me?"

"Truman says it's urgent, and you're all about speed. I also knew you were the best man for the job once Truman mentioned Africa. There's a chance this Saunders kid might have gotten himself mixed up in a scam. They found a letter."

"What kind of letter?"

"You know, Ryker, one of those crazy letters from some prince in Nigeria who needs your help unlocking a secret bank account?"

"Sure," Judd said, failing to hide his scowl. "Everybody knows about those scams. But you said London."

"The kid's gone *missing* in London. But these con games are global, and you know that the bulk of them emanate from Nigeria. Once I saw that, I knew it had to be you."

"But I'm no expert on Nigeria," Judd said. "I once spent a few days in Kaduna as an election monitor, but that's it."

"Didn't you meet your wife in Nigeria?"

"I met Jessica in Mali. Then, before we got married, we worked together in Niger. But never Nigeria."

"Niger? Close enough."

Judd wondered what Jessica would make of it all.

3

T he Bear," Jessica Ryker announced. On a large screen behind her flashed a grainy photo of a beefy man with a thick beard and long, wispy hair, his eyes covered by wraparound sunglasses. "This is our target," she explained.

Jessica's team had been reassembled for this project at the behest of the Deputy Director of the Central Intelligence Agency. *Unofficially*, of course, since Purple Cell didn't exist. That was the whole point.

The windowless chamber in the third-level basement where Jessica was sitting was blandly labeled *Conference Room B3-204/Logistics Assessments*. Her most trusted member of Purple Cell, an analyst named Sunday whose day job was inside the CIA Africa Issue team six floors up, sat at the laptop and ran the slides. The rest of the unit appeared only on screens, each of their faces beamed live via digital encryption from safe locations in Marrakesh, Jakarta, Shenzhen, Nairobi, Tikrit, Caracas, and Moscow. None of the Purple Cell members could see each other. In fact, none of them even knew about the others, only that they were part of something special, something exclusive.

Strict compartmentalization was one of the features that allowed Purple Cell to work anywhere, anytime, and to avoid detection. Purple Cell functioned completely black, off the books, with total deniability. Each operative reported only to Jessica, who in turn was accountable only to the Deputy Director. That was one of the benefits of Purple Cell. That was a big reason the Deputy Director had come to rely so heavily on Jessica Ryker and her team for his most sensitive assignments.

"The Bear operates a vast criminal syndicate from his base in St. Petersburg that extends around the world. His network has been linked to extortion, trafficking, sabotage, cyber-crime, and terrorism."

While Purple Cell was a favorite of the Deputy Director's, few other of the CIA's senior management even knew about it. For the Deputy Director, it was his secret weapon. For Jessica, Purple Cell was a high-wire act without a safety net. Her team was a ghost. Jessica was a shadow. If things ever went wrong, she was on her own.

"The Bear is running guns in Mexico, drugs out of Pakistan, and human organs in India," she continued. "He financed Somali pirates to capture Saudi oil tankers in the Gulf of Aden. He was behind the theft of smallpox from the Russian Zagorsk Laboratory and the attempted sale of the virus to an extremist group in western China. His empire operates a pipeline that kidnaps thousands of young women in Romania and sells them into the sex trade in Western Europe, the Persian Gulf, and even on the U.S. Eastern Seaboard."

Sunday flipped the slide to a cargo ship. "This is the *Ocean Constellation* in the Port of Baltimore last year," Jessica continued. The slide changed again to show a news file photo of an open shipping container lined with the bodies of dead girls. "Forty-four women suffocated to death. All at the hands of the Bear."

Jessica paused for a moment to let the photo sink in.

"The Bear is a monster. A savage. And he's becoming increasingly bold, expanding his reach into the United States," Jessica continued. "The Defense Intelligence Agency believes his hacker network was responsible for the breach of the Pentagon's personnel system last year. And last week the FBI traced a series of blackmail attempts against members of Congress back to a hacker group in St. Petersburg that's almost certainly working for the Bear."

Sunday clicked the slide to a photo of an old white man in a dapper business suit sitting in a chair, eyes wide, a bloody hole through the middle of his forehead.

"The Agency's Crime and Narcotics Center now believes that the Bear's expanding further by taking out other mob bosses and appropriating their businesses. This is James Wilbur-Wilcox, who ran heroin and crystal meth throughout southern England. Until last month, when one of the Bear's hit men did this. Now the Wilcox network works for the Bear."

Jessica faced her team. "The CNC says that this is a common pattern. Criminal organizations use the same tactics, the same network, the same facilitators, regardless of the commodity they're moving. Guns, drugs, uranium, girls. It doesn't matter. It's the network that matters. The only thing unique about the Bear is the scale of his operation. He's gotten bigger than anyone else, faster than anyone else. He must have help. High-level friends. But we don't know yet who."

The screen clicked back to the grainy photo of the bearded burly man. "We know what he's into. We know what he's capable of. But we don't yet know *who he is*. This was taken from a nightclub security camera in Istanbul." Sunday zoomed in, but the amplification didn't help make the face any more recognizable. "It's the best we have right now," Jessica said. "The Bear is clever. Every one of his businesses is run like an intelligence operation. His network is strictly compartmentalized. He uses multiple layers of shell companies and even other criminal organizations to provide cover."

Jessica cleared her throat. "He uses special contract assassins that report only to him. It's one way he maintains control of the empire."

Just like Purple Cell, Jessica thought, unsure of what Judd knew about Purple Cell—and what he did not

"As we speak," she continued, "there are multiple covert operations under way by a range of U.S. agencies to get underneath the Bear's skin. To figure out his network, identify him, and to take him down."

"What's our mission, boss?" asked one of the screens, her voice scrambled to protect her identity.

"Most Russian mob are linked to ex-KGB. We don't know yet about the Bear. He could be ex-KGB, he could be current FSB, he could be all on his own. We don't know if he's operating strictly for profit or with the collusion of someone high-ranking inside the Russian government. Our mission, for now, is to find out whatever you can about him and his dealings. You are each in a known location of his operations. Find the threads."

Jessica put her hands on her hips.

"Find the threads," she repeated, gritting her teeth. "And pull."

4

Judd Ryker calling me? *Dios mío*, this can't be good news," Isabella Espinosa giggled.

"I know. I owe you lunch, Special Agent," Judd said into the speakerphone, suddenly feeling guilty for not staying in closer touch with the Department of Justice investigator who had helped him on past missions. "How's my favorite monster hunter?"

Isabella Espinosa had midnight-black hair, fierce eyes, and a chip on her shoulder. She'd grown up in the worst barrios of East Los Angeles. Her mother, Florita, born in Chihuahua not far off the main highway into Ciudad Juárez, had made her way to California to raise her only daughter. Isabella had scrapped her way through overcrowded LA public schools, a training ground more for street gangs than the workforce, but with a firm mother's hand she had not only survived but thrived. Next was community college, a minimum-wage internship with a public defender, a transfer to UC Irvine, and eventually a full ride at UCLA law school.

"I'm keeping busy," she said.

After graduation, Isabella had been lavished with generous offers from California's most prominent law firms, and a bidding war had ignited for the Hispanic woman who'd come in top of her class. In the end, with the full support of her mother, she'd turned them all down for an entry-level civil service job in Washington, D.C., chasing down the worst that humanity had to offer. Isabella Espinosa had dedicated her life, not to money or prestige, but to justice.

"I've rotated off war crimes for a few months," she said. "They've got me chasing other ghosts now."

"Any news from Zimbabwe?" Judd asked.

"Nothing yet," she said. "The new government is still deciding whether to prosecute the general for war crimes or let him confess in exchange for immunity. Just like South Africa did after apartheid."

"After everything that happened? After all the suffering? All those people slaughtered? Are they seriously considering . . . *forgiving him*?"

"If Zimbabwe chooses truth and reconciliation—if the general admits in open court what he did—then, yes, they'll let him off," Isabella said. "They call it healing."

"I don't get it," Judd said. "I don't think I could forgive someone after all of that. If someone did that to my family—"

"It's not up to us," she said curtly.

"After we worked so hard to take the old man down and put his henchman in prison? After finally getting a decent election? After all we did together? That doesn't bother you if they let him off?"

"It's not about us."

"You're right, Isabella," Judd acknowledged. "That's not why I'm calling."

"So, *qué pasa*, Professor?"

"You know anything about advance fee scam letters? You know, the ones offering a big payout if you send money or your bank account details?"

"*Claro,*" she chuckled. "Don't tell me our Dr. Ryker fell for one of those?"

"No. Not me. I just need to know more about them."

"Law enforcement calls them 419, after the fraud section of the Nigerian criminal code. The bait, as you know, is any false promise, like a cut of a long-lost bank account or an unclaimed court settlement."

"Do you know how many people fall for it?"

"Thousands. Back in the 1990s, the FBI was getting dozens of reports every week. People kept calling for help getting their money back. But it's gotten a lot more sophisticated since. It began with simple letters, then graduated to email. Now the scammers deploy modern marketing software and big data. They use all kinds of lures to convince people to send money. Promises of jobs, fame, even marriage. And it's moved from a few con artists in an Internet café to a sophisticated international criminal operation. Don't think of some poor street kid. Think of Pablo Escobar. Or a modern business run by the Sopranos."

"A Nigerian Tony Soprano? Isn't that a bit dramatic, Isabella?"

"Nigeria has its mob bosses, its *peces gordos*, just like everyone else. But these networks have spread way beyond West Africa. Everyone loves to blame the Nigerians, but we're now seeing scams run out of Brazil, Russia, Madrid, Dubai. Ground zero for fraud today is London."

"London?" Judd's ears perked up. "That's a coincidence. That's exactly why I'm calling. I'm looking for a civilian who's gone missing *in London*."

"And you think he's caught up in a scam?"

"It's possible. Some business deal that was too good to be true, and now he's disappeared."

"Since when does S/CRU hunt for missing persons?"

"That's an excellent question, Special Agent Espinosa."

"But you're not going to tell me," she said.

"What's DOJ doing about all of this? Don't you have an antifraud task force or something?"

"We don't. But Nigeria does."

"Nigeria?"

"The Justice Department works with local authorities wherever we can. We can't police the whole world. We can't even respond to specific cases where American citizens have been taken in. So we've worked closely in the past with the Nigerian Crime and Corruption Task Force and they clamped down on the 419ers. They did a pretty good job. Executed raids, confiscated computers, blocked bank accounts, even put a few of the big bosses in jail. But it's whack-a-mole, Judd. The government moved on to other problems and the scammers came back."

"What about rumors in the press that senior Nigerian government officials are involved? I read a Nigerian state governor was arrested when one of his staff was running a hustle using official email and stationery."

"Yes, I remember that case in Oyo. They never proved the governor was aware. But the Nigerian government has much bigger problems these days. The price of oil is low. They've got terrorists in the north and militants in the south. If government officials are involved with organized crime, we don't know how high it goes. Just like in Mexico. We'll probably never know. There's a certain level of tolerance, if not outright complicity. All politics is local."

"If you believe that the Nigerian government is harboring organized crime bosses, how are you not running stings? Can't you beef up that task force again? Kick in some doors?"

"I can't talk about DOJ operations, Judd. You know that."

"Sure, but it seems wrong to just give up."

"Fraud is just way too low on the Christmas list these days. We're tracking terrorist finance. If we have time, we look into high-level political corruption. That leaves no resources for the little stuff."

"You just said it was organized criminal networks." Judd leaned forward in his chair. "Isabella, you said Pablo Escobar. You said Tony Soprano."

"If the crazies in Boko Haram were getting money from 419 letters, we'd take a different view. If we saw *al-Qaeda* making money off these scams, believe me, we'd have bodies on it. But as long as it's a naïve old lady in Oklahoma, we can't do much."

"Or a missing kid in London?"

"Sorry, Judd. You know how it is."

"What about . . . kidnapping?"

"Excuse me?"

"Or murder? What if the kid I'm searching for turns up dead? Would that make any difference?"

"Look, Judd. Let's not speculate. Go ahead and send over the missing person's details and I'll look into it for you. I promise I will. But don't expect me to find much. If he was sucked into a confidence game, this kind of thing has been going on since money was invented. *Dios mío,* they've found scam letters from the French Revolution. There's not much we can do to protect people from themselves. Cons work best on people who just want to believe."

"They *want to believe,*" Judd repeated. "Right. Special Agent Espinosa, how about I buy you that lunch?"

5

T he world is going to hell in a handbasket," the Congressman snorted as he threw the *New York Times* down on
the coffee table. Every time he opened the newspaper,
Shepard Truman, the three-term Representative for the Tenth
District of New York, winced at more bad news. Russian ag-
gression. Looming financial meltdown in southern Europe.
American soldiers dying in Afghanistan. The Chinese navy
saber rattling in the Pacific. It just never went away. Worst of
all, the New York Stock Exchange was spooked again. That
made him especially anxious.

"Sir?" asked a young staffer, the pretty twenty-something
daughter of a banking scion in his district.

"Going to hell," he repeated, taking a sip of weak black coffee. "And what is the State Department doing about it? They're looking into it. They're always *looking into it*. They're never solving any goddamn problems."

"You could call for a hearing?" the staffer suggested. "The National Security Oversight Subcommittee hasn't held any hearings on State Department operations for at least a year."

"Excellent idea. Our government should be creating jobs and keeping Americans safe. Instead, the State Department is running a goddamn travel agency. Everyone flying around, making speeches, having a grand old time. Do you know how much the State Department spends on airline tickets?"

"No, sir."

"Well, maybe you should go find out?"

"Yes, sir, I'll . . . I'll make some calls," she said.

"Give me the lineup."

"You've got the Cuba policy hearing at eleven, a call with the SEC Chairman at eleven-thirty, and a drop-in by Senator McCall at eleven forty-five. Then your private lunch at The Palm."

"Very good. What else?"

"You've got a group of pharmacists squatting in the lobby. They want to talk to you about drug pricing. And Mr. Holden is on hold on line three."

"Harvey's on the phone? Again?"

The aide nodded.

"It never ends, does it?"

The aide, unsure of the correct answer, smiled awkwardly.

"I'll need the room," he grunted. The staffer backed out of the Congressman's office and closed the door.

"Harvey! Good to hear from you," he said cheerily. "I see Brooklyn won big over the Lakers last night."

"It's all going to hell, Shep," said the man on the other end of the line.

"That's just what I was telling my staff. The world is a mess. I haven't heard anything yet from the State Department yet about your man missing in London. They assure me they are looking into it. I've been promised that they have their best man on it. We'll find him. Don't you worry, Harvey."

"I'm calling about another problem, Shep."

"You haven't lost someone else, have you? Good God, Harvey, maybe you should put GPS trackers on your employees?"

"Listen up, Shep. I just learned that Wildcat got beat on another oil license."

"Geez, I'm sorry. Where is it this time?"

"Block 24A offshore Sulawesi. That's part of Indonesia. Fucking Chinese swooped in and took it right out from under our noses."

"Gosh, how did that happen?"

"Fuck if I know, Shep. It's the third time this year. Do you know how much HHQ spent on Wildcat's seismic and pre-production in Sulawesi this quarter? More than what one of your fuckwit campaigns cost me!"

"I'm sorry to hear that, Harvey."

"It's not just the Chinese. Wildcat lost two contractors to

a pirate attack in January. You want to guess what that does to our insurance? And now this. You can hardly run an oil business anymore without getting shot at from all sides."

"Pirates, wow. I know it's tough out there."

"It's a war out there, Shep. A goddamn war. And what is our government doing about it? What do I pay my taxes for? Can't we get the Navy to patrol the Celebes Sea? Or the Gulf of Aden? Can't you get the FBI to investigate these Chinese oil contracts stolen right out from under American companies? What about raising *this* with the State Department? Isn't that why we have ambassadors in the first place?"

"Yes, Harvey."

"Isn't that why Congress responds to the needs of its constituents?"

"I always appreciate your support, Harvey. You know that."

"I mean, what the fuck are we doing here, Shep? Can't an American businessman get some goddamn help from the goddamn government these days?"

"I promise you, Harvey"—the Congressman cleared his throat—"I'm looking into it."

6

Jerry took a sip of the bitter instant coffee and thought again of Louisiana. When he got home, he'd hug his two beautiful daughters, eat a heaping bowl of his favorite crawfish étouffée, and sleep in his own warm bed for at least twelve hours, cuddled next to his wife.

Jerry was nineteen days into his current 20/20. The oil company's engineering teams worked on the platforms for twenty days straight in twelve-hour shifts. One more day and he'd be on a helicopter to Port Harcourt on the Nigerian mainland, a chartered airplane to Houston, and then a commercial flight to Baton Rouge. For twenty days off. The job was exhausting and often tedious. But it paid well enough to support his family back home. He'd worked like this in Brazil for Petrobras, in Indonesia for Total, in Kuwait for Chevron, and now in Nigeria's Mega Millennium Field for the Chinese oil giant Sinopec. And after eighteen years in the offshore oil rig business, Jerry had gotten used to being a petroleum nomad. An engineering mercenary. It was his life.

Jerry refilled his coffee mug from the canteen and scanned the Quaker Oats instant oatmeal boxes for his favorite flavor. Still none. He made a sour face. If he had to endure eating breakfast at dinnertime, they could at least give him the oatmeal he wanted.

"Hey, Abdul, where's my apple cinnamon?" he called out.

"No supply boat today" came the reply from the back room.

"Aw, come on. It's already after six o'clock. I'm back in the box in, like, twenty minutes."

"Aaay, oh," said the impatient voice. "No boat."

Jerry snatched a packet of strawberry Pop-Tarts and brushed past the other workers, an eclectic mix of Germans, Scots, the occasional American, and a growing number of Chinese sent from company headquarters.

Jerry headed outside with his coffee to catch the West African sunset one more time. He pushed the heavy door open and felt the pressured air *woosh* as he stepped onto the steel deck, sixty feet high over the open water. All the operational and residential cabins on the oil platform were kept at a pressure slightly above the atmosphere. This ensured any toxic gases that might have leaked would be quickly expelled rather than silently kill the crew. It was just one of the safety features of the high-tech offshore complex, which had been prefabricated in Shenzhen and hauled by ship for reassembly here offshore Nigeria at the recently discovered but highly productive Mega Millennium Field.

Jerry squinted at the orange fireball touching down on the horizon and drank his coffee, watching the sky turn from yellow to pink. As the last of the sun dropped out of sight, he spotted off in the distance a single bobbing light approaching the platform. His mood brightened. Maybe he would get his breakfast after all. He downed the last of his coffee and did a quick mental calculation of the time required for the boat to land, the supplies to be off-loaded and brought upstairs to the canteen. The oncoming boat was getting closer. Cooking time for his instant oatmeal was just two minutes. He noticed the boat was approaching more quickly than usual. Maybe they were running late, so they used a faster vessel? That might be good news.

Or maybe not. Jerry's pulse quickened. It wasn't one ship oncoming but three smaller boats in a triangular formation. And instead of the bulky shape of the usual cargo boat, these were low, sleek, and open-bow, with huge dual outboard engines. His spine tingled as he realized the lead boat had a tripod with a mounted weapon. The outlines of the shadows were unmistakable: Each boat bristled with heavily armed men.

Jerry spun and rushed inside. "Pirates!" he shouted. "Fucking pirates!"

A shrill alarm sounded, along with a monotone voice blasted over the loudspeakers: "Emergency procedures. Emergency procedures. Execute immediate lockdown. All crew report to secure room in sixty seconds. . . ."

Jerry raced down the corridor, where men were coming out of their cabins, one man hopping on one leg as he pulled on his pants. The seconds ticked by quickly.

"Safe room lockdown in fifty seconds. . . ."

As he scurried down a flight of stairs, Jerry wished he had his old Colt .45. He knew no weapons were ever allowed on an offshore oil platform. That would be suicide.

"Safe room lockdown in forty seconds. . . ."

Rat-tat-tat-tat! echoed loudly through the complex. "What the . . . !" Jerry yelled to himself. Live automatic-weapons fire? This was new. Not like last year, when a payment was quietly negotiated and the pirates never even came aboard the rig. This was serious. *Don't those bastards know live fire could blow us all up?*

"Safe room lockdown in thirty seconds. . . ."

Live weapons on a platform filled with explosive oil and gas was an outrageous safety risk. But so, too, was sitting out here alone and unarmed. The oil company had dissuaded the Nigerian navy from patrolling too close to the facility for fear of stray fire or an accident. Friendly fire from the local security forces was an even bigger risk than pirates. But not today.

"Safe room lockdown in twenty seconds. . . ."

Jerry kept moving. He had to make it to the secure room where he and the rest of the crew could sit and wait it out.

They had drilled for emergencies dozens of times and he knew exactly where he was going. He turned a corner and could now see the reinforced steel door.

"Safe room lockdown in ten seconds. . . ."

Jerry pushed his way in. He exhaled deeply. He was safe. It looked like everyone was there. Once the lockdown was complete, there was no way for the pirates to get inside. The security door would seal and they would all live.

"Five, four, three . . ."

The entire operation was designed to run remotely in just such a situation. The company could shut down production and call the authorities, and the sixty-four men on board would survive in the secure rooms until the pirates were killed, paid off, or just gave up. They could last for days in the bunker if necessary. Then a jarring thought hit Jerry: unless this was resolved quickly, he'd miss his flight home tomorrow.

"Two, one . . . executing lockdown."

Jerry cursed to himself at the thought of being stuck there, in that box with all these men, while the airplane, *his fucking airplane*, flew back home to America. How would he explain it to his girls? Would they even believe him if he tried to blame . . . pirates?

Then Jerry had an even more frightening realization. Where was the lockdown confirmation? Where was the security officer instructing them what to do next? *What the heck was going on?*

That's when the shooting erupted again.

7

Have you got OCD?"

"What are you saying?" Sunday responded, without bothering to turn around.

"Obsessive compulsive disorder. OCD. Is that what you've got, S-Man?"

"Go away, Glen," Sunday huffed at his colleague, who was always hanging around his cubicle.

"There's really no other way to explain it, Sunday. Every desk here in Africa Issue is a mess. I mean, mine is a total shithole. Every single one. *Except yours.*"

Sunday waved Glen away and narrowed his eyes on his classified computer screen. He'd spent most of the day creating a database of every attack on oil facilities over the past ten years. It was part of a project he was working on for Jessica Ryker, the head of the covert Purple Cell. No one at his day job as an analyst at the Africa Issue office—not Glen, not even his office director—knew the truth about his special assignments.

"But, no, not Sunday," Glen continued. "Your little cube here is just perfect. Not a piece of paper out of place. No dust, no crumbs. I'll bet you've even lined up all the pencils in your drawer, haven't you? It's all just so . . . spiffy."

"No one says 'spiffy' anymore, Glen," Sunday said deadpan, his eyes focused on the first item on the list:

> Kuwait, small arms attack, 6 dead, suspected
> terrorist

"You think that it's true what they say about the analysts?" Glen kept talking. "That we take on the characteristics of our regions? You know, that the analysts working East Asia become hyperefficient. The Latin Americans are laid-back, you know, '*Mañana*, man.' And those up in Western Europe are a bunch of uptight snobs?"

"I wouldn't know," Sunday mumbled.

"We hate those pricks," Glen said.

Sunday ignored his colleague and continued reading:

> Venezuela, small cell raid, 2 kidnapped, confirmed
> criminal

Algeria, large-scale assault, 17 dead, confirmed
   terrorist al-Qaeda in the Islamic Maghreb
South China Sea, small cell raid, 4 dead, suspected
   criminal
Nigeria, small cell raid, 16 kidnapped, suspected
   criminal
Turkey, pipeline sabotage, confirmed terrorist
Equatorial Guinea, small cell raid, 2 kidnapped,
   suspected criminal

"Maybe that's why Africa Issue is so lovable and chaotic," Glen said. "We're becoming like the countries we follow. Kinda like how people start to look like their pets. You know what I'm talkin' about, S-Man?"

"No," Sunday said. He was searching for some pattern in the attacks. Oil rigs had been targeted by criminals and competing governments ever since the first oil well. But lately the number of such incidents had spiked. NSA had passed on a series of top secret SIGINT hits that suggested Russian gangs were now specifically targeting foreign oil facilities. Jessica asked Sunday to follow the data, to see where it led. He was already working on African petroleum forecasts for a report going up to the Director of National Intelligence, the very top of the U.S. intel pyramid. It provided a perfect cover for this latest Purple Cell assignment.

"I don't have a dog," Glen said. "But if I'm right, and we're all becoming like our target countries, then how do we explain *you*? Why are you such an immaculate neat freak living here among us slobs?"

"I don't know, Glen."

"You don't fit in, Sunday. That's what I'm saying."

"Maybe there's a flaw in your theory. Something fatal."

"OCD. That's the only way I can explain it. I'm sorry to tell you this. You've obviously got a disorder, Sunday."

"Are you sure I'm the one with the disorder, Glen?"

"Come on!" Glen chortled. "That's the best you can do, S-Man? Your desk looks like it fell out of an Ikea catalog and you're Nigerian."

"I'm American," Sunday corrected. "How many times must I tell you? I grew up in LA."

"Well, you know what I mean. Your family is Nigerian. Haven't you ever been to Lagos? I mean, good Lord. It's total chaos, five, ten, maybe twenty million people all crammed together on those islands. People living under bridges, on floating platforms. No one even knows how big that city really is."

Sunday spun around and locked eyes with Glen. "My father is from a small village up north. Kano State. Then he worked in the Delta in the south. My mother is from Zamfara. My grandparents still live there. None of my family has ever lived in Lagos. Most of them are now in southern California."

"What's your point, Sunday?" Glen shrugged innocently.

"You have no idea what you're talking about." Sunday

shooed away his colleague and spun back to his computer. "Now, go away. I have work to do."

He shifted his eyes to his unclassified computer and opened up a database of Russian oil companies and their investments around the world.

"Whatcha working on?" Glen asked.

"Even if I was allowed to tell you, I wouldn't," Sunday said.

"Well, finish up quick. Arvind, Blessing, and a few of the others are heading down to the Blarney Stone for burgers and beers. You should come. You could obviously use a break. And Lucy's gonna be there."

Just then a news item flashed on Sunday's screen:

Nigerian Mega Millennium oil facility overrun, multiple casualties reported.

"I think I'm going to be here late."

8

Jessica admired her husband's profile as he stood at the kitchen sink, finishing the dishes. Judd wasn't traditionally handsome. His nose was a little crooked and his hair was usually a mess. Tonight his faded jeans hung too low on his hips and his T-shirt advertising Long Beach Island, New Jersey, was so wrinkled it looked like it had been rolled into a ball.

But watching Judd merrily scrub their children's plastic soup bowls, she felt bone-deep attraction. It was the same feeling she'd gotten when she first met Judd twelve years ago. Before the three proposals that changed everything.

———

Judd and Jessica had both been graduate students working for Professor BJ van Hollen in the very far north of Mali, deep in the Sahara Desert. Neither knew it at the time, but BJ had specifically selected each of them. He was their match-maker. The professor was confident they would work well as a team on the Haverford Foundation's clean water research project, but BJ's motivations at the time had been on behalf of neither science nor Cupid. He was, Jessica now knew, recruit-ing for the Central Intelligence Agency. That was Jessica's first proposal, long planned by BJ van Hollen, perfectly exe-cuted by the professor, and accepted without hesitation.

The second proposal had taken more time. From the mo-ment Jessica stepped out of the Land Rover that day in Kidal and seen the scruffy brown-haired boy from Vermont with the uneven smile, she knew he was the one.

Judd didn't stand a chance. A tall, slender beauty, her sul-try dark-brown eyes, her mocha-colored skin against a pure white blouse, the kickass black boots. *An angel in the desert.* The searing heat and desolation of the landscape only made her all the more alluring. All the more irresistible. Jessica knew that any man would notice her under such conditions.

Van Hollen knew it, too. That was one of the reasons he had engineered for his two brightest students, his most prom-ising recruits, to meet on an extreme expedition in the rolling dunes of the Sahara. It was just such an encounter that he was certain would create tight bonds and lifelong loyalty. Shared hardship was the best recruitment tool, and it was especially powerful when paired with raw sexual attraction. It was almost too easy.

Yet BJ couldn't predict then that one of his favorite targets would accept the offer, while the other would veer in another direction, away from government service, choosing instead the genteel seclusion of academic life. And the professor certainly couldn't have known that animal attraction would become true love.

After that first trip to West Africa, Judd courted Jessica long-distance for months. Then one day he showed up in Madison, Wisconsin, where she was completing a doctorate in arid climate agronomy. Judd had no idea what he was doing. But when graduation arrived, so, too, had Jessica's second proposal.

Judd got down on one knee, presenting a silver Tuareg ring smuggled back from West Africa, and asked her to marry him. He'd been offered a plum tenure-track assistant professorship at Amherst College in Massachusetts, with housing and a generous research budget. He promised to help her find a job at one of the many colleges nearby or perhaps consulting for a charity planting trees in the driest parts of Africa. Judd's offer was to settle in the foothills of the Berkshire Mountains together, to build their careers, eventually to raise a family.

This proposal was a tougher decision for Jessica. Yes, she loved him. Yes, she wanted to marry Judd. Yes, she wanted children. But rural Massachusetts? What about her job? What about her commitment to BJ van Hollen? What about the

CIA? Jessica had already made plans to move to northern Virginia to begin her training in the Clandestine Service. She had already signed the paperwork, already been assigned a start date at the Farm, already chosen a career of espionage.

The wise professor had foreseen this dilemma and was ready with a solution: Do both. BJ advised Jessica to accept Judd's marriage proposal and move to Amherst, and the CIA would arrange a part-time agronomy position with the Haverford Foundation. It was a perfect civilian cover for traveling around the world while stealing information for the United States government. It was ideal. It was also a perfect commitment to a double life. A life of secrecy. A life of lies.

The third proposal that had created Jessica Ryker had been hers to offer. Early in her career, she'd been assigned to a Red Cell, a special analytical intelligence unit that solved problems by thinking like the enemy. A Red Cell operated by gathering all new people, starting fresh, and working in isolation, outside of the regular bureaucracy. She loved it. But as a rookie case officer, Jessica saw much of the same groupthink and dysfunction in the Clandestine Service. She shared her observations with BJ van Hollen and pitched him on a new type of isolated operational model. BJ took the idea straight to the CIA's Deputy Director. Purple Cell was born.

The only problem was . . . Massachusetts. How to run a new off-grid supersecret CIA cell from the Berkshires? And how to maintain her cover without destroying her marriage?

That's when BJ van Hollen, just weeks before his death, had one last match to make. The professor arranged for Judd to be invited to share his research at the State Department and quietly pulled strings to encourage the creation of an experimental new office at State for crisis response. That was the origin of S/CRU, and Judd jumped at the opportunity—with a subtle push from Jessica. It was almost too easy.

Standing in the kitchen of their home in Georgetown, admiring her husband, Jessica knew that BJ had been right all along. Everything had come together. Husband, two beautiful young sons, fulfilling careers, bright prospects, most of all the deep-down warmth and comforting tingles of true inner happiness. Judd had learned that Jessica was more than an agronomist, that she had a second unspoken career, and that she'd been secretly helping him. But he didn't know everything. They had agreed to a set of rules to keep their marriage and their work apart. So far, it was working. All was well in the Ryker home.

If only the lies could be kept at bay.

Jessica cleared her throat.

"Hey, sweets." Judd closed the refrigerator and spun around. The fridge door was covered in photos of their young boys at the beach, scribbled crayon drawings, and the season schedule for the Boston Red Sox. "All done here. Kids asleep?"

"Two boys down," she said, and flashed a double thumbs-up. "You could go back in and read it one more time."

"*Where the Wild Things Are*?" he asked, with a faux grimace.

"Every night this month."

"I can't read that book again," he said. "Maybe tomorrow."

"You'll regret it, Judd. They're growing up fast."

"I don't know how these kids can listen to the same old story every single night," Judd said, cracking the top off a bottle of beer.

"Familiarity gives children comfort," Jessica said. She snatched the beer with a cheeky smile, took a healthy drink, and set the bottle on the counter.

"I guess so."

She moved closer to him and slipped her arms around his waist.

He gave her a gentle kiss.

"Knowing what comes next helps to clear their minds," she said, closing her eyes and kissing him back.

"Clear minds, deep sleep," he mumbled.

"That's right. And not just for the kids."

"Okay," he said, taking a slight step back.

"I take comfort when I know what's coming next. I sleep better, too."

"Where are you going with this, Jess?"

"Nowhere," she kissed him again. "So . . . what are you working?"

He let out a forced chuckle. "The office?"

"Judd, you know the deal. Our work-life balance depends on it."

"The Ryker rules of engagement," he said, grabbing the beer bottle. "Avoid, assist, admit. I know the rules."

"I know you hate it. But they're for our own good," she said. "It's the only way our family is going to be able to keep a slice of normality. To maintain trust. We have to make sure we don't get caught on the same thing."

"Again, you mean."

Jessica frowned. "Yes. *Again*. We can't get entangled. That's why we have the rules of engagement."

"I get it, I get it," he said. "We avoid working on the same problem. On the same countries. We assist each other where we can. And if those fail, then we just have to admit it. I was there when we made the rules, remember?"

"So that's why I'm asking, Judd. I want to stay out of your hair and maybe even help you." She shrugged. "So, what are you working on?"

"I was creating a new contingency strategy for the South China Sea. A sort of diplomatic Red Cell, just in case things get hot."

"A diplomatic Red Cell?"

"That's what Parker wanted. New ideas outside the usual bureaucratic box."

"You said 'was'?"

"Pushed to the back burner. Just this morning," Judd sighed. "Friend of some congressman got lost in London, so Landon Parker asked me to look into it. That's what I'm working on now."

"You got pulled off the South China Sea, something that could lead to World War Three, for . . . a missing person?"

"Nuts, huh?" Judd shook his head. "I was embarrassed to even tell you about it."

"You can tell me anything, sweets," she said.

Judd shrugged.

"Maybe he's someone important?" Jessica offered. "Maybe he's really a VIP?"

"Or maybe he's just some punk with a rich uncle who got drunk and fell in the Thames."

"But then why would Parker give it to you, Judd? Why pull you off something substantial to do something trivial? That doesn't add up. What do you know about him?"

"The missing guy works for some hedge fund in New York. Parker says his bosses think he may have been caught up in an advance fee scam."

"A 419?"

"Yeah. Parker says he wants me involved because he thinks I know—wait for it . . . Nigeria."

"Niger, Nigeria, Namibia." Jessica arched her eyebrows. "Narnia."

"Right," Judd laughed.

"Maybe I can help you," Jessica said, trying to keep a straight face. "Most of those hustles aren't even run out of Nigeria anymore."

"That's what Isabella at DOJ says, too."

"So let me dig around. Maybe I'll find something you won't."

"Don't waste your time, Jess. I'm going to spend a few days on it, probably go nowhere, and then kick it over to the embassy so I can get back to the South China Sea. I can't just keep sitting around, waiting for Landon Parker's next whim. I was onto something."

"Good idea," she said. "You've got to make it happen."

"What are you working on, Jess?"

"Not the South China Sea. And not Nigeria."

"That's all I get? 'Not Nigeria'?"

"It's enough to be sure we aren't crossing wires. Avoid is enough."

"You can't tell me anything?" he asked. He set the beer down and gave her a soft kiss behind her ear.

"Judd, don't do this."

"China?" He kissed her neck.

"Stop."

"Iran?" Another kiss. "Mexico?" *Kiss.* "Luxembourg?" *Kiss.* "Russia?" *Kiss.* Judd cocked his head to one side. "That's it," he said, stepping back.

"What're you talking about?"

"You tensed up when I said 'Russia.' You're working on . . . *Russia.*"

"Don't be ridiculous."

"It wasn't much, but I could feel it. You flinched. When I said 'Russia.'" Judd grinned from ear to ear.

"I don't flinch," Jessica insisted.

"Well, I felt it, Jess." His face brightened. "How about that?"

"Judd, don't be ridiculous. You think your lips are a poly-graph?"

"Maybe. Are you denying that I'm right?"

"It's not funny. Let's talk about something else. Who's pitching for the Sox tonight?"

"Russia is dangerous, Jess."

"Change the subject. I want to talk about baseball."

"That's a first. You working on Russian oil?" he asked.

"Stop it. I'm not going to say any more, Judd."

"Arms trafficking? The military? The Kremlin? Organized crime?" Judd paused. "I saw that," he whispered.

"What?" she snapped.

"You twitched when I said 'organized crime.' You just gave away that you're working on . . . the Russian mafia."

"Fuck," she hissed.

"It's fine." Judd took her hand. "Don't worry about it."

"I can't have a tell."

"It's just me, sweets."

"I. Can't. Have. A. Tell," she repeated.

"It doesn't matter, Jess," he said, suddenly feeling badly. "I was messing around. I shouldn't have even asked you. It's me. Your husband. I know you better than anyone. I'm sure no one else could do that. I'm sorry. I won't ask you any more about the Russian mob. Or anything about work."

She scowled at him.

"But," Judd hesitated. "Maybe there's an upside?"

"An upside? A tell can get you *killed*, Judd."

"Not in a marriage."

"What are you talking about?"

"I've accepted that you have another life. We've got our rules of engagement. We've both made our peace with it. All of it," Judd squeezed her hand. "But a little part of me always wonders what I don't know about you."

"I've told you about my family," she said impatiently. "About being adopted from Ethiopia. I've told you what I can about my life. You know all that. I just can't tell you *everything*."

"I can live with that," Judd said. "But it still feels good knowing that I can figure you out once in a while. That I can put one more piece in my Jessica puzzle."

Jessica squeezed his hand back.

"And," he continued, "it's even better if I'm the only one that can read your mind."

"I want to share more about me," she said. "I really do."

"I want to know more, Jess. Whatever you can tell me."

"Like what?" she asked.

"You said a tell could get you killed. Have you ever, I don't know . . . almost . . . died?"

Jessica shrugged.

"How many times?"

"I'm a professional, Judd. I know what I'm doing." She looked away. "I don't take unnecessary risks."

"How close?" Judd asked.

"I know how to protect myself in a dangerous world."

"What's that mean?"

"If someone's coming to kill me. Or my team. Or hurt my

family," she raised her eyebrows. "I'm trained to react. I know what to do. I won't hesitate. I won't have any regrets."

"No regrets? What are you trying to say, Jess?"

"What are you asking, Judd? Are you asking me if I've ever killed anyone?"

"You're the mother of my children. You just read them a bedtime story. I probably don't want to know the answer to that question."

"You just said you want to know more about me. That seems like a pretty big thing," she said.

"I don't need to know that."

"Have you ever killed anyone, Judd?"

"Of course not. I've never even fired a gun."

"So don't you want to know my answer? Whether I've ever killed anyone?

"No, I don't want to know," he said. "I choose not to know."

"Don't be naïve, Judd. People get killed every day."

"What does that mean, Jess? Are you saying that you have no qualms killing people for your country?"

"Are you asking what bad things your wife may have done, Judd? Or do you want to debate the morality of U.S. national security policy? The world is messy and dangerous. More dangerous than you know. More dangerous than I hope our children will ever know. That doesn't change, whether I'm in Washington or Moscow or Kandahar."

"Of course it does, Jess."

"Is it really so different to press a button that sends a missile into a truck ten thousand miles away or if you twist the knife into a man as you look into his eyes as he sucks in his final breath?"

Judd swallowed hard.

"I don't think so," she said matter-of-factly.

"Well, I couldn't do it," Judd said.

"What about for your family?"

"I don't know," he whispered.

"Back in Cuba, don't you think I would have slit Oswaldo Guerrero's throat right there if I needed to save your life?"

"I guess so."

"Of course I would have. With no second thoughts. No regrets. Same goes for how things went down in Mali. And in Zimbabwe. Don't you know that I would have done whatever it takes to keep those I love safe?"

"Of course I do. I just don't know"—he cleared his throat—"if I could kill someone face-to-face."

"We never know our inner bravery until we need to," she said. "You'll know when you have to. And when your moment comes, you won't hesitate. And you won't have regrets."

"I just hope I never have to kill someone to save your life, Jess."

"So do I," she said. "But the world—"

"I know, Jess. The world is messy and dangerous."

DAY TWO

TUESDAY

9

D ead," said the Bear, stroking his bushy beard.

Despite the dark hour, the burly man wore his usual wraparound sunglasses as he stood in front of a large picture window. The view was of twinkling lights along the black Neva River that ran through the center of St. Petersburg. Vibrations from the nightclub two floors down pulsated through the room like a beating heart on speed. "Zhang-tao is supposed to be . . . dead."

"Aye, boss," replied a muscular bald man in a tight black suit standing at attention. "Should I bring in Yuri?" he asked, with an accent that could come from nowhere except the streets of London's East End.

"You see the Neva, Mikey?" the Bear said, ignoring the question and gently tapping a long finger on the window. "The water of the Neva comes from Lake Ladoga, where my grandmother was born."

Mikey nodded enthusiastically, even though he had heard this speech many times before.

"The Neva pours from there through our glorious city out to the sea. The Neva flows to Finland, to Sweden, to Denmark. It surrounds Great Britain. My family's water floods the Atlantic. It goes wherever the ocean currents take it, to Africa, to Asia, to America. From my small village at Tuloksa, the Neva touches the entire world."

"That's right, boss."

"Everyone is drinking the water of Mother Russia."

"'At's it, boss."

"It's invisible. No one sees it. No one knows. But the water flows from me." He smacked his hand on the window. "To everywhere."

"You's everywhere."

"From nothing. From nowhere. We are everywhere. We have built an empire." The Bear spun to face Mikey. "And how did we do this?"

"Crackin' skulls."

"No!" the Bear growled. "Any man can just kill another man. That is nothing. Violence alone cannot build an empire. That is a recipe for savagery. To build an empire, you need savages, yes."

"You have me, boss," Mikey offered.

"But more than brute strength, we must create fear and respect. That's how our business works. That's how the world works."

"'At's it."

"When we see something we want, a snake that is feeding, how do we make that snake our own? We can cut off the head. But for the body to live, for the body to thrive, for the snake to truly become ours, we need fear and respect, Mikey."

"Fear and respect, boss."

"That's how we profit from every kilo of opium from Afghanistan, every Kalashnikov on the streets of Mexico City, every whore in Romania. And that's how we will profit from every barrel of oil."

"Truth."

"How are we supposed to create fear and respect if Zhang-tao defies me? If he's allowed to live?"

"It's bang out of order."

The Bear pulled a compact comb from his pocket and slowly groomed his beard. "Bring the boy here."

The bald man opened the door and led in a younger man with a brush cut and wide shoulders. The new arrival saluted the Bear.

"We aren't in the army anymore, Yuri," the Bear said. The man raised his hands in apology as Mikey placed a hand on his shoulder and forced him down into a chair.

"What were your orders, little Yuri?" the Bear demanded.

"Get to Zhang-tao," Yuri said.

"And?" Mikey demanded, looming over the younger man.

"I put our very best on it," Yuri said nervously, looking back and forth between the two bigger men.

"So how did Evgeny see Zhang-tao drinking champagne in Manila yesterday?"

"I don't know, boss. Queen Sheba has never failed us before. Maybe Evgeny is mistaken?"

"Is he dead or not?"

"I don't know, boss."

"Show me your hands," said the Bear. The young man hesitated, then extended his arms and rested his palms on the coffee table. "The world is a rough and filthy place. Men have to be this way to survive. Are your hands rough and filthy, Yuri?"

"Yes, boss," the man said.

"The world is a terrible place, full of monsters. Strong men have to be terrible and sometimes inhuman. Can you be inhuman when I require it?" the Bear asked.

"Of course," Yuri said, a quiver sneaking into his voice. "I follow orders. You know that. I always follow orders."

"Do you know how our organization works?"

"Fear," the younger man said. "You told me yourself."

"Correct," said the Bear. "How do we maintain our empire?"

"Respect."

"Correct again," said the Bear, sinking his hands into the deep pockets of his overcoat. "But, Yuri, do you know what separates us from the beasts?"

"I . . ." the man looked to Mikey who offered no assistance. "I don't understand."

"I said: Do you know what separates men from animals?" the Bear repeated. As the man shook his head, Mikey lunged forward and pinned Yuri's left arm. In that instant, the Bear swung a meat cleaver high over his head and whacked it down on the table like a guillotine, severing Yuri's left thumb. Bright red blood spurted across the room. Yuri screamed in pain and clutched his hand.

The Bear calmly wiggled the cleaver to remove it from the table, wiped it off with a white handkerchief, and replaced it in his coat pocket.

"Thumbs," said the Bear. "Now bring Queen Sheba to me."

10

The sun was shining and the band was playing Louis Armstrong's cheery version of "What a Wonderful World." The crowd chatted excitedly in the State Department's south courtyard while they sipped orange juice and tall flutes of champagne.

"*I see trees of green, red roses too . . .*" the music blared.

The courtyard featured a bronze-and-glass sculpture of a superhuman ten-foot giant riding atop a spinning planet. Marshall Fredericks's *The Man and the Expanding Universe* was a fitting image to celebrate Tunde Babatunde, the seven-foot-two-inch star center for the Brooklyn Nets basketball team.

"The colors of the rainbow so pretty in the sky . . ."

Judd Ryker snagged a glass of bubbly off a tray and stood toward the back, watching the gray-suited Americans mingle with the Nigerians in multicolored robes and wraps. Several of the women were adorned with *gele*s, elaborate traditional cloth head wraps that added at least a foot to their height. He scanned the crowd for a face that matched the photo Serena had showed him a few minutes earlier. *The ambassador's not here yet.*

Judd checked his watch just as the song came to an end.

"Yes I think to myself what a wonderful world . . ."

"It's indeed a wonderful world," announced a beaming Secretary of State. "On this beautiful day, we are so honored to have Tunde Babatunde with us to celebrate his achievements, his generosity, and his enduring commitment to an even more wonderful future. Like many of us here today, Tunde came from humble roots. But he worked hard, he believed in himself, and he succeeded. And now Tunde is giving back. To make the world a better place. To build bridges between the country of his birth and his adopted homeland. To bring Africa and America one step closer together."

The Secretary paused to allow the crowd to clap and cheer. "Tunde is a model for all of us. And the work he is doing with the Tunde Babatunde Foundation, in collaboration with the U.S. embassy in Nigeria, is a model for the public-private partnerships that the State Department is building to leverage the unique capabilities of philanthropy and diplomacy." She paused again for another round of polite applause. "I'm so very pleased to introduce our special guest today, a great symbol of the pursuit of excellence and our common humanity, Tunde Babatunde!"

Judd moved toward a gap in the crowd to get a better view just as a gigantic man dressed in an elegant pin-striped suit stepped into the courtyard. He flashed a wide smile at the cameras, bent down to embrace the Secretary, and then accepted the microphone.

"Thank you, Madam Secretary of State," he said in a deep, froggy voice. "Thank you, Ambassador Katsina, proud representative of our great and beautiful country." Babatunde nodded deferentially toward an older woman standing in a black dress and head scarf, with a large oval diplomatic pin on her collar. "I will be brief. As a small boy on the streets of Lagos, I was the tallest of all my friends. I always dreamed of playing basketball in America. I idolized Michael Jordan and Patrick Ewing. I sold oranges with my friends on the street to earn one naira so I could pay to watch American basketball games on a black-and-white television running on a car battery."

Judd edged closer toward the front.

"As a boy, my true hero was Hakeem Olajuwon, who had made the unimaginable journey from Nigeria to Texas. Olajuwon was Nigeria's biggest star who moved to the biggest state in the biggest country."

"Big is good!" someone shouted from the back of the crowd.

"Yes, yes, in Nigeria, big is good," Babatunde replied. "Back in Lagos, we all wanted to be like Hakeem Olajuwon. We all wanted to play basketball in America. The trouble was that my school had no books, no desks, no basketballs, and no basketball court. We had nothing but our dreams."

Babatunde continued, "One day I was messing around outside the American consulate with some friends. I won't tell you what trouble we were really up to."

He smiled cheekily, eliciting a round of forced laughter from the crowd.

"But one of the Marine guards called me over. 'Come here, little man,' he said. I was scared and thought he was calling me for a beating. But I obeyed his order. Instead of a beating, the Marine handed me a basketball. He said I was so tall that I should learn the game and one day come to play in America. He made me promise that if I did make it, that I would become a Seminole." The crowd hooted and whistled.

"I didn't know what a Seminole was, but I wanted that basketball, so I agreed! I played with that ball every day in the street on a hoop and backboard that my friends and I rigged up from scrap wire and asbestos sheeting. I slept with that ball in my bed. Eventually I got better, and one day I met a visiting high school coach who told a college recruiter about me. I kept my word to the Marine, insisting that I was a Seminole. Eventually word got back to Tallahassee and Florida State University offered me a scholarship. After taking the Seminoles to the Final Four"—cheers and whistles from the back again—"I was so blessed to be drafted in the first round by the Brooklyn Nets. I had always known that Texas was the biggest state, but I was going to New York, the biggest city."

Babatunde bowed his head. "I've been so fortunate. I will never forget that Marine guard. And I will never forget the streets of Lagos where I come from. Where my career and good fortune all began. And I cannot also forget all the other children of Lagos who were not so lucky. Big is good, but small is good, too."

Babatunde took a deep breath and raised his head, opening his arms to his full wingspan. "So I am very pleased today to announce that the Tunde Babatunde Foundation will tomorrow break ground in Lagos on the Babatunde Hospital for Children."

Clapping erupted from the crowd. The Secretary of State handed Tunde a shovel with the State Department logo on the blade. He held it high over his head, igniting another round of cheers. He held the Secretary's hand in triumph and they posed for the cameras before the Secretary was pulled away, back into the building.

Once the formal presentation was over and the crowd broke apart, Judd beelined for his target.

"Ma'am, I'm Judd Ryker."

"Very pleased to meet you," said the older woman in the black dress and head scarf. "It is a wonderful day for Nigeria. We are so proud."

"I'm with the Crisis Reaction Unit here at State," Judd said.

"I am Ambassador Katsina. From the Federal Republic of Nigeria," she said, handing him a card, but not making direct eye contact.

"I know you don't have much time, Madam Ambassador. We're working on a special project to combat international fraud that may be of interest to your country," Judd explained as he fished his own business card out of his wallet.

"Those 419 Yahooze Boys were a terrible nuisance." The ambassador clicked her tongue. "But we have dealt with them harshly. You know about the sweep last year? Our federal police. With your FBI."

"Yes, Madam Ambassador, I know your government has cracked down on con artists. But there are some new cases that we're looking into. I'm wondering if your embassy is seeing a resurgence in fraud activity."

"No matter how hard we try, there will always be bad apples," she tsked. "A few bad people ruin our nation's image."

"I'd like to come over to the embassy to talk with your justice ministry liaison. To find out more about these new cases and get any data that you may have."

"I'm sorry, Babatunde is leaving now for Lagos," she said as she backed away. "I must escort him to the airport. Please excuse me."

"Ambassador Katsina, can I call your office to talk more about 419?"

"It is a terrible problem and we are trying our best, yes. But there is nothing more I can do."

11

Where are you with the Bear?" the Deputy Director demanded, swiveling in the chair behind his desk on the seventh floor of the CIA's old headquarters building.

"Purple Cell is on it," Jessica Ryker replied. "I've got all my people turning over rocks. The pieces are starting to come in. It's still early, but we'll get a line on him. One of my team has identified a pattern of attacks in the oil sector that could give us a new way to predict the Bear's next move. He's working on an algorithm as we speak. Once I have—"

"No, no, no, sweet Jesus, no," said the Deputy Director, waving Jessica's answer away. "New direction. Your computer hacker isn't going to find the Bear. And enough of this sneaking around, hunting for clues like Sherlock Holmes. This isn't an investigation. It's an intelligence operation. Old-school, with a twist. Time to go straight to the source."

"What do you mean, sir?"

"It's time for you to meet the Bear."

"I don't understand," she said, folding her arms. *I don't like where this is going,* she thought. "Purple Cell just started on the Bear yesterday. I'm throwing lines into the water. I don't even know where he is yet."

"That's correct, Jessica. You don't understand," he said, deadpan. "I've been working an operation against the Bear for years. Now I'm close."

"You're close?" she snapped. "Then why did you have me starting fresh? I just pulled some of my best people off—"

"Enough," he held up his palm. "You know how this works, Jessica."

"Yes, sir."

"May I continue?"

"Yes, sir," she conceded, but inside she was steaming.

"The Bear prefers to use outside contract hit men to take out his rivals. That has been one of his protective tactics, but it's also a weakness we've been trying to exploit. After years of hard work and lots of failures, we are finally close."

"You've got a man inside the Bear's operation?"

"Not exactly. And not a man. We persuaded one of his key lieutenants to hire an assassin code-named QUEEN SHEBA, who is really one of ours. Over the past six months, we've made sure that each hit goes smoothly, and thus the Bear keeps coming back to Queen Sheba."

"You're right, I don't understand, sir," she said. "Are you telling me the Agency is assassinating the Bear's competitors in order to get close to him?"

"In a way. Not only are we getting one of our people closer to the Bear's inner circle but he's inadvertently handing us his priority hit list. Queen Sheba is giving us a window directly inside his operation. We can see exactly where he's headed next. We haven't yet figured out why."

Jessica took a step back from the Deputy Director. "Do you have a presidential finding for this operation?"

"Don't get your panties in a twist," he said with a scowl. "We don't need White House authorization because we're not whacking anyone. I can't tell you details, but we've staged a series of hits to convince the Bear that Queen Sheba is for real."

"Decoy kills."

"You could call it that."

"I thought the Agency halted decoy kills after the congressional inquiry."

"Correct."

"They were too risky. People got hurt. Things got out of control."

"Yes, I remember. I was there," the Deputy Director said impatiently.

"But you just said you're doing decoy kills again?"

"No I didn't. You did."

"If you're faking assassinations, that means you need forged proof of death, black-site safe houses, new identities, the whole show. I don't understand how they're not decoy kills."

"You don't need to understand, Jessica. You only need to know that we're running an operation to show the Bear that Queen Sheba is the most efficient contract killer he's ever seen. We've made sure of that."

Jessica let that sink in. "You're running decoy kills so your operative gets the most important assignments," she said.

"That's it," he said.

"So you know the Bear's top targets."

"Now you've got it. I thought you'd be faster than that." He snapped his fingers. "But I knew you'd come around."

"So, why did you have Purple Cell chasing this guy?"

"I wanted you up to speed on the Bear because I knew sooner or later this operation would come to a head and that I'd need you."

"Me?"

"And that moment is now. The Bear wants to meet Queen Sheba."

Jessica narrowed her eyes.

"*You* are Queen Sheba."

"Excuse me?"

"You're going to meet the Bear. In St. Petersburg. You leave tonight."

"If you need someone to take the Bear out, get White House approval, task Purple Cell, and I'll make it happen. But

I'll do it my way. I've got one of my best operatives in Moscow right now. Give me the green light and I can have her in St. Petersburg by nightfall. Give me the meet location and she can—"

"No, no, Jessica," the Deputy Director interrupted. "It has to be you."

"Why me?"

"Queen Sheba is an ethnic Somali operating out of Djibouti. I need a light-skinned black female operative just about your size who speaks Arabic, Portuguese, and Russian."

"How convenient," Jessica said through gritted teeth.

The Deputy Director grinned.

"You built a fictional assassin for hire from scratch," she said. "You could have created any profile you wanted. A blond Norwegian. A Pakistani woman with a British accent. Anything. But you chose a specific profile that could only have been . . . me?"

"We needed Queen Sheba to stand out in order to make her credible with the Bear. She had to be something special."

"I don't buy it, sir."

"The Bear needed the best. Just like I need the best. The Bear needed you. And I needed you. That's why her profile matches you. That's why you are running Purple Cell in the goddamn first place. And that's why, Jessica, *you are Queen Sheba*."

"Who do the Bear's people think they've been meeting?"

"No one in his organization has ever physically met her. Not yet. They've been communicating entirely through encrypted electronics. Technically, that means Queen Sheba is a former Army Ranger computer whiz from Oklahoma who is, at this moment, working nine floors down in a secure room. We can't send him. It has to be you."

"You want me to go to St. Petersburg, meet the Bear, and eliminate him?"

"Negative," he said. "Do not eliminate the Bear. Your immediate task is to convince him that Queen Sheba is for real. We believe he's on the verge of a major new expansion and we want to know what that is. Is his next move into heavy arms? Biological weapons? Uranium? Is he only interested in business or is he plugged into the Kremlin? We need you to go see him to get your next assignment. That's it. You get the target and pass it to me. We'll handle the rest."

"My whole mission is to acquire Queen Sheba's next target?"

"That's it," he said.

"Get the target, then . . . come home?"

"In and out."

"Why does the Bear want to see me now? Why would he take the risk?"

"We don't know for sure."

"What aren't you telling me, sir?"

"The last operation didn't go exactly to plan. The target was a Chinese tycoon based in the Philippines and things got a little messy."

"So you're sending me into a trap."

"No. It's all under control. The problem in Manila has

been taken care of. All you have to do is go to St. Petersburg and convince the Bear that you're authentic. You've just got to con him. He has to believe beyond any doubt that you are Queen Sheba."

"And how do you suggest I do that?"

"You have to believe that you are Queen Sheba."

"I can do that."

"Here's the dossier." He held up a thumb drive. "Everything you need to know is in here. Queen Sheba's backstory, details on all the hits, anything that he might ask you. Read it, memorize it, then fry it."

Jessica nodded.

"And you'll need this," he said, handing her a small blue velvet box.

"A ring?" Jessica asked.

"Not exactly."

12

Judd sifted through the tall stack of fraud reports received by the U.S. embassy in London. American citizens abroad had fallen for just about every trick on the planet: real estate swindles, counterfeit currency, identity theft, fake insurance rackets, bogus investments, and elaborate Ponzi schemes. A thick file detailed the sad victims of dating and marriage scams. Another file documented the dozens of young American citizens who got stuck in London after spending all their money chasing false promises of a West End acting career. *People will fall for anything.*

The fattest file from the embassy, however, was for advance fee fraud. People just couldn't help themselves when offered the chance at a big payout in exchange for a seemingly modest up-front fee. Judd found a recent consular report about $22,000 sent by a retiree in Buffalo, New York, to an account in East London that was supposed to unlock $40 million in unclaimed lottery winnings. Another complaint was filed by a dentist in Orlando who wired $15,000 as a down payment for half of an unpaid $70 million legal judgment against the Queen of England. *Who could believe this stuff?*

The Jason Saunders case was not too different. Landon Parker had sent down a copy of the original letter that Saunders' company, Holden Harriman Quinn, had received. Fortunately, the hedge fund scanned all incoming mail as part of its compliance and security procedures.

The outlines of the case were pretty simple. The approach was an offer from a fictitious firm called Global Allied Financial to help manage a $2 billion account comprised of assets allegedly recovered by an international court from Syria's ruling family. The lure was a four percent annual management fee, unusually high, but supposedly endorsed by the Bank of England. The hook was a face-to-face meeting in Canary Wharf. That was where Jason Saunders had supposedly disappeared. The airline records showed he had landed at Heathrow on a British Airways flight from JFK four days earlier. That was the last anyone heard of him.

If the basic facts were clear, the case left many unanswered questions. Why would an associate of a well-known New York financial firm travel all the way to London for a deal with an unknown company that was obviously too good to be true? Judd deduced there was probably a pretty good answer to this one: *$80 million a year.*

But what motivated the scammers? Why would anyone lure a low-level hedge fund employee from New York all the way to London to just kidnap or kill him? What was the payout? Was that the plan or did something go wrong at Canary Wharf? Were they specifically targeting Saunders, or HHQ, or was it just random? Was Saunders just unlucky or was he caught up in something larger? Was HHQ?

The security office at One Canada Square reported that the lobby's closed-circuit cameras weren't operational that day and the visitor log was lost. They claimed some software glitch shut down the system. It was suspicious yet plausible. But it meant that there was no record of whether Saunders had ever arrived at the meeting or not.

London Metropolitan Police hadn't recovered a body, either, and there were no reports of any John Does matching his description at any London hospital. So, where was Jason Saunders?

And the biggest question of all that nagged Judd, which he couldn't yet answer: Why was S/CRU given such a case?

"Dr. Ryker is unavailable," Judd could hear Serena insist in the outer lobby.

"Oh, I don't think so" came the brash reply of a familiar voice.

"I'm sorry, but you can't just walk in there," Serena shouted. "If you'd like to leave a message . . ."

"You tell Dr. Ryker that it's me and I'm here to see him now."

"He's in the middle of an important—hey, you can't go in there!'

"Judd, darling!" said the voice as his office door was flung open.

"Hello, Mariana," he said, looking up from his papers to see Mariana Leibowitz, five foot two inches and 106 pounds of well-toned twisted steel in an immaculate Versace pantsuit.

"I'm sorry, Dr. Ryker," Serena apologized, scurrying to put herself between the intruder and her boss. "I've called Diplomatic Security."

"It's okay, Serena," Judd said. "I'll see Ms. Leibowitz now."

"Of course you will, darling," Mariana announced with a smile as she straightened her jacket. The super-lobbyist was in her late forties but still knew how to leverage her charm and beauty inside the hallways of Washington, D.C.

"Security can stand down, Serena. Apologize for me," Judd said. "Again."

"I'll be at my desk if you need anything, Dr. Ryker," Serena said with a scowl before shutting the door behind her.

"She's very good," Mariana said.

"Yes, she is," Judd replied.

"But she clearly hates me."

"Serena is just doing her job."

"Maybe I should hire her."

"You can't keep busting in here, Mariana. Why can't you make an appointment like everyone else?"

"I don't make appointments, Judd dear. That would ruin all the fun."

"This is fun?"

"Do you think I'd be where I am today if I made *appointments*?"

Judd blinked.

"Do you think my clients expect me to just—good God, no—*wait in line*?"

"I don't know, Mariana," Judd said. "Why are you here?"

"Haven't you learned anything from working with me yet?"

Judd couldn't tell if she was annoyed or if this was part of the setup. "I see you're back from Zimbabwe," Judd offered.

"President Mutonga is well on her way. Gugu doesn't need me anymore. At least not until she runs for reelection. Don't you worry, I'll let you know when the time comes."

"So you're here today because you're now working for . . . ?"

"Judd, I was just *delighted* that I could help you out in Florida. You know, when you called me all the way in Africa when I was crashing with Gugu in the very first days of her administration. When I took your call and time out from what I was doing just to get you into that little party. Miami, was it?"

"Las Olas."

"Oh, right. Las Olas. I'm sure it was a lovely party. And I was very happy to do that favor for you."

"Yes, thank you, Mariana," Judd said. "I owe you a big one." Judd was genuinely grateful. He just could never tell Mariana how crucial getting Jessica into the political fundraiser had been to unraveling the entire Cuba puzzle.

"How long did it take me to get you an invitation for your friend?"

"Five minutes."

"Five minutes!" she bellowed. "I just love it when things work out like that. You make a call." She snapped her fingers. "You need help." Another *snap*. "And then your friends come through for you." *Snap, snap, snap.* "That's what having friends in the right places can do. That's how Washington works."

"And that's why you aren't in handcuffs right now, Mariana," Judd said. "Or being waterboarded in the State Department basement."

"That's not funny, Judd. I've been waterboarded. It's not pleasant."

"You have? I'm so sorry."

"No." Mariana shrugged. "But you see how I disarmed you? I've still got tricks to teach you, Judd dear."

"How does your husband react to such tactics?"

"Divorced. Twice." She held up a well-manicured but ring-less left hand. "Neither of them could handle me. They thought they could. But they were wrong."

"Why are you here, Mariana?"

"Bola."

"What's Bola?"

"Not what. Who. Judge Bola Akinola."

"He's your new client?"

"Not a client, a friend. I would never accept money from an angel like Bola."

"So, who is he?"

"Bola Akinola is the head of the Nigerian Crime and Corruption Task Force. He was a police officer, then a criminal defense lawyer, then became Nigeria's youngest ever Supreme Court judge before taking over the CCTF."

"I've heard of the CCTF. They just arrested one of the governors, right?" Judd asked.

"The Kwara state governor. For stealing highway funds to buy himself a private jet. Bola wrote the sealed indictment and his team executed the arrest. They grabbed the governor as he was trying to escape on a motorcycle—get this, Judd—while *wearing a burka*."

"Sounds like a Hollywood movie," Judd said.

"That's not all. Bola was the one who prosecuted the energy minister last year for taking bribes from Chinese oil companies in exchange for offshore rights in the Gulf of Guinea. Then Bola was offered five million dollars in cash to let the minister go."

"So, what happened?"

"Bola taped the conversation, confiscated the five million dollars, and used both as evidence for additional charges of attempting to bribe a public official!" she announced with glee, dancing a little jig in place. "The energy minister's case goes to trial next month. How's *that* for integrity?"

"An energy minister's a big fish, Mariana."

"That's Bola's problem, Judd. He's too good. He's been investigating Nigeria's top politicians. He keeps turning over rocks and finding worms. *Snakes* is more like it."

"Sounds like J. Edgar Hoover keeping dossiers on all his enemies."

"Wrong analogy, Judd. He's not blackmailing politicians to expand his power. He's more like . . . Eliot Ness and the Untouchables. A lone wolf fighting for justice in a corrupt system."

"You called him an angel."

"Bola's a motherfucking superhero, Judd."

"So, what happened? Why does your superhero need me?"

"I don't quite know yet, Judd," she said, lowering her voice. "I don't want to know. But I think Bola must have discovered something he didn't want to find. Whatever it is, he's under tremendous pressure."

"Death threats?" Judd asked.

"Yes, but he gets those all the time. Something's changed. He sounded different on the phone. For the first time since I've known him. Bola sounded, I don't know, *scared*."

"So, what do you want from me?"

"Make some inquiries, Judd. Look into it. Watch his back for me. Bola Akinola is a patriot. He's a good man trying to help his country. He's sure as hell good for the United States. He's trying to clean up Africa's biggest country. Africa's biggest market. The biggest oil producer. I need you to make sure the U.S. government doesn't let a good man go down."

13

Big judge man, how you dey? God don butta my bread me to see you."

"I'm very happy to see you, too," said Bola Akinola through his open car window to a boy in a dirty white T-shirt, holding up a sack of oranges.

"You buy dis?"

"No, thank you. No oranges for me today," said the judge.

"I dey hungry. I wan chop. You fit buy DVD?"

Bola's driver, Chuku, waved the boy away as he nudged the vehicle, an aging black Mercedes E-Class sedan, through the crowd. "Tsah! Go!" Chuku hissed.

The hawker ignored the driver and jogged cheerily along-side the car in bare feet.

"You aren't trying to sell pirated merchandise to a judge, are you, son?" Bola asked.

"Oh, no, big judge man. Dis good movie. First-class. You wan Yankee Hollywood? *Iron Man*, *Star Wars*, *Happy Feet Two*," said the boy, flashing the plastic cases. "You wan Nollywood film? *Last Flight to Lagos*. Dis ha fine film. Funke Kanju dey inside. Dey ending too funny. Laugh wan kill me die. Good price."

"Do you have any children's books?" Bola asked as they pulled slowly through a gate and into the courtyard of his office block.

"Abeg, wait me, big judge man," the boy squealed, then disappeared.

Chuku eased the Mercedes into a space underneath a palm tree and then sprung out to open the rear door. Bola emerged from the car, sprightly for a man in his early fifties, wearing an *agbada*, a huge free-flowing robe, all white with fine gold trim, matching white trousers, and well-worn brown leather sandals. On top of his head, a matching embroidered soft *gobi* cap flopped to one side.

He eyed the line of people that had formed outside his office, a whitewashed concrete building that had once housed a mission boarding school for girls.

"Many people again today, Chuku," Bola said, stroking the wisps of gray hair in his goatee.

"I'm sorry we are late, sah. The traffic on the bridge was too go-slow, eh. I will drive better tomorrow."

"It's not your fault, Chuku. The governor should have finished the new bridge by now. Life in Lagos will be better when the bridge is open."

"Eh, chief. Soon life will be better."

Bola handed his briefcase to the driver. "Take this to Mrs. Oshinowo. I will be inside in a moment." He wandered over to the crowd outside his front door. "It's a beautiful morning," he said to the woman at the front of the line. "Why are you here today, my friend?"

"Doctor judge man, my sister has moved in with a bad man who is trying to steal our father's land," she said. Bola nodded and moved on to the next person.

"I have information about the Senator from Lagos East," whispered an old man.

"De *Oga* in Ikeja. Dey resell subsidized fuel," reported an elderly woman. "De police, dey no care."

"We seek your wise advice for our marriage," said a young couple holding a newborn baby.

Next in line were three young men huddled together. "Chief, we have a business proposition. A big idea. Very big." And on to the next, and the next.

When Bola had finished hearing from each and every person waiting in line to see him, he thanked everyone for coming and begged for their patience. Waiting by the door was the street boy who had been selling oranges and DVDs.

"I sell you dis, big judge man," said the boy excitedly, holding up several books, a dog-eared used mathematics textbook, a tattered German romance novel, and a shiny new copy of *Green Eggs and Ham* by Dr. Seuss.

"How much for the green book, my friend?"

"Good price," said the boy. "Three thousand."

Bola tsked at the offer, about fifteen American dollars, and walked away. "It's not worth more than five hundred."

"I have to eat. I wan chop. You wan big man to beat me? Two thousand." The boy chased after him, thrusting the book into Bola's hand. "You take dis, big judge man. Pay me tomorrow. Any price you wan."

Bola accepted the book and walked into his office. The air was hot and humid, like breathing spicy peanut soup.

"Good morning, Mrs. Oshinowo," he said to the woman sitting at the reception desk. "How is Timi?"

"He's better, Judge Akinola. Thank you. He was able to go to school today."

"Very good. I have this for him," he said, handing her the Dr. Seuss book. "It's very popular with children in America. I think he will like it."

"I am sure he will, Judge Akinola. Thank you and God bless."

"Give me a few minutes to read the newspaper and have my tea, then send in the first person. There are many outside today. It's going to be a long day, Mrs. Oshinowo."

"Just like yesterday. You have calls from the attorney general, the governor of Cross River, the police commissioner, and your cousin Ife in Greenwich."

"Ife!" Bola snorted. "I will call them all back after my tea."

"And Funke called twice. She wants to interview you again for the show. In studio, tomorrow."

"Of course," he said. "Call Funke back and tell her yes."

Bola stepped into his office, which was even hotter than the reception area. He flipped on the air conditioner, but nothing happened. He tried again, with no result.

"Mrs. Oshinowo!" he called out. "The AC is out again."

"No power today," she replied.

"Tell Chuku to turn on the generator."

"No diesel," she said.

Bola slumped into his chair and exhaled. "Where is Chuku?"

A few moments later, the driver appeared in the doorway.

"Where is the diesel?" Bola asked patiently.

"No fuel in Ojota today, sah. I tried Ikeja, too, eh. No luck."

"Can you go to Victoria Island?"

"Eh, chief. But it's extra money. The rich people on the island pay too much."

"That's fine, Chuku. We need diesel today. It is too hot," he said, handing Chuku a thick wad of local currency.

"Yes, sah. Right away."

"And on your way out, there is a small boy. White shirt, no shoes."

"The area boy selling books?"

"That's the one. Give him this," he said, handing Chuku three thousand naira.

"Okay, chief. Right away."

14

Judd had been feeling cooped up in his office and needed fresh air, so he decided to walk the seven blocks from the State Department to the White House. The traffic was heavy for midday. Herds of taxis, government-plated vans, and diplomatic limousines crowded the streets around the World Bank.

As Judd crossed 17th Street near the Eisenhower Executive Office Building, a huge black SUV with the telltale red-white-and-blue diplomatic license plates came to a screeching halt, nearly hitting him. Judd jumped back onto the sidewalk but kept moving.

After skirting the crowds of tourists wandering by the front gate to the West Wing, he cut across Lafayette Park, past the bright yellow stucco of St. John's Episcopal Church across H Street, to McPherson Square. As he strode across the grass, he spotted Isabella Espinosa seated at a table on the sidewalk. Underneath the bright orange umbrellas of Siroc, the Moroccan-Italian restaurant she had suggested, Isabella looked serious in her sunglasses and tapered dark-blue business suit. As usual, she was thumbing fiercely on her phone, her lips pursed.

"You cut your hair," Judd said, still catching his breath from his hike.

"You're still wearing the same suit," she said without looking up.

"Good to see you, Isabella. I've missed this."

"Me too," she said, slipping the phone into her pocket and flashing a warm smile. "I did cut my hair. *Mi madre* hates it. Says I look like a boy."

"I think it makes you look younger. More intense," Judd said, taking a seat at the table.

"That's what I'm going for. Justice Department youthful intensity. How's the family?"

"Boys are good. Jessica still busy. She sends her best. Thanks for asking."

"Any word from our Colonel Durham?" Isabella asked.

"Not lately. Last I heard, he was deployed overseas again. I'm sure I'll hear from old Bull once he's back in the States.

But he goes through these periods of total radio silence. It's normal for the Special Ops guys to disappear."

"And then they just reappear. I dated a Green Beret once. I know all about it."

"You dated a Green Beret?" Judd raised his eyebrows and smirked.

"Forget it, Judd." She shook her head.

"Was that back in LA? Before or after law school?"

"I'm not talking about it. Let it go."

"You brought it up."

"No I didn't," she insisted. "I just agreed that it's strange when people close to you have secret lives. When they suddenly appear, then disappear. It makes life complicated."

"You talking about this boyfriend or your mother?"

"I said forget it. I hate talking about my personal life," Isabella said.

"Me too," Judd said. "Speaking of disappearances, you find anything on Jason Saunders?"

"I looked into your missing person. FBI's got nothing. Looks like he vanished without a trace. The Metropolitan Police in London have opened a file at our request, but I don't expect them to find anything. Do you know how many people go missing in London every year?"

"I'm at a dead end," Judd said, scanning the menu.

"I would drop it. You're a strategist, not a private detective."

"You're probably right. S/CRU isn't built for this."

"Good idea, Judd. I'm sorry I can't help you more."

"One thing is bugging me, Isabella."

She took a sip of her drink. "Shoot."

"I can't help but wonder if Jason Saunders was just very unlucky"—Judd winced—"or if he was targeted for some reason."

"If this kid was caught up in a scam—and that's a big leap, Judd—it's almost certainly random. That's how those advance fee scams work. They throw out as many lines as they can and wait for someone naïve enough to reply. They spray and pray."

"If you say so."

"I do. I hope you've got another reason for buying me lunch." She looked up with a mischievous grin. "I'm ordering the lobster cavatelli special."

"You mentioned on the phone something about the Nigerian Crime and Corruption Task Force. Tell me more."

"Nigeria?" She sat back in her chair. "What's the angle with Saunders? The CCTF can't help you find him, even if he disappeared in Lagos instead of London."

"Unrelated," Judd said, shaking his head. "You told me that DOJ worked with the task force. You know anything about this Judge Akinola?"

"Bola Akinola," she said. "Smart guy. Highly capable. Akinola set up the CCTF. We helped him do it. He spent time in New York working with the FBI and DOJ teams, learning how we trace fraud, how we gather evidence, how we execute takedowns. He took our advice to heart and hasn't looked back. The student became the master. Why are you asking about him?"

"Just checking him out. I've heard he's impressive," Judd said.

"Akinola's been building cases and kicking in doors. He even took down a corrupt governor in Nigeria who was skimming millions off the state budget. You might have heard about it. Akinola's built a little anticrime empire over there."

"So Bola's succeeding in fighting corruption?"

"He's made a dent. He's uncovered links between politicians and Russian arms traffickers. He was behind the Interpol warrant for the Director of Customs after he traced funds back to a Colombian cocaine cartel," Isabella said.

"Bola was behind that case? I remember reading about it in the paper."

"Yes. He's certainly spread fear into the political class."

"So he's making enemies, too," Judd said.

"Any time you target powerful political elites, you put a bull's-eye on your back. That's rule one of corruption hunters: Corruption fights back. He's been investigating who's behind the pirate attacks and pipeline sabotage. He's gone deep into the Niger Delta militants. He's playing a very dangerous game."

"What does that mean?"

"Bola Akinola is in the devil's den," Isabella whispered.

"Are you saying that Bola's too close? That he's becoming corrupt?"

"You ever see the movie *Donnie Brasco*?" she asked.

"A mafia movie, I think." Judd tapped his fingers on the table. "What's your point?"

"Johnny Depp plays an undercover FBI agent who befriends a mobster played by Al Pacino. Depp's character goes deep inside the family. So deep that the line between criminality and justice becomes blurred. That's a very thin line."

"Are you saying that Bola Akinola, the head of the Nigerian anticrime unit, is becoming a criminal himself?"

Isabella shrugged. "To accomplish what he's done, Akinola needed to build relationships. He needed to get close to some very dangerous people."

"So DOJ thinks he's too close?"

"I couldn't say. But it's a good question, *amigo*." She picked up her menu. "What are you having for lunch?"

Judd stared down at the menu but wasn't seeing the words. Questions about Jason Saunders, Landon Parker, Bola Akinola, and Mariana Leibowitz all spun around inside his head. *Was Mariana handing me a valuable lead? Or sending me into a devil's den?*

"Who's your friend?" Isabella asked.

"What?" Judd cocked his head, confused.

"The SUV with foreign diplomatic plates," she said, keeping her eyes low. "The driver in the alley has been watching us."

Judd spun around just as a black Chevy Suburban bolted out of a side street and roared away.

15

R *ussia.* Sunday checked his data again and it kept coming back to . . . Russia.

The big question was why. And now Jessica Ryker was going to St. Petersburg. She hadn't told him more than she would be gone only a few days. While the rest of Purple Cell was digging for leads on the Bear, Sunday's clear instructions were to keep looking for patterns in the attacks on global oil facilities.

Kuwait, Venezuela, Equatorial Guinea, Iran, Algeria. He added the latest attack on the Chinese-operated platform offshore Nigeria when the control room was overrun and the staff all murdered. All sixty-four men. *What was the point of killing everyone?* Sunday thought as he typed.

In isolation, each incident could be explained. Business disputes. Organized criminal extortion. Local politics. Pirates.

Sunday knew the Nigeria flare-up was being blamed on militants in the Niger Delta. That oil-producing region was a maze of swamps and creeks that had long been a hot spot for armed groups. The trouble had all started as a legitimate complaint against oil pipeline leaks destroying the fishing grounds that local people depended on for a living. When their grievances were ignored, the protests grew over the lack of development. It wasn't lost on those who actually lived in the Niger Delta that the oil, *their oil*, was making lots of people rich in London, Dallas, and Lagos. But no one in the Delta. Even the regional capital, Port Harcourt, was shoddy, with potholed roads, unreliable electricity, and a broken water and sewage system. People were pissed off and fed up.

The Niger Delta militants gained notoriety after they began sabotaging pipelines and kidnapping oil workers. Groups started taking celebrity hostages, too, including the Delta state governor's daughter, the wife of the Port Harcourt Police Commander, and the star goalkeeper of the national soccer team, the Super Eagles. Each was released after a ransom was delivered, but the real payout was the front-page headlines. They justified their actions as fighting for a fair share and bringing attention to their plight.

Like so many rebellions that Sunday had analyzed, legitimate complaints turned to greed. The noble cause gave way to a petty thirst for cash. Militant groups morphed from freedom fighters demanding justice into criminal bands running extortion and smuggling rings. Gang leaders savored interviews on CNN, BBC News, and Al Jazeera, their faces hidden by ski masks, their pleading voices cut over dramatic clips of high-powered speedboats with mounted machine guns racing thorough the creeks. Email blasts sent to reporters around the world claimed attacks were on behalf of the Movement for the Emancipation of the Niger Delta, or MEND.

Locals, the Nigerian government, and the CIA all knew MEND was a public relations cover for any and every illicit activity in that part of the world.

But so far, Sunday concluded, attacks in the Delta were consistently for money or notoriety. No one had ever slaughtered a whole team. What would be the point of that? In fact, mass murder would make the oil companies invest more in private security and be less likely to pay future ransoms. The deaths would almost certainly force the Nigerian government to react even more strongly. They'd be obligated to deploy the Joint Task Force, the Nigerian military's special counterinsurgency unit with a notorious reputation for scorched-earth tactics. The Joint Task Force took no prisoners. And an American engineer, a father of two from Louisiana, was among the dead. This might get the U.S. Congress asking questions, which, Sunday knew, would mean that the Pentagon would be forced to get involved one way or another. Was that the reason Purple Cell was on this project? In anticipation of a

U.S. military deployment? To secure oil facilities? No, that didn't make any sense either, Sunday decided.

Whatever the rationale, Sunday knew that this latest attack on the Chinese platform was a clear escalation. *But it made no sense.*

Unless it wasn't the MEND or local militants after all? The brutal tactics were closer to those used by Boko Haram. That radical Islamic group operated mainly in Nigeria's northeast, far from the oil zone. They slaughtered young men and kidnapped girls as part of a terror campaign to chase away the central government and attempt to create an Islamic caliphate. Boko Haram might wantonly murder dozens of people, but . . . *why this?* They had never gotten involved in the oil-producing region before. And the Delta was a largely Christian zone, so the chances of expanding a caliphate there were close to zero. The tactics fit, but not the motivation.

Before she left, Jessica had insisted that Sunday try to find a link to Boko Haram. While the Pentagon shied away from getting sucked into the Delta, they were increasingly involved in counterterrorism operations in West Africa. The United States Africa Command, based in Stuttgart, Germany, had even sent a special operations team to Nigeria to help coordinate intelligence-gathering and kinetic operations against Boko Haram. If the extremist threat was spreading from the northeast corner of the country to the oil region in the south, then the U.S. government needed to know about it.

If true, Sunday's project would no doubt be quickly taken away from Purple Cell. This would go higher than AFRICOM.

If Islamic radicals connected to al-Qaeda and the Islamic State were now attacking Western oil facilities and killing American citizens, this was a major escalation that would pull in the Joint Chiefs, the Director of National Intelligence, the White House.

Jessica Ryker had been very clear that the Deputy Director wanted no stone unturned on this. If Boko Haram was involved in oil attacks, the CIA needed to know about it first.

The problem was that Sunday had found no such evidence. Nothing whatsoever pointed to Boko Haram.

Sunday's investigation had, however, found something unusual about this particular platform. It was situated in the middle of the Mega Millennium Field, which had been the subject of an unusually fierce bidding war because it was adjacent to a known geological formation that had already proven to be exceedingly profitable. While it was always in bidders' interests to hide the true value of an exploration block, it was clear that the Mega Millennium Field was a prized concession. In the end, the Chinese oil giant Sinopec had won after beating out bids from Italian, Russian, Norwegian, and American companies. The local papers were filled with accusations of impropriety, one paper even publishing photos of Chinese workers building a luxury villa on land owned by the energy minister.

Sunday's alternative theory was simpler: *business*. What if the attacks were part of a protection racket? Or a scheme to chase away competitors?

Sunday ran a statistical analysis on his database and calculated that Chinese companies like Sinopec and PetroChina had a seventy-two percent higher chance of suffering an attack than companies from other nations. Were the Chinese investing in especially dangerous places? Or were they being specifically targeted? If the latter, by whom? That would take more digging.

As Sunday stared at the data on his screen, he suddenly had another question. What nation was least likely to be attacked? Sunday typed a few keystrokes and the result popped once again onto his screen: *Russia*.

16

Mother Russia," said the Bear. "That is who we serve."

"Yes, of course, sir," the soldier snapped. He was standing at attention in a neatly pressed dark-green military uniform, a matching flat-top hat with red trim, and a gold leaf pulled low on his forehead.

The Bear was losing his patience. He shot a look of irritation toward Mikey, his bald British henchman sprawled on a white leather couch at the back of the room.

"Then why are you late?" Mikey asked, sitting forward and folding his hands on his knees.

"The train from Moscow, sir. There was a . . . delay," the soldier said.

"Bollocks. You having us off?" Mikey shook his head.

"Do we need to go back to Moscow?" the Bear growled. "About you wasting my time?"

"You wasting the boss's time?" Mikey parroted.

"No, sir. Perhaps next time we have urgent business that cannot be conducted over the phone, you could"—his Adam's apple bounced as he swallowed hard—"come to the capital?"

The Bear gazed out the glass window to the city lights below but said nothing.

"You suggestin' the boss should come to see *you*, my son?" Mikey sneered.

"I mean, sir," the soldier stammered, "I know the general would like to host you at his club in Red October. He has France's finest champagne. Moscow's finest girls. You could meet with the commissioner. Maybe the minister, too."

The Bear spun back to face the soldier. "Tell him," he said, gesturing toward his sidekick.

"The boss don't go to you," Mikey said. "The general, the commissioner, that wanker of a minister. That's why they send a mug like you. If they want to see him, they come *to the Bear.*"

"Yes, sir," the soldier snapped to attention. "I will report back that you prefer to continue to communicate through a liaison or to meet in St. Petersburg."

"The whole bloody Kremlin will come here if we want," Mikey said. "You tell them all who's boss."

"Yes, sir."

"You tell them to remember who made them rich."

"Yes, sir."

"You remind those tossers about who started this business and how it works."

"Um, yes, sir."

"Vodka and toilet paper," the Bear muttered, his eyes again locked on the twinkling lights outside.

"Sir?"

"Vodka and toilet paper," the big man bellowed. "That was the beginning. The commissioner issued the vouchers and I made them sell. I made them all sell *to us*. From the center, to the people, to us. That's how we built this. That's how it worked for the vodka distilleries and the paper mills."

"Yes, sir."

"And that's how it worked with steel and shoes. And that's how it's working with heroin and whores. Now that we're a global enterprise, our business model doesn't change."

"Yes, sir."

"They do their jobs and I do mine."

The soldier nodded and bowed his head.

"Now the boss has set you right straight, what do you want?" Mikey snorted.

"The general wants to know where we stand with the concession. Are we expanding or not?"

"Working on it," Mikey said.

"I don't think the general is going to be pleased. He sent me down here to get some answers about the next phase. Is Shenzhen accepting our offer?"

"We're taking care of it our way," Mikey said.

"So . . . no deal with the Chinese?"

"Wot did I just fuckin' say?" Mikey barked. "You fuckin' deaf? I just said *our way*. I just said there's no fuckin' deal."

The soldier cleared his throat. "I believe the general would prefer—"

"You tryin' to have a laugh? Do you know who you're messin' wif?"

"No disrespect."

"Didn't the boss just get done telling you how our business works proper? You tell Moscow we're doing it our fuckin' way."

"So . . . when?" the soldier asked. "The general already assured the minister the concession acquisition would be complete by now."

"We've had a minor setback," Mikey said smugly, sitting back in the sofa and putting his feet up on a zebra-skin ottoman. "Couldn't be helped. But now we're back on track. No more cock-ups. Our best man will be here soon to deal with Zhang-tao. A real proper naughty geezer. The Chinaman'll be sorted by end of this week. You tell Moscow there's nuffink to worry about."

"Mother Russia," the Bear mumbled to himself.

"What about the Americans?" the soldier asked.

Mikey forced a smile. "Them Yanks haven't got a fuckin' clue."

17

t's time to get funky!" the woman sang as she gyrated her hips to a heavy bass rhythm mixed with West African drumming. "Hello, world. Hello, my people. It's me, Funke Kanju, and it's time for the latest episode of *Let's Get Funke!*"

She danced to the music in a bright-red dress for a few more seconds in front of a green screen, one of her most beloved moves that had helped turn Funke Kanju into an Internet sensation across Nigeria and the diaspora communities in London, New York, and Houston.

This was the point in the show when the producers would insert her regular opening montage: Funke with a microphone weaving through the crowded streets of Lagos, Funke playing electric guitar, Funke sipping tea with the Nigerian President, Funke kicking down a door with jackbooted police officers, Funke smiling mischievously at the camera.

"Hello, world! Hello, my people! I'm sure you have all seen the news by now that the Lagos commissioner of culture and tourism has been arrested by federal police. I had the displeasure of meeting Mr. Kingsley Oluwa just last week. Ah-ah! What a man!"

The screen cut to a shaky single camera. Funke was standing in an orange-and-pink print dress outside a brightly lit hotel just as a long black Mercedes pulled through the security gate.

"Commissioner Oluwa, Commissioner Oluwa!" she shouted at the car, waving a bulbous microphone. "It's me, Funke!" The car slowed and the back window lowered.

"Mr. Commissioner, have you seen my latest movie, *Last Flight to Lagos*?"

"I wouldn't miss it," said a chubby face in the window. "I see all your films."

"Mr. Oluwa, what should government be doing to support Nollywood directors like me?"

"We are very proud of you," said the commissioner. "Nigerian movies are seen all over Africa. All over the world. Soon we will overtake Bollywood. And one day Hollywood!" he declared, flashing a two-fingered victory sign and a toothy grin.

"Ah-ah! So, what happened to the cultural arts fund?" she pouted.

The commissioner's smile evaporated.

"Where are the four hundred million naira allocated to the film festival at Benin City?" she demanded, shoving the microphone into his face. "How can you spend the festival fund but have no festival? How does that happen, Commissioner?"

The man tried to close the window, but Funke stuck her arm deeper into the vehicle.

"Is that how you afforded this car, Mr. Commissioner? With the money meant for Nigeria's young filmmakers?" she asked as the car rolled forward. "Have you spoken yet with the Crime and Corruption Task Force? Has the CCTF questioned you about the missing money? Have the police?" she shouted as the Mercedes sped away.

The shot cut back to Funke Kanju in the studio. She looked directly into the camera and scrunched her face. "Well, my people, what do you think of that? My interview with the commissioner of culture and tourism didn't go too well, did it?"

She shook her head and clicked her tongue. "I guess Mr. Kingsley Oluwa can now answer those questions for the police." A still shot of the commissioner in handcuffs appeared over her shoulder. She flashed a devilish smile at the camera.

"Well, enough about politics. It's time for the Nollywood Beat, oh! The most popular films produced in Nigeria this year . . ."

The show continued with its usual mix of popular culture, news, and the signature of *Let's Get Funke*, the peppy host's

muckraking confrontations with public officials. Funke's guer-
rilla journalism tactics had made her an online pop star. Her
TV show had also helped turn her into one of the country's
most admired filmmakers and a cultural icon for millions of
West African youth.

"Tomorrow is a big day," Funke declared. "Tunde Babatunde, the pride of Nigeria, will return home from America.
Fresh off signing a new seventy-five-million-dollar five-year
contract to play basketball for the Brooklyn Nets in New
York City! That's a lot of American dollars," she said, shaking her hand like it was on fire. "I'm going to meet him, oh!"
She smiled and stuck out her chest. "Our hometown hero is
sharing his success by donating the new Babatunde Hospital
for Children in central Lagos. *Let's Get Funke* will be there
for the opening ceremony. . . ."

But Funke's greatest success was far outside the public eye.
Her cell phone was flooded every day with tips about missing
money, government scams, and other boorish behavior of the
country's elected officials. She had become, more by accident
than design, one of the most valuable sources for criminal
investigation. And that had made her a secret ally of Judge
Bola Akinola's.

"Here is a question that all of us should be asking," she
said with a cheeky grin into the camera. "How many planes
does the office of the president require? Five? Six? Seven?
No!" she said, wagging a stern finger at the audience. "Eight,
chai!" She covered her ears and shook her whole body. "It
cannot be! But that's the truth. Eight airplanes for one presi-

dent! What do the men at Aso Rock have to say about this? Aah, notin'. But they cannot escape the truth forever!"

Funke passed on some of her juiciest tips to the Judge's Crime and Corruption Task Force. Bola would return the favor, pointing Funke to a particular piece of evidence that he couldn't reveal but that might, were it to somehow wind up on popular television, create a stir.

"I'm Funke Kanju and that's the end of another episode of *Let's Get Funke,*" she sang as the theme music began.

"That's a wrap," she said curtly as the camera light turned from green to red. "Good show, everybody. See you tomorrow."

A crowd quickly formed around her. Funke handed over her microphone to one aide and accepted a bottle of bright-orange Fanta. In among the staff a young man with bloodshot eyes held out a piece of paper and a pen.

"Sista', autograph?"

She smiled back at him. "How did you get in here?"

The man replied by pulling a snub-nosed pistol from his pocket and—*bang-bang-bang*—putting three shots into her chest and, once her body hit the floor—*bang*—one more bullet through Funke's forehead.

18

Jessica packed light, as usual. One change of clothes, toothbrush, passport, cash, three cell phones. That was plenty for a quick trip to St. Petersburg. Going via Paris, Dubai, and Istanbul was an inefficient route but necessary under the circumstances. Jessica threw the items into a shoulder bag and walked downstairs.

"I'm going now, sweets," she called out. She *hoped* it would be a short trip. Get in, meet the Bear, convince him that she was his secret assassin Queen Sheba, get the next assignment, and then get the hell out. Quick, painless, and back home before anyone even noticed.

She checked her carry-on again, finding a baggie of stale Cheerios and a copy of *Treasure Island*. Items left over from a past family trip to Fort Lauderdale. That was one hell of a vacation. Everything had nearly come crashing down in Florida.

J essica had the confidence of a tightrope walker. As long as she looked ahead and kept moving, all was fine. But if she tried to peek down, to contemplate everything she was doing and how it was affecting others, she would start to wobble. She'd start to wonder about her choices. Even worse, if she glanced backward, she would certainly topple over.

Her past was one of the secrets Jessica kept from her husband. She had told Judd about being born in Ethiopia, about witnessing her parents being murdered right in front of her eyes, fleeing to America, being raised by adopted parents. Revealing all that was unavoidable after the events in Zimbabwe. She'd had little choice but to explain to him why she'd gone to such lengths. And why she had had to manipulate her own husband into abetting murder.

And then there was Florida and their close call on a Cuban naval ship. Judd now knew about her role in all of that, too.

What she hadn't told Judd was how this all was affecting her. How revenge, which had burned inside her for decades, when it finally came, brought no relief. Jessica had, since the moment she watched her mother die, been deliberate in everything she did. Planning her every move, stripping sentiment away, doing whatever had to be done without emotion. She was cold and calculating. She was a machine on a mission. That was how she lived. That was how she thrived.

But now Jessica wanted to stop. Learning to be a mother and a wife was nothing like her other vocations. To her total surprise, neither serving her adopted homeland nor satisfying her personal bloodlust was ever as nourishing as creating a family. *How clichéd,* she scolded herself. But it was the truth.

Jessica was still accepting this realization. She decided that she needed to show her feelings. Exposing weakness was okay. Having doubts was normal. Emotions were human. She now wanted to be passionate, even if it meant being less effective. Being less perfect. She told herself: *Be more like Judd.*

Judd appeared in the doorway of their home office. "You're going already?"

"I'm late," she said.

Judd frowned. "I didn't realize you were leaving so soon. I hoped we could have a quick dinner before you go."

"Sorry," she pouted. "Maybe you can order pizza for the boys."

"Sure."

"I won't be long, Judd. The sitter arrives in the morning. She'll make breakfast, get Noah and Toby to school and back, and then watch them until you get home from the office. I've arranged everything."

Judd was trying to hide his disappointment that she was leaving. He knew the deal.

Jessica had supported him at every stage in his career. She had followed him to Amherst, she had adapted to the genteel rhythms of family life, and she had even agreed to the abrupt move to Washington, D.C., on short notice, all in good humor. Jessica had made endless compromises for him. She allowed—encouraged, even—her data geek partner to take a major gamble by leaving the safe and cozy life of academia for the trenches of the U.S. government. She encouraged him to test his ideas in the real world, to take some risks.

Ever since his move to the State Department, Jessica had been his advisor, his gut check, and, when necessary, his cheerleader. Even as Judd learned the ways of Washington, and his Crisis Reaction Unit was racking up small victories, he was never quite comfortable. He was never sure what was real and what was theater. Was he really succeeding? Was S/CRU pulling strings behind the curtain? Or was Judd a puppet in some larger game?

Jessica was always the analytical one. She was thinking three steps ahead, laser-focused on helping Judd achieve his goals, always keeping him on track. Judd was too emotional, too seat-of-the-pants, too filled with self-doubt. Judd was too willing to let his emotions cloud his judgment. He knew that he needed to be a bit more cold and calculating. He told himself: *Be more like Jessica.*

A re you listening to me, Judd?"

He snapped back to the present. "Yeah, I got this."

"If you have to work late tomorrow, just let the sitter know. She can sleep over if you get in a real jam."

"I'll be fine. The kids will be fine," he said. "When did you say you'll be back?"

Jessica shrugged. "I'll text you when I know. If I'm not home by Saturday, Toby has T-ball at nine, Noah's swimming lesson is at eleven. Got it?"

Judd nodded. "And *where* did you say you're going?"

She gave him an exaggerated scowl.

"If it's an evening departure from Dulles, then you're probably going east. To Europe." He scratched his chin. "I'm guessing . . . Moscow?"

"Don't do this, Judd."

"If you're still working on Russia and it's not Moscow, then somewhere warm and wonderful. Siberia?"

She kissed him on the end of his nose. "I promise not to have any fun without you."

"I'll take what I can get," he said.

"Every place has its charms," she said. "Even Siberia."

"Or, everywhere is dangerous."

"Most places are both." Jessica played along. "The world is wonderful and dangerous at the same time. That's how it is."

"Well, I'll be right here in warm and wonderful Washington, D.C. I'm not going anywhere with this London missing persons case."

"I'm glad that you'll be home, here with the boys, while I'm traveling," she said. "They need some time with you. You need it, too."

"Just be safe," he said, giving her a kiss on the lips. "I told you, Jess. I got this."

DAY THREE

WEDNESDAY

19

LAGOS, NIGERIA

WEDNESDAY, 10:44 A.M. WEST AFRICA TIME (5:44 A.M. EST)

The homecoming celebration had begun at sunrise. The party was in full swing for hours by the time it approached the big moment. A semicircle of young, muscular boys pounded a frenetic hypnotic rhythm on goatskin drums shaped like giant hourglasses. In the center, a dozen women danced, their hips shimmying impossibly fast, cheered on loudly by the audience. A banner overhead declared "Opening Ceremony of the Babatunde Hospital for Children: Investing in the Future Means Investing in Our Children."

Overlooking the ceremony was an implausibly tall man watching from an elaborate throne underneath a white sun umbrella. Throngs of people in Nigerian traditional clothing and Western business suits surrounded him. Cameramen wandered through the melee, logos emblazoned on the cameras from several local television stations, CNN, ESPN, and the publicity department of the National Basketball Association.

At a break in the dancing, a rotund fellow in a traditional flowing Yoruba *agbada* robe seized the microphone. "Ladies and gentlemen, notables, friends. We are here to celebrate the greatness of Nigeria!" The crowd roared its approval.

"Before I turn to our guest of honor," the man bellowed, "I want to acknowledge all of the people who made today possible and who bless us with their presence." The emcee went on to thank the governor of Lagos state, the minister of health, the minister of public works, a long list of local councilmen, the head of the women's league, the ambassadors from Switzerland and the United States, and most of all the Almighty God.

A special thanks was then provided to a heavily perspiring white man in a black suit, the vice president for emerging market product development at the Muller BioTechPharma Corporation. The Geneva-based company had pledged to donate free antibiotics to the new hospital as part of its global corporate social responsibility campaign. The pharmaceutical giant was thanked for this investment in Africa's children and also for sponsoring the jollof rice and mango juice for today's party.

"All protocols observed," declared the emcee. "Now I want to bring onto the stage our guest of honor and the reason we are all gathered here today. For those of you who do not speak the Yoruba language, you will not know that 'Babatunde' means 'the Father has returned.' Indeed, today one of Nigeria's great patriots has returned to open the Babatunde Hospital for Children. The Oba of Lagos has declared a new chief of this area. Ladies and gentlemen, notables, friends, I give you our son, our father, our newest ambassador to the world, the NBA Eastern Conference's leading shot blocker for three years in a row, our nation's shining light, the patron of the hospital we are opening here on this blessed spot. . . ." The emcee took a deep breath for his big finish. "I give you Chief Tunde Babatunde!"

Tunde stood up to his full towering height of seven feet two inches and waved to the applauding throngs. He read a brief prepared speech about the importance of children, why youth are the future, and how he always wanted to give back to his country of birth, to the land of his parents. He ended his moment onstage with an enormous smile for the cameras and a ceremonial cutting of a red ribbon across the front door of the hospital. A long line of well-wishers and VIPs then took turns posing with Tunde for the cameras, each hoping that their photo with the famous giant would be the one shown on television.

A picture of Tunde Babatunde surrounded by a crowd would indeed soon be in newspapers and televisions across the world.

After festivities wound down, Tunde folded himself into the back of a limousine and sped off to his hotel on Victoria

Island. The big man relaxed, stretching his legs as far as he could, exhausted but satisfied with the day's events. He was sure the Babatunde Hospital would be a success and confident the media coverage in Lagos and New York would be positive. Maybe he'd parlay the publicity to finally launch the line of designer sportswear he'd always dreamed of. Maybe basketball shoes, too?

As Tunde's limo crossed over one of Lagos's many bridges, something hit the windshield with a *splat*. A bird? A rotten papaya? The driver tapped the brakes and jerked into another lane.

"What the—" Another quick *splat, splat, splat* hit the car until the entire front glass was covered. The windshield wipers strained against the debris, smearing the muck and making visibility worse. Now driving blind, the driver veered the vehicle sharply to the side of the road, screeching to a halt.

"Sorry, sorry!" the driver yelped. Then Tunde felt a violent jolt as the limousine was forcefully rear-ended, catapulting the basketball player onto the limo floor. Shouting erupted outside the car, deep voices barking orders in a language Tunde didn't know. As he tried to regain his bearings and sit back up, the rear passenger door flew open.

A masked man aimed an AK-47 at Tunde's head. "Chief, you are now with us."

20

I t's an honor to be able to speak at the Council on Foreign Relations," Congressman Shepard Truman said, opening his breakfast comments. He was perched at the head of a long U-shaped conference table packed tight with council members, the business and political elites of New York who regularly assembled there to get the inside scoop on world affairs. "I'm always pleased to speak here, just a stone's throw from my own district, New York's proud Tenth. As a member of the House Energy and Commerce Committee as well as the House Oversight Subcommittee on National Security, I want to talk this morning about the future of global energy markets. And how American policy is falling short."

Truman sat up straight in his chair, his dark-gray suit highlighted by a round red-white-and-blue medallion on his lapel, his official congressional pin that allowed him to walk freely into the Capitol Building. "I recently led a congressional delegation to visit with parliamentarians in our emerging energy partners in the Caribbean, West Africa, and the South China Sea," he said. "And I didn't like what I found. I didn't like it at all."

Truman waved away a waiter offering him coffee and a cheese Danish.

"First, I saw a shortage of American companies in the places where our future energy will be produced. Oil, natural gas, and geothermal are all expanding as the technologies are being deployed to find and exploit resources in new places. Countries that had never before been energy suppliers are now entering the market as a result of rapid advances in modeling, detection, and extraction technologies. But I didn't see many companies from New York, Texas, or elsewhere from these great United States. Our energy companies should be out there, at the cutting edge. But I didn't see them," he said, shaking his head.

"Second, I did see China. Our Chinese competitors are aggressively expanding their presence into the emerging energy regions of the world and securing long-term contracts to ensure supply for their growing middle class, their burgeoning cities, and their escalating energy demands."

The Congressman cracked the knuckles on his left hand.

"It wasn't only China. I saw companies from Russia, Turkey, India, and across Europe, all making strong plays for new energy resources. It's clear that our competitors are all pushing hard to magnify and diversify their energy supplies. Now, we are fortunate in the United States to have been blessed with our own energy bounty. We have oil, gas, coal, hydro, wind, and sun. We are fortunate to have every kind of energy source that you can imagine right here at home. But, at the same time, we still do not produce enough energy to meet all our needs. And therefore we cannot concede every promising new global energy source to our competitors." He looked sternly around the room. "Our national security depends on it. Our future prosperity depends on it."

The Congressman held up three fingers. "Third, I heard terrible stories of corruption. Oil and gas concessions are sold under the table. Decisions are subject to influence and extortion. Deals are signed on the basis of greed and graft rather than open, competitive markets. The bottom line is that the playing field is tilted and our companies are losing out. *America is losing out.*"

Truman pointed out the window toward Park Avenue. "I regularly hear from investors right here in New York who cannot get a square deal, who cannot protect themselves from the racketeers. We expect the highest standards from U.S. companies. We expect them to compete fairly, to pay their taxes, to adhere to the Foreign Corrupt Practices Act, to represent the United States proudly wherever they operate. But in too many places, this is becoming impossible because of the action and behavior of corrupt foreign officials."

He placed both palms on the cherrywood conference table. "To combat this growing scourge, I will soon be introducing new legislation in the House of Representatives. The Truman Amendment will require the U.S Department of Energy, the State Department, and the Department of Commerce to jointly issue an annual scorecard on the business practices of our major energy trading partners. In the most egregious cases, the legislation will allow for sanctions and other punitive steps to be taken against those who are stealing the future. Stealing *our* future," he said.

"The intention is to name-and-shame the countries where under-the-table contracts have become the norm, to focus our own government on the threat this poses for U.S. national security, and most of all to shine a bright light on the cancer of corruption. When business must operate in the shadows, we get shady deals. When business operates out in the open, in fair, transparent, and competitive markets, then we see how market capitalism works best. As Supreme Court Justice Louis Brandeis once said, 'Sunlight is the best disinfectant.'"

"The Congressman has to catch the shuttle back to Washington in a few minutes," interrupted the host, a woman sitting next to him with well-coifed black hair and a freshly pressed designer suit. "But he's generously agreed to take a few quick questions. Please remember, we are strictly *off the record.*"

"Thank you, Congressman," said an elderly man in a faded gray suit. "Those are some pretty strong words about

China, which is still our most important trading partner and the second-largest economy in the world. Aren't you concerned about igniting a trade war?"

"We're already in a war. I met with a senior executive at Wildcat Oil just the other day. They are one of the innovative American companies using the latest in seismic sensors and big data processing to hunt for new oil reservoirs in locations where oil has never been found before. He told me that they've lost four contracts over the past twelve months to unscrupulous foreign rivals. They just can't compete in places where government officials allocate licenses based on gifts and bribery. We cannot stand for this. If this ruffles feathers in Beijing, I can live with that."

The host pointed to a young woman at the far end of the table. "We've seen a crackdown on corrupt practices in Thailand and Nigeria recently. What more can the United States do to support those efforts?"

"They don't go far enough. The Justice Department has assisted police departments overseas on select cases. But these don't begin to scratch the surface. I'm talking about a global system that's rotten to the core. Not a few bad apples. I grew up right here in the city, you know. And in New York you don't bring a flyswatter to a knife fight."

"Are you proposing a budget plus-up for DOJ's foreign anticorruption support programs?" she asked.

"That's something we'll be looking into," Truman answered. "If the Justice Department needs more resources, we'll just have to find them."

"Final question before the Congressman has to run," the host said, pointing to another council member.

"Sir, we've seen a spike in attacks on American civilians abroad over the past twelve months. According to a recent report from the Council's Center for Preventive Action, overseas civilian kidnappings are up forty-two percent over last year. Will your legislation boost the capacity of the United States to respond to such incidents?"

"It's an epidemic and an outrage," he said, slamming a fist on the table. "More and more Americans are disappearing. Petroleum engineers, humanitarian workers, bankers, even tourists. That's something that we all need to take a close look at. What's driving the attacks? Who's behind them? How can we prevent kidnappings? And especially what new steps must our government take when such incidents occur. We all have a right to demand some answers from the Justice Department, the State Department, the White House. Just this morning, before I came here for breakfast, I spoke with a senior official at the State Department about just such a case. I can't go into any details, of course, but rest assured that I demanded that no effort be spared. All American hostages must be brought home quickly and safely."

21

Ryker!" Landon Parker barked. The Secretary of State's chief of staff was standing again in Judd's doorway. "I've gotten another call from Congressman Shepard Truman. You need to go to Nigeria," Parker ordered.

"I'll have an update for you soon on Jason Saunders. I don't think going overseas will be necessary. I've spoken with the FBI, consular services, and the embassy in London. It seems his employer HHQ—"

"No, no, no," Parker interrupted, shaking his head. "Truman didn't call about that, Ryker."

Judd cocked his head to one side and winced. "Not Saunders?"

"Keep working on that case. Sure. Keep at it. But right now I've got another one for you. This is strictly close-hold for now."

"Another one what?"

"Tunde Babatunde has been kidnapped."

"The basketball player?"

"In Lagos. Roughly three hours ago. It hasn't hit the press yet, but when it does, they'll go bananas. The team's owner called Truman, and Truman called me."

"And that's why you're here now," Judd added.

"Exactly. I need you to get Babatunde back before anything goes public. Let's end the story before it starts. Seal it before it leaks. Kill it before it crawls."

"So Saunders bumped the South China Sea, and now Babatunde is bumping Saunders? Is that right, sir?"

"You're my firefighter, Ryker," Landon Parker said, taking a seat and shoving a stick of gum in his mouth. "I need someone who can handle hostage negotiations without getting the press involved, without creating some interagency circus that gets bogged down. We're going to need Shepard Truman on the House Oversight Subcommittee. I'm sure you understand how important it is that he knows State is being helpful on this. So that's why I need you."

"Got it."

"One of the owners of the Brooklyn Nets, Harvey Holden—

"Harvey Holden from HHQ?" Judd interrupted. "The same firm where Jason Saunders works?"

"I don't know."

"Isn't that a coincidence?" Judd scowled.

"Ryker, I've been in government too long to believe in conspiracies. All I know is that Holden wanted to bring in a private security outfit to handle hostage negotiations and execute the exchange. But I told him no ransom, no outside contractors. Let us get him back safely. Give State a chance to turn this disaster story into one about a hero. He's given us forty-eight hours."

"Two days? That's impossible."

"Well, that's what you've got, Ryker. Until Friday morning. The team wanted to call in the newspapers and the mercenaries. Truman promised the owner that we would handle it quickly *and quietly*."

"And that's why you're here," Judd said.

"That's why I'm here," Parker repeated. "Get Babatunde back before anyone knows he's gone."

"No press, no interagency, no circus," Judd said.

"And no ransom," Parker said, popping in a second stick of gum. "The United States government doesn't pay ransom."

"Hostage negotiations aren't my expertise. You know that, right, sir?"

"You got the four soccer dads back from Cuba. Just do it again."

"Don't you think that this would be better handled by the FBI—"

"The FBI's out," Parker said dismissively. "They already screwed the pooch on this one."

"What do you mean, 'already'?"

"I can't share any details. Hell, I'm not even supposed to know. But I think you should know. The FBI has been conducting a sweeping covert investigation of corruption in foreign embassies here in Washington. Ambassador Katsina, Nigeria's representative here in D.C., is one of the targets. It's damn inconvenient timing."

"Ambassador Katsina? Is she corrupt?"

"Who the hell knows?" Parker shrugged. "But we sure as shit need the Nigerians right now. With Boko Haram. With these attacks on oil facilities. The peacekeeping operations in Sudan, Kosovo, and Lebanon. They're rotating onto the UN Security Council next year. We're going to need Nigerian cooperation on about a dozen critical issues of national security. Guns, drugs, terrorism—you name it and we're working with the Nigerians on it. The FBI's timing is total shit, Ryker. Whatever has the FBI all spun up about Katsina, it can't possibly be as important as what we're trying to do. I need Ambassador Katsina right now."

"You need her? On what?"

"On everything, Ryker. She's my backchannel to Aso Rock, to the Nigerian President. When I need to talk to him, to get something done, I call her, and she makes it happen. You get that, right?"

"Of course, I do, sir. We're going to need the Nigerians to help get Babatunde back, too. If the FBI wraps up Ambassador Katsina, that'll definitely complicate matters. I wouldn't expect any cooperation if we detain their ambassador."

"Exactly my point, Ryker. You get it. That's why it can't be the FBI on Babatunde. It has to be you."

"Can you get them to delay any arrests, at least until we've got Babatunde home safely?"

"The FBI Director is going to throw a shit fit if another department tries to tell him how to run a criminal sting. I'm not even supposed to know about it. But I'll find a way to hold them off. I'll buy you a day or two, but probably not much more."

"I can't do this by remote control. I'll have to go to Nigeria," Judd said. He'd turned on the mental faucet, his mind filling with a long list of people he'd need to speak with before he was wheels up: *the Nigeria desk officer, the hostage specialist at the crime bureau, the regional security officer, Jessica, Sunday, and* . . .

"That's what I said when I walked in here, Ryker," Parker said, standing up to leave. *"You need to go to Nigeria."*

"I'm ready. But I don't think I have enough time to get to Lagos, even if I catch the flight—"

"Already thought of that. You're going private."

"A private plane?"

"Courtesy of Harvey Holden. His long-range Gulfstream is already on its way. It'll be at the executive terminal at Dulles and ready for the flight to Lagos at noon. That's in three hours."

"Is that even allowed? Can a State employee take a private plane on official business?"

"Unclear," Parker said. "But if we wait for the lawyers to

give us a ruling, it'll be too late. Sometimes it's better to ask for forgiveness than seek permission."

"Yes, sir."

"I knew you'd get it, Ryker. Let my office know if you need anything else."

"Just one thing, Mr. Parker," Judd said. "My chances of success—*our* chances of success—would be greatly increased if I had a capable partner."

"Who? You want Gordon from policy planning?"

"No. I need someone from law enforcement."

"I just told you that the FBI is out, dammit." Parker spit his gum into the wastebasket. "Weren't you listening, Ryker?"

"Not the FBI. Someone from the Justice Department."

"Justice? Who?"

"I need someone special. I need Special Agent Isabella Espinosa."

22

Don't drive so fast, Chuku," Judge Bola Akinola instructed, pulling one of his four cell phones away from his ear.

"Yes, sah," replied the driver, swerving aggressively through traffic.

"Don't be nervous, Chuku. We are safe."

"Eh, chief. We are safe. But this is the bridge where Tunde Babatunde was kidnapped this morning. I'm not going to stop."

"That has nothing to do with us, Chuku," Bola said, tightly gripping the car's backseat handle with one hand and his phone with the other. "My greater concern is that you're going to crash. Or kill someone."

"Eh, chief. I will get us there safe."

Bola turned his attention back to his call. "Yes, Minister. I understand," he murmured. "But once an official inquiry is opened, there is no way it can be closed without cause. It has to be completed all the way to a conclusion. . . . Yes. . . . Yes, of course. . . . I assure you that will happen. . . . Yes, I will personally share your concerns with the lead investigator. Thank you for your call, Minister."

Bola hung up and picked up another phone.

"Chuku!" he shouted. "Slow down! You are a greater danger than the area boys."

"Yes, sah. . . ."

"This is Judge Akinola," Bola spoke calmly into the phone. "The police commissioner is expecting my call. . . . Yes. . . . This is the time. . . . No, I'm calling for the update on the Funke Kanju murder. . . . I demand to know what's happening. . . . Yes. . . . Yes. . . . Well, this is very pressing, too. Tell him I called again and I'm expecting a reply within the hour."

He changed phones and the tenor of Bola's voice shifted. "Eh, Zina, I hear you have gotten yourself into trouble again, my friend. . . . No, no, no, you have a choice, Zina. . . . You can let me help you or you can take your chances in the creeks. . . . It is up to you, Zina: You can let me help you or you can choose a long, slow, painful death. . . . Those are your only choices, Zina. . . . Eh, I will send one of my people to meet you. Azikiwe Street, by the entrance to the university, she will find you there. In exactly one hour. Be there or there is nothing I can do to save you."

Bola swapped phones again, not noticing a yellow minibus taxi that was lurching forward alongside his car. "Mama, how are you today? Is Auntie with you—"

"Crazy *danfo*!" Chuku shouted as the taxi swerved with several young men hanging menacingly off the side. The van's side door slid open, revealing a masked man shouldering an assault rifle.

"Go, Chuku, go!" Bola shouted and ducked.

A slight merciful pause, then the attacker unloaded his weapon, raking Bola's Mercedes with bullets, *rat-tat-tat-tat-tat-tat-tat!* The windows exploded over Bola's head and showered him with glass. The vehicles around them screeched their brakes, but Chuku didn't slow down. He jerked the wheel sharply and stomped on the accelerator, crashing into the side of the minivan. The traffic came to a halt and an eerie silence fell over the scene.

The next sound Bola heard was a spine-tingling shriek of metal scraping metal as Chuku forced the Mercedes along the minivan until the car finally pulled itself clear. By this time the armed man had gathered himself and stumbled out of the taxi. He moved in front of the van, taking aim for another round of shots at Bola through the rear window.

"Go, Chuku!" Bola yelled from the floor of the backseat. But rather than drive forward, Chuku yanked the transmission into reverse and accelerated backward. The Mercedes crunched into the van, crushing the shooter between the two mangled vehicles. Chuku then slammed the Mercedes back into drive, sideswiping cars as he sped away. Bola lay on the backseat, the only sensations the sound of his pounding heart and the smell of burning rubber.

The next thing Bola Akinola knew, Chuku had pulled the car through the security barrier of a gated shopping mall and come to a steaming stop. Bola tried to catch his breath.

"Eh, chief. We are safe."

23

'll be right back," Judd told the driver. He jogged from the waiting taxi into his house to grab the things he'd need. As he tore around his bedroom, Judd ran a mental checklist of what to take: emergency short-trip go-bag from the front hall closet, passport, BlackBerry, wallet, a roll of mints, and a packet of beef jerky. And his Boston Red Sox cap. That was plenty.

A horn blared from outside. "I'm on my way!" he shouted. What else did he need to do? He'd already called the sitter to watch the boys for a few days, cleared his schedule with Serena, and canceled the *Washington Post*. What was left, other than going to Nigeria to rescue a kidnapped basketball star?

And then get back home before . . . *Jessica.*

Judd pounded out a quick text:

> All good. Boys fine.

> Gotta quick trip 2Nigeria. Sitter moving in.
> Back before u. See u @home.

Then one last gesture.

> sorry xoxo

As he pressed SEND, the doorbell rang.

"I'm on my way—" Judd huffed, opening the door and reaching for his carry-on.

"Hello, darling," said an unexpected voice.

"Mariana? What are you doing here? I'm on my way out. Wait . . . how'd you know I was even home?"

"You promised me the United States wouldn't let a good man go down."

"What are you talking about, Mariana? I've got to go."

"Bola Akinola. You promised me you would help him."

"You're tracking me?"

"Bola's in trouble, Judd. That's why I had to find you."

"Look, Mariana. I've been looking into Bola and what's going on in Nigeria. Just like I promised. I'll push the crime unit at State and I'll do what I can with the FBI, too. But I can't do it right now. I've got to go."

"You're leaving?"

"I'll call you the minute I'm back," he said, trying to brush past her. "Something urgent's come up."

"It's urgent for Bola," she insisted, and stepped in front of him, blocking his path. "They're trying to kill him."

"Who?"

"I don't know who. Bola's got plenty of enemies. Maybe one of the governors or ministers he's put away. Or someone he's investigating. He's probably getting too close. But *who* doesn't matter now," she said, waving away his question. "Bola was ambushed today. They chased him down in traffic and shot up his car. He barely made it out alive."

"What happened?"

"I don't know details. They aren't important. But you can see I need your help." She took a deep breath. "Bola needs your help right away."

"Where is Akinola now?"

"He's gone underground. Into hiding."

"And what do you want me to do?"

"Help, goddammit!" she snapped. "Call the FBI. Call the CIA. Get the ambassador to storm into the presidential office at Aso Rock and demand they stand down! Go down and bang on the fucking front door of the Secretary of State's house if you need to!"

"Mariana, I'll make some calls—"

"The Nigerian government has to know that America cares about this," she demanded, grabbing Judd by both shoulders. "They have to know we aren't going to just sit by and watch them destroy a good man!"

"Have you spoken with Ambassador Katsina?"

"Katsina?" Mariana scowled. "The Nigerian ambassador is no help at all. I don't know what she's up to. But she's not going to help Bola. He needs *you*, Judd."

"How about I go to Nigeria and tell them myself?"

"You'll do that?"

"That's where I'm headed," he said, motioning toward the taxicab idling by the curb.

"You're going now? To Nigeria?"

"Nigeria." He nodded. "Right now."

24

Easy, chief. Easy, eh," said the voice. A firm hand gripped Tunde Babatunde's tree trunk of an arm, pulling the big man to his feet. The hand shifted to Tunde's back, leading the blindfolded basketball star out of the van and down a muddy path.

"Where are you taking me?" Babatunde demanded. This was their third change of vehicles since Tunde was kidnapped from his limousine in Lagos nearly five hours earlier. He could hear multiple footsteps around him. He could tell that the gang that had taken him was well organized and highly disciplined, like a tightly knit team of elite athletes who knew each other's rhythms. Or brothers. They had struck with smooth military precision and near-total silence. Only one man spoke.

"Keep walking," said the voice.

"How much do you want?" Tunde pleaded. "This is about money, right?"

"You know our fight, chief. We want justice, eh."

"I can get you money," Tunde said. "My agent in New York. Let me call him. He can get you whatever you need."

"Ehe. There is plenty of money right here in Nigeria. We only want what is ours," the voice said.

"Who are you? MEND? Are you taking me to a MEND camp?" Tunde asked as the ground under his feet changed from soft mud to a hard wooden surface.

"MEND is nothing," scoffed the voice. "They have become corrupt. Just like the others."

"Who are you?" Tunde swallowed hard. "Boko Haram?"

"We are the true freedom fighters, eh. For the people." A hand shoved Tunde forward. "For Nigeria."

"Maybe I can help you? Promote your cause. Get you training in America. Get you on TV."

"New York City?" asked another higher voice.

"Eh, yes, I can do that," Tunde said.

"Silence!" shouted the first voice, followed by a loud slap.

"If you let me go," Tunde said gently, "I will bring you to New York City. Courtside seats. Free tickets. Cash. School. Whatever you want."

The hand grabbed Tunde's shoulder, stopping him in his tracks. "Texas?"

"Texas? Yes, I go there all the time. Dallas, San Antonio. I go to Houston."

"Hakeem Olajuwon?"

"Yes, of course. I know him."

"You know Shaq? Kobe? Do you know . . . Michael Jordan?"

"I've met them," Tunde said. "Yes, if you let me go, I will take you to America. To Chicago. To California."

"Houston," said the voice. "I want to go to Houston."

"After New York City, we can go to Houston. If you let me go, I'll take you to Texas."

"There are many Nigerians in Houston, eh?"

"That's right. Plenty of Nigerians in Texas."

"The boys. They all root for you, chief," he said, his voice softening. "We watch you on the satellite. You are a hero to the boys in the creeks."

"Is that where we're going? To the creeks?"

"We are taking you somewhere safe. No one can find us there. Until they pay."

"Who will pay?"

"The president. The governor. The minister. The ones who steal our oil and give us nothing. They must pay. They have two days."

"Or what?"

"Or they will be sorry."

"Brothers, I am like you," Tunde pleaded. "I'm not a big man. My papa was a kerosene hawker. My mama brewed *ogogoro*. You know, push-me-push-you. You drink that?"

"Ehe."

"See? I come from the streets in Lagos. I am like you. I can help you, my brother. I can help you tell the world about the problems in the Delta. We're all in this together. I am Nigerian."

"You are American," said the voice. "Get in," he said, pushing Tunde onto a plank that ran from the wooden dock down into an open-bow wooden boat. Once all the men had climbed in, the voice demanded, "No. You cannot trick us with your false promises. You cannot take us to America. No. *They must pay.*"

The outboard motor fired up and roared away, deep into the creeks of the Niger Delta.

25

hy would Russian oil companies be immune from attack? Sunday had run statistical analysis correlating the locations of Russian oil blocks with known areas of violence and found nothing out of the ordinary. He had examined Russian security protocols at their facilities and found nothing unusual there, either. If anything, Russian petroleum assets around the world seemed to rely on low-quality private contractors who applied especially lax protection measures. That should make them more vulnerable. But it wasn't showing up in the data.

By contrast, Chinese companies utilized extra layers of security: more men, tighter procedures, top-of-the-line monitoring, larger physical buffer zones. The Chinese assets were hardened targets.

Yet the database that Sunday had built showed exactly the opposite—that Chinese facilities suffered the most. Why wouldn't militants choose the soft targets?

Could it be fear of Russian military? Moscow had once responded to an attempted seizure of a Russian oil compound in Azerbaijan by sending in a special forces Spetsnaz kill team that retook the site. A classified CIA report concluded that the Russians executed all the attackers on the spot.

The Chinese or Indians or Turks would never be able to deploy such a force or get away with such tactics. Neither could the Europeans. The U.S. military had bases in the Persian Gulf and plenty of forward operations near oil regions of the Middle East, but they had not been directly involved in rescue operations for private companies. For years the U.S. Africa Command had run war game simulations for the potential capture of oil assets in Nigeria. But AFRICOM had never come close to real-life deployment. Neither the Africans nor the oil companies themselves had ever wanted American boots on the ground.

But that still didn't answer Sunday's question. *What was the Russian connection?* At that thought, Sunday's phone rang.

"Aaay," he answered.

"This is Judd Ryker," said an impatient voice on the other end.

"Dr. Ryker, um." Sunday paused. "Nice to hear from you.

I still owe you a favor for connecting me with your friend over at the Justice Department."

"Yes, sure, Isabella was happy to help," Judd said quickly. "I'm sorry to call out of the blue, Sunday, but something's come up."

"Of course. Why don't you come over to Langley? I won't be able to say much over an open line, you know."

"I can't. I'm at Dulles already. On my way to Nigeria."

"Very cool. But you know I never work on Nigeria, right? On account of my parents being from there."

"Yes, I know. But I'm sure you follow Nigeria's politics closely."

"Of course."

"You know anything about advance fee fraud?" Judd asked. "You know, 419?"

"I get those emails like everyone else. Don't tell me you fell for a scam, Dr. Ryker?"

"Ha. Of course not, Sunday. Do you know how they work?"

"The Yahooze Boys work in teams. They send out thousands of letters and emails and then wait for someone to respond to the bait. They're just fishing for easy marks."

"So it's random?"

"Usually."

"What about aiming a 419 at a specific target?"

"I've heard rumors of crime cells creating a shadow list, but I've never seen any evidence that it really exists."

"A shadow list?"

"Target lists. But that's just Nigerian street folklore. It's probably nothing."

"What about kidnapping for ransom?"

"Sure, it happens sometimes in Nigeria. Just like Mexico and Colombia and the Philippines."

"You ever analyzed kidnapping patterns in Nigeria? Or ever worked on a case when the U.S. government tried to get hostages back?"

"I'm sorry, Dr. Ryker. That's not the kind of thing they usually ask of an Agency analyst."

"That's fine, Sunday," Judd said. "Just one more question before I let you go. You ever heard of Bola Akinola?"

"Judge Akinola?" Sunday nearly squealed. "Are you going to Nigeria to meet the judge?"

"So you do know him?"

"Judge Akinola's famous in the anticorruption world. He's taken on some of the most notorious criminals. And politicians."

"So I've heard. He's supposed to be Nigeria's modern-day Eliot Ness. You know, the cop who got Al Capone."

"*The Untouchables.* I've seen the movie."

"Is Akinola solid? I mean, do you think I can trust him, Sunday?"

"Nigeria is . . . a complicated place, Dr. Ryker. I couldn't say for sure without doing a deep dive. Is that what you're asking me to do? Dig into Bola Akinola?"

"That would be great. Don't go out of your way, but anything you can do to help would be appreciated, Sunday."

"Sure."

"I'm sorry I can't tell you exactly why."

"I'm used to it. I guess we're even now."

"Thanks, Sunday. Text me if you find anything."

"Dr. Ryker, um . . ."

"What is it, Sunday? I've got to go."

"You know what happened to Eliot Ness's colleagues, right?"

"No, I don't remember," Judd said, with a slight hesitation.

"They all died."

"What's your point, Sunday? Are you saying he's in imminent danger?"

"Akinola is always in danger."

"Should I be worried? Is that what you're saying? That I'll be in danger if I meet Akinola?"

"Do you know what happened to Funke Kanju?"

"Who's that?"

"You're going to Nigeria to meet with Bola Akinola and you don't know Funke Kanju?"

"That's why I'm calling you, Sunday. Spill it."

"She's the investigative journalist with the TV show that's always exposing corrupt officials. It's very popular among young Nigerians. I watch her all the time."

"Should I go see her, too?"

"You can't. She's dead."

26

Jessica strode off the Air France flight and beelined for her next meet. The Dubai airport's hallways were jammed with Western businessmen and Arab families. She brushed past a cluster of women in all-black Saudi *abaya*s, peeping through their veils into a brightly lit shop window displaying handbags by Prada and Louis Vuitton.

Jessica entered the duty-free store and found the sporting goods section, which was packed to the ceiling with jerseys and fan gear for the 2018 FIFA World Cup in Russia. She paid cash for a green backpack emblazoned with the Brazilian flag and then quickly moved on to her next stop.

Without slowing down as she walked, Jessica slipped her

passport, wallet, and air ticket into the backpack and slung it over one shoulder. When Jessica arrived at McGettigan's Irish Pub, she took a seat at the bar and placed the backpack on the stool next to hers.

"Grey Goose, rocks," she said to the barman.

"Hendrick's and tonic, twist of lemon," called a voice next to her in an elite British accent. The man was South Asian, probably Indian, wearing an expensive and finely sculpted business suit. "Do you mind?" he said apologetically, signaling to the stool.

Jessica shrugged and moved the backpack to the floor between them.

"So you fancy Brazil?" the man said, settling into the seat.

"Desculpe, senhor," she said in perfect Portuguese, without looking at him.

"No time to chat. Very well," he said in the Queen's English.

"I'm late for my flight," she said.

"England is looking mighty good for Russia, don't you agree? This is our year to win the World Cup. Just like '66."

"You won't get through the group stage," Jessica said matter-of-factly in English with an accent that hinted of the favelas of Rio de Janeiro. "England was a disappointment in Brazil in 2014. I predict it'll happen again."

The man was about to reply when their drinks arrived. "I've got these, love," he said, slapping down a fifty-pound note. "Cheers."

Jessica held up her cocktail, nodded, and sipped her vodka.

"The world's gone mad," he said, setting down a carefully folded newspaper on the bar. She glanced at the business section of that day's edition of the *Times*. A headline caught her eye:

Another US Oil Co Withdraws from Indonesia

JAKARTA—*Texas-based Wildcat Oil LLC announced today that it has relinquished its controlling interest in an offshore oil license in Indonesia following a series of attacks against its employees. This is the third overseas operation that the privately held Wildcat Oil has closed this year. Analysts suggested a deteriorating environment for frontier market prospects. . . .*

Jessica drained her drink. "*Obrigada*. Thank you. Good luck to England in Russia." She slipped the man's newspaper under her arm and stood to leave without the backpack.

"Anytime, love. Good luck to Brazil," he called out.

Jessica walked briskly along the airport corridor, then into the women's restroom and directly into a stall, where she locked the door. Sitting on the toilet, she tipped the contents of the newspaper onto her lap: an envelope stuffed with euro notes, an Emirates Airline first-class ticket to Istanbul, and a new Brazilian passport. She flipped to the passport's photo of herself and quickly memorized the name and birth date.

Time to go. She stood to leave, when she had a second thought. Jessica pulled a BlackBerry from her jacket pocket and powered it up. The lights flickered, a few moments later the phone connected to the local network, and then the phone pinged three times with text messages, all from Judd.

> All good. Boys fine.

> Gotta quick trip 2Nigeria. Sitter moving in. Back before u. See u @home.

> sorry xoxo

Fuck, she hissed to herself. *Judd's going to Nigeria?*

She quickly flipped through the *Times*, searching for anything on West Africa. In the World News section, she found only two minor items.

Crime Wave Hits Nigerian Metropolis

LAGOS—*The murder of Internet television star Funke Kanju is the latest attack on prominent Nigerians in the past month. The Lagos Deputy Inspector General of Police released a statement denying any connection between Kanju's death and the disappearance of football legend Nuhu four weeks earlier. . . .*

Jessica's eyes moved on to the next item.

Nigerian Judge to Face Corruption Charges

ABUJA—*Nigeria's attorney general today announced a formal inquiry into the business dealings of a former supreme court judge charged with leading anti-corruption investigations. The surprise move was sparked by allegations in the local press that Judge Bola Akinola, chairman of the Nigerian Crime and Corruption Task Force, had failed to accurately account on his asset disclosures for luxury properties held in Monaco, London's posh Mayfair neighborhood, and a villa in the Cayman Islands. The attorney general declined to provide any further details of the inquiry, but sources within the Ministry of Justice confirmed that the judge was being suspended from the CCTF and that criminal charges were expected soon. Akinola could not be reached for comment. . . .*

Jessica tossed the newspaper into the trash and ran for her gate.

27

Judd squirmed in his seat, thinking about the long flight ahead. He'd just finished sending a text to his highly capable assistant Serena, asking her to dig around discreetly for more on Ambassador Katsina. He needed to know what Landon Parker was really up to. He tucked a pillow behind his back and tested out the recliner. The soft leather seat went fully flat, perfect for sleeping.

"Hey, not a bad way to fly," he said, bringing his seat back upright. "Beats cattle class."

Isabella sat across the aisle, peering out the window and ignoring him. She was steaming.

"If you have to go to Lagos at the last minute, this is the

way to go." Judd nodded to himself. "You ever flown in a G550?"

Isabella still didn't reply, her eyes laser-focused on the truck outside refueling the plane.

"Isabella, I'm sorry to pull you into this. But I need your help. I wouldn't have asked for you if I didn't."

"Do you have any idea what you've done, Judd?" she turned on him. "I'm in the middle of something big. Probably the biggest case of my entire career. Months of work. It's all coming to a head. Everything I've been working for. It's all building up to right now."

"And I messed it up?"

"My team was saddled up and ready to roll. Three, two, one, and . . . the phone rings. The goddamn attorney general's office telling me to stand down. My whole operation is on hold because someone needs me to go to . . . where? Nigeria. *Qué jodienda!* Why? For some State Department *pendejo*. I just knew it had to be you."

"I'm sorry, Isabella," Judd said.

"Liar," she hissed. "You're not sorry."

Judd knew she was right. "What's the case?"

"I can't say. You know that."

"If it helps, this will be a quick trip."

"I've heard that before. How quick?"

"I don't know."

"Of course you don't."

"If we can sort everything out in Nigeria and get back

here, then you can get back to your case. And I'll be moving onto something big. Landon Parker has—"

"It's not all about you, Judd," she snapped. "There are other people in this town trying to do their jobs, too."

"How could I know? You should have just said no."

"I can't say no to the United States attorney general. Just like you can't say no to Landon Parker."

Judd knew Isabella was right. He was doing Parker's bidding yet again. "So, what happens to your case now?"

"The AG put Donatella Kim in charge while I'm gone."

"Is that bad?"

"She's fine. Donatella's a Special Agent like me. We came up through field training together. She's good. But she's not me. It was my case. And I'm on this stupid plane with you going to West Africa."

"Well, I'm glad you're here," Judd said.

"You haven't even told me *why* we're going to Nigeria."

"I will. Once we're wheels-up." Judd put his hand on her arm. "I'm sorry I pulled you off your case. Let's go to Nigeria, fix the problem, and get back here so you can rejoin your friend Donatella."

"You should have asked me before you had Parker make the call," she said in a low voice. "We could have avoided all of this with a little backchannel communication. If you need me, *you call me*. You don't have your boss call my boss. That's not the way this is supposed to work."

Judd was deciding how to respond, when his phone rang.

"Speak of the devil," Judd said, and pressed the answer button. "This is Ryker."

"You on schedule?" Landon Parker snapped.

"Yes, sir. On the tarmac now. They're just refueling and then we'll be en route to Lagos."

"Excellent, Ryker. Do us proud. Bring Babatunde home safe and sound."

"I will, sir."

"I'll let Congressman Truman know you are on schedule."

"One more thing . . ." Judd hesitated.

"Make it quick, Ryker. We've got the Chinese foreign minister here today. It's a cluster and I'm late."

"I need your preauthorization for political asylum for Bola Akinola. It's spelled A-K-I—"

"Who the fuck is that?"

"A Nigerian judge. He's been working with DOJ helping to uncover corrupt government officials. But now he's going to need U.S. protection. So I need you to tell the ambassador—"

"Is the judge already in the embassy? Why haven't I heard about this?"

"No, sir. He's in hiding. But he's going to come into the consulate in Lagos once I'm in country—"

"No, no, no," Parker interrupted. "Tell him not to do that. No way."

"Excuse me?"

"Call him off. We can't get entangled in Nigeria's domestic

politics. Not right now. Not while we've got these other problems," Parker said. "Ambassador Katsina—"

"Katsina? What does she have to do with this?"

"Ambassador Katsina has been extremely helpful. I told
you already. If we start meddling in their internal affairs, it's
going to throw everything off. Think about the optics, Ryker.
The timing is for shit. We can't do this right now."

"I need it, sir."

"Hell, our ambassador's not going to like it, either."

"That's exactly why I need you to preclear Akinola's asylum. The embassy will slow-roll and then it'll be too late to
help him. You have to authorize it before I land."

"Why exactly would I do this, Ryker?"

"His life is in danger."

"And I care about this judge why?"

"Bola Akinola is one of our allies. He's the one fighting
against the cartels and the corrupt politicians. He's standing
up for democracy. For everything we're trying to do in Nigeria. We can't give up on him now that his own government is
trying to kill him."

"Christ, Ryker! His own government? What is going on in
that place? Kidnapping, scams, corruption. Now we have to
save this judge from himself? Is everything falling apart over
there?"

"Things fall apart. That's why you have S/CRU. That's
why you're sending me. I need this."

Judd listened to Parker's breathing, waiting for a reply.

"Sir? Can you hear me? I need you to send a cable to our embassy in Nigeria. I need you to ensure that we can give sanctuary to Judge Bola Akinola when he shows up at the consulate."

"What do you suggest I tell Ambassador Katsina?"

"Tell her whatever you want," Judd said. "Horse-trade. Give her something she needs. Maybe make her think we have some dirt on her to buy some time."

"*Do* you have dirt on her?"

"I need asylum for Akinola, sir," Judd said, intentionally avoiding an answer to Parker's question. *Better to let him wonder,* Judd decided.

Parker paused, then groaned. "Okay, Ryker. I'll do it. I'll have my office alert the consulate. But don't let this judge business sidetrack you from your mission. You're going to Nigeria to find Tunde Babatunde."

"Thank you, sir."

"And, Ryker, be careful."

The pilot arrived in the cabin. "We're ready to go now, sir."

Judd nodded back.

"I will, Mr. Parker."

"Your mission is hostage recovery. Don't forget that. You can help this Judge Bola-whatever, but nothing gets in the way of rescuing Babatunde. I'm counting on you."

"Yes, sir," Judd said, and hung up the phone, a satisfied smirk appearing on his face.

Judd Ryker had gotten what he wanted from Landon

Parker by keeping his boss happy, by projecting a convincing pretense of compliance that was *just good enough.* Judd knew Parker was almost certainly doing the same thing with Shepard Truman, keeping the Congressman off his back by providing assurances, by promising that he was doing everything possible. Parker was probably on the phone with Truman already, reporting that the special State Department rescue team was on its way.

And then the game of favors and façades would be passed down the line. Judd wondered who Truman would be calling next, running the same line of assured promises. Everyone was pursuing their own goals, playing each other in a dense web of confidence games and smoke screens. Judd was getting the hang of it. And that begged the question: Who was playing *him?*

As the jet engines revved up, Isabella Espinosa's face softened and a tiny smile appeared at the edges of her mouth. "We're going to see . . . Bola Akinola?"

28

Huan was dying to get out. He'd been inside the compound walls for more than a hundred days straight and was feeling claustrophobic. Company rules dictated that all senior employees stay on campus unless escorted by an armed security detail. Many of the engineers got out regularly, Huan knew. They inspected the pipeline, visited with their local counterparts, and occasionally stopped at a restaurant for grilled meats and a cold beer. Sometimes they even met local women.

But not Huan. As the company's senior on-site account manager, his job was to stay in his office and oversee the money. He paid the salaries of local workers. He procured food, drinking water, and whatever else the teams needed to keep producing in the heat of tropical Nigeria. He also ensured that cash payments were made on time to ensure the safety of his colleagues and the continued flow of oil. This all meant staying put. Staying inside the walls. The most exercise Huan had gotten for the past three months was a morning routine of tai chi and an occasional ride on his bicycle around the dirt path just inside the compound perimeter.

But today Huan needed to be free. The office felt like a prison cell. He needed to breathe the air on the other side of the walls, out in the open, just for a few minutes. That had worked in Venezuela, Turkey, and Algeria. Why not Nigeria?

Huan locked his office door and grabbed his bicycle. He rode around the usual path, stopping at the main security gate to light a cigarette. The security guards barely noticed him. They also didn't notice Huan and his bicycle slip behind a departing supply truck and out the gate.

Once on the other side, Huan felt a surge of adrenaline. He stood up high on the pedals and raced the bike like an excited schoolboy along the road into town, a cigarette dangling from his lips. As soon as he was far out of sight of the compound gate and confident he'd gotten away cleanly, he slowed his pace to take in his surroundings. The colors were brighter and the sounds sharper than he remembered. He passed hawkers' stalls selling green fruits and rainbow mounds of used clothes, a crowded petrol station, a buzzing taxi stand, a bright yellow-and-red Mr. Bigg's fast-food restaurant.

An Asian man on a bicycle in the middle of town might have turned heads ten years ago. But the presence of so many Chinese in the country lately had transformed him into just another part of the new Nigeria. While Huan was trying to absorb everything around him, to enjoy his brief moment of freedom, none of the locals paid him much attention.

Except one boy on a cheap motorbike who had followed Huan from the gate.

After twenty minutes the accounts manager decided it was time to head back. He pulled off the busy main road and down a residential street. As he did, the motorcycle cut him off.

"Hello, Chinaman," said the boy, his narrowed yellow eyes projecting menace.

"What you want?" Huan scowled.

"Where you going, Chinaman?" the boy asked, stepping off his battered Jincheng two-stroke.

Huan tried to pedal away, but the boy grabbed his handlebars.

"I say, where you going, eh?" the boy huffed.

"What you want?" Huan repeated. "No trouble from me."

"No *wahala*, Chinaman." The boy pulled a pistol from his waistband and pointed it at Huan's chest.

"No money! No money!" Huan shouted, holding up his hands and letting his cigarette fall to the ground.

"No robbery, eh," the boy laughed. "I work for Oga."

"Oga?" Huan lowered his arms and bent down to pick up

the smoking cigarette and put it back between his lips. "Which Oga?"

"The big one. The boss man," he said, waving the pistol.

"I already pay Oga. Every month."

"You pay?"

"I pay! I pay! You call Oga. He tell you I pay already. That's the deal. We pay. No one bother us. You keep the company safe."

"You have cigarette?" the boy asked, with a nonchalance that made Huan nervous.

Huan pulled a packet of imported Chinese smokes from his pocket and tossed it to the boy. "Take it. No gun!" he pleaded. "We have a deal."

"I know you pay," said the boy. "Oga tell me. Oga send me to find you, eh."

"What?"

"Someone else pay more."

"What?" Huan winced. "Who pay more?"

Pop, pop, pop. Three bullets fired from the gun burst into the Chinese man's stomach. Huan crumpled to the ground, bleeding from the holes in his gut.

"You pay. Someone else pay more, eh."

29

I brought you Chinese food," Serena announced with a smile, holding up a paper bag. "Pork lo mein and those shrimp dumplings you like."

"Oh, that's my favorite," said the executive assistant from behind her desk in the outer lobby of Landon Parker's office. "You spoil me."

"Yes, I do," Serena said. "That's what old friends are for. I haven't even begun to pay you back for all you've done for me."

"Well, thank you. You're sweet." The assistant lowered her voice. "You heard about what happened in London? With Ambassador Tallyberger?"

Serena shook her head and leaned in close.

"There was an incident at the Dorchester. That's one of those fancy hotels near the embassy. The police had to be called."

"What happened?"

"Diplomatic security is hushing it up, but I heard from one of the public affairs officers that they had to drag him out of the dining room." She cupped her hand and mimed like she was drinking from a bottle.

"That's too bad," Serena shrugged. "He seemed like a nice man."

The assistant sat back and contorted her face. "Puh-leeeze! Old Arnold Tallyberger? He's been nothing but trouble. Don't you remember what happened in Haiti?"

"That was terrible. I'm trying to forget what you told me."

"It's the forgetting that lets someone like that go to London, and then we have the police coming to drag him out. It's undignified."

"Some things are better not gossiped about."

"You probably got that right. Let's talk about something else. I heard Dr. Ryker is on his way to Nigeria. You got some peace and quiet, I guess."

"Nah. Not too much," Serena said casually. "Always chasing things no matter where he's at."

"I know that."

"Right now I'm trying to chase down the Nigerian ambassador. You know her?"

"Ambassador Katsina? She's a funny one. Real quiet, but

she knows what's going on. She was just here." The assistant jerked a thumb toward Parker's office door.

"Here? Seeing Mr. Parker?

"Uh-huh."

"And I missed her?"

"Uh-huh."

"I know Dr. Ryker was hoping to get a meeting with her once he's back. That's why I'm chasing. But she's slippery." Serena put her hands on her hips. "She might just be avoiding me."

"Could be." The assistant flashed a sassy smile.

"Is Katsina in here often? To see Mr. Parker, I mean."

"Four times in the past month."

"Four times? For the ambassador from Nigeria? That's an awful lot of face time for the chief of staff to give one ambassador, don't you think?"

"Could be."

"Any idea what they're talking about? Maybe it's relevant for what Dr. Ryker's working on?"

"I wouldn't know," the assistant said, opening the lunch bag that Serena had delivered. She stuck her nose inside and inhaled deeply. "It's all closed-door. But they're definitely up to something."

30

In her sixth-floor office, Mariana Leibowitz pressed the button on her treadmill to accelerate the speed. Forty minutes in, she was drenched in sweat and her heart was racing. But it wasn't the workout that was elevating her heartbeat.

Mariana was comfortable in high-pressure situations. She thrived on stress. The lobbyist had built her practice exactly by taking on some of the toughest clients in the tightest jams. At twenty-two, she'd moved from Miami to the nation's capital with bright eyes and brighter ideals. She wanted to use her publicity training and natural negotiating skills to make the world a better place. Mariana had gotten her start as a junior associate with a big public relations firm that represented foreign banks and embassies in Washington, D.C.

From the inside, she saw how the firm collected hefty fees but didn't deliver much for their clients. They arranged meetings, often with the wrong officials. They wrote press releases and, for a large bonus, placed op-eds in the newspapers, but usually to no effect. It was *a con*.

She increasingly realized that her own firm was taking on wealthy problem clients, but mostly playacting because actual resolution meant the end of the contract. They didn't want to solve clients' problems. They wanted those problems to drag on forever, along with a robust retainer. All the commotion was a series of clever diversions. *A con.*

The senior partner, a former intelligence officer who had lost his security clearance from drinking on the job, called them *decoy kills*. It was macho nonsense. The PR firm was generating a lot of activity, pretending to be working hard to eradicate a problem but leaving the actual source untouched. It was all theater to keep the cash flowing. It was all a confidence game. It was *all bullshit*.

Mariana held her nose and tried to learn the ways of Washington. But when her company declined to take on a jailed journalist in Egypt because the fee was too low, that was the final straw. Mariana quit to break out on her own.

Leibowitz Associates International, her new one-woman

shop, agreed to take the Egyptian case pro bono. She made a few phone calls, stopped by a few offices unannounced. She argued, cajoled, flirted, and horse-traded. Mariana triangulated between the State Department, the Pentagon, and the White House. She worked her meager contacts on Capitol Hill and in the newspapers. In the end, Mariana managed to get her client's plight into the talking points of the Undersecretary for Political Affairs during a stopover visit to Cairo. *Voilà*, two days later the journalist was free.

For that first client, Mariana had stumbled upon a winning formula. Make friends, collect information, trade favors, and, most of all, play American officials off each other. Turn the dysfunction and infighting inside the U.S. government to your advantage. If State and Justice won't talk to each other, if the Pentagon and the White House are bickering, that was exactly where a well-connected outside force could exert maximum manipulation. This was Mariana's secret to success. And fighting like a pit bull for your client.

Over the years, she'd created a successful lobbying business at a prestigious K Street address all on her own. She'd built a reputation as a D.C. operator par excellence. That's how she'd once gotten a private meeting with the Secretary of State for a no-name freedom fighter in the Congo. That's how she'd repeatedly managed to ensure that specific spending items would be quietly inserted into the annual 1,200-page appropriations bill. That's how she'd gotten the State Department to be aggressive after a coup in Mali that deposed the

President, Boubacar Maiga. And how she convinced Judd Ryker to work behind the scenes in support of human rights lawyer Gugu Mutonga in Zimbabwe. And that's how she planned to save the life of Bola Akinola.

As Mariana ran on the treadmill, she surfed the cable news channels. None of them were running anything on Nigeria. CNN was leading with the Secretary of State meeting with the visiting Chinese foreign minister to reduce tensions in the South China Sea. The screen showed U.S. naval warships on patrol, oil platforms under construction, and remarkably sharp Google Earth satellite photos of artificial islands the Chinese had built. Mariana grabbed the remote and changed the channel. *Flip.* MSNBC was reporting on the same story with the same stock video. *Flip, flip, flip.* Ditto over on the three networks. *Flip.* BBC News was running a special report on the end of the construction boom in Dubai. *Flip.* Fox News was airing a talk show arguing about the fortunes of potential future U.S. presidential candidates.

"A few months ago, I would have bet my left foot that our Secretary of State would be the next President of the United States," declared the on-air pundit, a balding man with tiny round spectacles in a split-screen box. "But after the foreign policy debacles in the Middle East, Mexico, and now the South China Sea, her candidacy is all but dead."

"I don't think the Secretary's quite dead yet," argued a tall blond woman in another box on the screen. "But she's on life support."

"If she's going to turn her fortunes around, we're going to need to see some progress with China during the foreign minister's visit today. I think this is do-or-die for the Secretary," said a third talking head.

"What happens with China doesn't matter as much as her ability to rally her own party. I mean, come on! How is she going to respond to the challenges coming from the governor of Idaho and Senator McCall from Pennsylvania?"

"What about Shepard Truman? The Congressman from New York is starting to gain attention. Politico is reporting this morning that he's met with key party donors to explore a Senate bid. Truman's a rising star—" *Flip*.

Mariana changed back to CNN and put the television on mute.

She decided to try again, sticking headphones into her ears and pressing REDIAL on her phone while she ran. The phone clicked, bleeped, and finally rang.

"Hello?" said a familiar voice.

Mariana punched the emergency stop button on the treadmill and tried to catch her breath. "Bola!" she gasped.

"Yes, Mariana. It's me."

"I've been trying to reach you for hours. Are you okay? Are you safe? Where are you?"

"I'm very okay," he said calmly. "Don't worry, my friend."

"But *where* are you?" she pleaded.

"I cannot say on the phone."

"Who's listening, Bola?"

"I cannot say. But I am somewhere safe. I have many friends and they are protecting me."

"For now!" she snapped. "I have someone coming to help you."

"Don't say anything more on the phone."

"He's a troubleshooter. He'll help. He'll give you refuge. At the place I mentioned before."

"Thank you. Again. But I don't need help," Bola said.

"He's already on his way. Maybe you can help him, too."

"Mariana, do you know about the tortoise and the crab?"

"What crab?" She wiped her face with a towel. "What are you talking about?"

"It's an old Yoruba creation story. The tortoise and the crab."

"Folktales?" Mariana exhaled. "Bola, you know it's a terrible cliché for an African to tell wildlife fables to his white friends."

"The crab and the tortoise are enemies. Everyone knows that."

"Of course, everyone," Mariana said sarcastically.

"Well, one morning the crab and tortoise are on the beach. It is a beautiful day and they both feel very good. The tortoise says, 'I am the strongest in the world.' The crab says, 'No, I am the strongest in the world.' They fight to decide who is strongest. But because both have hard shells, neither can hurt the other. The fight ends in a stalemate."

"Are we talking about Nigeria or Washington, D.C.?"

"Let me finish the story," Bola says. "So the tortoise says to the crab, 'We are both very strong, but our shells are so hard that no one can hurt us.' The crab says, 'You are correct. We are both so strong and well protected.' The tortoise agrees: 'We are both the strongest in the world.' 'Yes, yes,' says the crab."

"Is that it?" Mariana asks.

"Almost," Bola says. "Just as the crab and the tortoise are feeling good that they are both the strongest creatures in the world, a small boy walks past. He picks up the crab with one hand and the tortoise with the other. He takes them both home and boils them for dinner."

"Okay, Bola. I get it."

"I knew you would."

"Sure," she lied. "But I'm still sending my friend to help you."

"If you must."

"He's *our friend*. You can trust him."

"Very well."

"You have to be careful, Bola," she said. "They're going to try again to kill you. They won't give up."

"Someone is always trying to do that," he chuckled.

"You're laughing? You're telling animal stories? This isn't a joke, Bola!"

"This is Nigeria, Mariana. We laugh. We tell tales. We celebrate life. That's how we survive. Don't you remember?"

"I don't remember making jokes while someone was trying to kill me. What happens to all your hard work if you die? You aren't going to let them win. I won't let you let them win."

"Thank you, my friend."

"What for?"

"For sticking with me. For fighting for the truth. And for sending our new friend to me. As you wish, I will meet him."

"That's what I do, Bola. I'm not going to allow Washington to let a good man go down."

31

You're a good man, Shep," said the man raising a tumbler of special reserve Kentucky bourbon. "Here's to the next senator from the great state of New York."

The private room off the main dining area of the steak house was adorned with dark heavy wood panels and nineteenth-century antique lighting. The table was a heavy oak replica of one used by James Madison at the 1789 Constitutional Convention in Philadelphia. It was already laid out for the VIP and his seven guests with German steel steak knives and crystal wineglasses filled with a chewy single vineyard Napa Valley cabernet sauvignon.

The other men, all late middle-aged and silver-haired in

finely tailored gray suits, held up their pregame cocktails in agreement. "Hear! Hear!" they chanted.

Congressman Shepard Truman clinked his glass with the others and took a hearty gulp. "Thank you, Larry," he said, nodding toward the man who initiated the toast. "But it's still very early. This is only an *unofficial exploratory* committee. I haven't even gotten Barbara to agree yet. I'm working on my wife." He winked. "But I'm going to need all of you and your help if we're going to do this. That's why Bob's invited you here. To help me think through the options and the timeline. Bob, why don't you run through the agenda?"

"Let's get the business out of the way before the steaks arrive," said a skinny man in tortoiseshell glasses at the other end of the table. "I've already established the political action committee, the Friends of Shepard Truman PAC. For now, that will run out of my law firm's office and will be managed by Fred Faulkner. We're in the early stages of starting to gather initial donations from Shep's closest friends and family in case he decides to make a run. Shep's most likely opponent, District Attorney Arturo Osceola, already has the police union and that prick governor on his side. So, gentlemen, we're going to need deep pockets right out of the gate. The next steps are to identify leads to build the legal, financial, strategy, and communications teams. That's why I've asked each of you to be here today. You're being volunteered."

"What about oppo?" one of the men asked.

"Opposition research is quietly under way." Bob got up and closed the dining room door. "I don't want to say who just yet, but we've engaged a real bloodhound. We're also starting counter-oppo. Sorry, Shep, but it's unavoidable these days. Our bloodhound is digging into your life, too, searching for anything that Osceola might find first. If there's anything that we all need to know, Shep, now would be a good time to share it."

"Nope. I've got nothing to hide. Squeaky-clean. Bring it on," the Congressman said.

"'Bring it on,'" Bob repeated. "I like that. Larry, make sure you send that catchphrase over to the comms team."

"Before we go any further, Bob," interrupted one of the men, "why don't we hear from Shep about his platform? Before we jump into campaign strategy and mudslinging, I want to hear about motivation and messaging. That's what the big donors are going to want to hear before they write checks. What's the Truman vision? Are you running on taxes, health care, or terrorism?"

"Good idea, Ralph," the Congressman said. "I'm going to run on three issues: corruption, corruption, and corruption." Shepard expected this would come as a surprise, but none of the guests reacted. "I know most campaigns are about what the candidate can deliver to constituents. It's all about favors. It's all about pork. 'What can you do for me?' Whose back can you scratch? Well, I'm sick of it. I'm sick of how Washington works. I'm sick of taking phone calls from demanding donors. You can't believe some of the nonsense I do for them. And that's just for a House seat. It'll only get worse in the Senate."

Truman took a deep breath. "So I want to run in exactly the opposite direction. I'm going to run a pork-free campaign. No favors. No deals. I'm going to run against corruption in the Senate, like selling earmarks to the highest bidder. I'm going to run against corruption at home, like no-bid construction contracts. And most of all I'm going to run against corruption overseas. I'm going to stand up for American companies to force a level playing field in foreign markets."

"So it's a pro-business campaign?" asked one of the men. "That'll play in the city."

"I've had enough of watching Chinese oil companies steal contracts out from under the noses of American companies by cutting crooked backroom deals," Truman continued. "I can't talk about it, but you wouldn't believe what I've seen. Bribery, extortion, kidnapping."

"Kidnapping? What are you talking about, Shep?"

"I think the American people have had enough of this crime and corruption, too. I want to put a stop to it. To kick things off, I'm going to introduce the Truman Zero Tolerance Amendment on the House floor. It's a series of reforms at home and abroad to reduce the ability of criminals to poison our country. We're going to start by limiting political contributions to curry favor."

"Law and order hits in the polls," said one of the men. "It'll play upstate and on Long Island."

"Sure, you run with the kosher thing, Shep. No one's against that. But how about we hold on domestic campaign finance and lead with foreign corruption?" suggested another. "That's less sensitive."

"Yeah, I'm with Fred. An earmarks ban'll be a heckuva tough sell with many of the party contributors. No one likes horse-trading, except when they're doing it. Don't quote me on this, old boy, but the whole point of political donations is to curry favor."

"Larry, you had the restaurant swept for bugs, right?" Truman joked. "You never know who's listening, boys." Truman then turned serious. "I know this might present a problem for some donors. But I believe we can rally support for zero tolerance. If we stand up for what I believe, the money will come. I think the electorate is ready. I think this is what ordinary people want."

Just then, a team of waiters invaded the room. Eight martini glasses piled high with jumbo lump crab were placed in perfect unison in front of each guest. "We begin with Maryland's finest," said the headwaiter. "For the main course, will it be the usual?" he asked.

Truman nodded. "Eight cowboys, José."

"Very well. Eight thick-cut bone-in rib-eyes. I will tell the chef," the waiter said.

"And another round of bourbon. We'll save the wine for the steaks."

The waiter bowed and led the staff back out of the room and closed the door tight.

"Before we go any further," said one of the guests, sitting

back in his chair, his arms crossed over his belly, "I think Shepard has to address the elephant in the room."

"Which elephant is that, Mort?"

"We're all adults here. We know how it works. Money doesn't just magically arrive because people like your speeches or some legislation. You'll be lucky if five percent of the electorate even knows about your zero tolerance bill. To win, you have to cultivate donors. You have to make promises." He sat forward. "If you want to win this thing, you have to cut deals."

"What are you saying, Bob?" Shepard asked.

"We've all read *Politico*. Hell, it's been on Fox News all morning. Everyone in this whole town knows that Shep wants to run for Senate. And we are all here today because we believe Shepard Truman would be the best candidate for the party and a great senator for the state of New York." Mort looked the Congressman directly in the eye. "But what we don't yet know is how you'll be competitive. If you go squeaky-clean, where will the money come from?"

DAY FOUR

THURSDAY

32

After twelve hours in the air, it felt good to escape the tube of the private plane. Judd poked his head out of the aircraft door. At the bottom hummed a huge black SUV and a thick-necked security officer with a wire in his ear.

"Welcome to Lagos, sir."

A quick passport check at the VIP lounge, a handshake with the airport manager, and an exchange of gifts with a mid-level foreign ministry official, and they had arrived. Judd Ryker and Isabella Espinosa were in Nigeria.

The moment the embassy vehicle slipped through the airport gate, the sirens began. A three-car police escort led the way, clearing the road like a snowplow in a blizzard.

"Is this necessary?" Judd asked the security officer, holding on tightly to the side handle as the SUV veered aggressively between two trucks.

"Lagos protocol, sir. The Nigerians don't want a visiting VIP stuck in traffic."

"Traffic? At this hour?"

"It's for your own safety, sir," he said as they nearly sideswiped a crowded minibus jam-packed with commuters.

Isabella eyed the security officer. "Tell him to slow down, Officer. We can live with a little traffic as long as we get there alive."

"Not here, ma'am," he said. "This stretch of the highway is a hotbed for carjacking and kidnapping."

Judd and Isabella looked at each other.

"Don't worry," the officer tried to reassure them. "Kidnapping has become big business in Lagos. Just like Caracas, Mexico City, and Baghdad. Every wealthy Nigerian is at risk, as are most of the expats."

"Tell me again why we shouldn't worry," Isabella said.

"The embassy's never lost anyone."

Judd was deciding whether this was good news or not when his phone buzzed with a SMS from Serena.

LP 4 mtgs w Katsina in 4 wks. Something up.

Judd swore to himself under his breath.

"What is it?" Isabella asked.

"I don't know. Not yet."

Forty harrowing minutes later, they crossed the bridge onto Victoria Island and pulled through the security barriers at the U.S. consulate. Once the Marine guards had sealed the gate, German shepherds had sniffed the car, and the all-clear was given, the security officer opened the rear doors of the SUV.

"Welcome to Lagos," he said. "The ambassador is tied up in the capital, Abuja, and the Consul General is back in Virginia on medical leave. I'll be your control officer. I'm under instructions to assist you with whatever you require."

Judd and Isabella glared at each other again.

"I'll need an office with a secure line to Washington, a discreet vehicle with driver, and I want to see the senior political officer here at the consulate as soon as possible," Judd said.

"Done."

"I need to speak with the FBI liaison ASAP," Isabella said.

"Vacant." The security officer shook his head. "There's a DOJ detailee in Abuja on a short-term TDY, but no one posted here in Lagos right now."

"No one?" Judd asked.

"No, sir. We're short-staffed at the moment."

"That'll be all, Officer. Thank you."

"What about your guest, sir?"

"Guest?"

"He's waiting inside."

D r. Ryker!" announced the man sitting on the couch in the reception area. He was in his fifties, with a gray goatee, wearing an immaculate white Nigerian robe and a matching floppy hat.

"Judge . . . Akinola? Is that you?"

The man stood and gave Judd a bear hug as if they were old friends.

"I thought I was going to have to find you," Judd said.

"You have just arrived and Nigeria is a complicated place, my friend. How could you possibly know your way around Lagos?"

"I don't," Judd said.

"That's why you need a guide. That's why our good friend Mariana Leibowitz called me and asked me to help this important man, this Judd Ryker. That's why you need me. Any friend of Mariana's is a—"

"I thought I was coming here to help you, Bola."

"True, my friend. We will help each other."

Judd gestured toward Isabella. "Bola, this is my colleague from the Justice Department, Special Agent Isabella Espinosa. Isabella, this is Judge Bola Akinola from the Nigerian Crime and Corruption Task Force."

Bola shook Isabella's hand politely. "Pleasure to meet a fellow law enforcement officer," he said.

"It's a great honor to meet you, Judge," she said.

"You two don't know each other?" Judd asked.

"I know about Judge Akinola's anticorruption work," she said. "I know from my FBI colleagues that he built the CCTF and it's doing valuable work."

"Mariana didn't give me many details," Judd interjected. "What have you gotten yourself into?"

"Ahhh, Mariana. She is a good one."

"She's worried about you," Judd said. "She said your life is in danger."

Bola laughed aloud and shook his head. "Ahhh, Mariana. People are getting nervous, eh. I'm getting too close to make people comfortable." Bola faced Isabella. "But that is our job, no? To make the criminals uncomfortable?"

"Judge, we have authorization to provide you with immediate political asylum and transportation out of the country."

"Go to America?" Bola scowled. "Now?"

"Yes, sir," Isabella said. "You only have to make the formal request for political asylum and you'll be with us on the plane back to Washington."

"Just say the word, Bola," Judd said.

"Leave for the U.S.A.? Now? That is impossible," Bola said, shaking his head. "There is too much to do. I still have work here. I'm about to release my final report on who is behind the pirates. Perhaps one day I will need to escape. And I will need your help. But that day is not today, my friend."

"So, why are you here at the consulate?" Judd asked.

"Mariana said you need my help. Perhaps you are here for the basketball player, eh?"

"How do you know about that?" Judd hurriedly shut the door.

"Nigeria is my country. I know about the politicians, the criminals, the celebrities. I know the chiefs in the villages, the confidence artists on the streets, the boys in the swamps, the Ogas in the palaces."

"What's an Oga?" Judd asked.

"Oga is a big man, a boss."

"I see."

"Nigeria is full of many Ogas," Bola said. "That's why you need me."

Judd looked at Isabella, who raised her eyebrows in agreement.

"Tell me how I can help you, my friend," Bola said.

He took a deep breath. "Yes, you're right. We're here to try to rescue Tunde Babatunde. He was taken—"

"Yesterday morning. From the Third Mainland Bridge. I, too, was attacked there yesterday. But I escaped."

"I need him back. I need Babatunde free by tomorrow."

"You're in quite a hurry, my friend."

"Yes, I am."

"Just like Mariana," he smiled. "She's always rushing, this way and that."

"That's how we are. But I need Tunde Babatunde back by tomorrow. Can you do it?"

"How much?" Bola asked.

"How much what?"

"How much can you pay? That's how we get him back."

"The United States doesn't pay ransom. It's our strict policy. It's not the American way. We need another way to get him back. If this kidnapping gang is well known, maybe we'll get lucky and they're already under surveillance. What does the Nigerian intelligence service know? The President's national security advisor? The head of the police?"

Bola smiled reassuringly. "I will handle this the Nigerian way."

The judge pulled out a phone and turned his back to the Americans. He mumbled in a local language. He grunted, laughed, mumbled some more, then hung up. "It's done. Now we wait."

"Done? What do you mean?" Judd was aghast.

"Babatunde will be free. I'll have him for you tomorrow morning. The exact time and location will need to be confirmed. But as you wish, you'll get him tomorrow."

"How did that happen?" Judd's eyes narrowed. "What did you just do?"

"You want Tunde Babatunde back. I will get him back."

"But how?"

Bola took a deep breath. "Is it not better that you do not know, my friend?"

"How did you have the phone number of the kidnappers? I mean, how did you even know whom to call?"

Bola only smiled back.

"What are we supposed to tell Washington?" Judd asked.

"You will tell them you got their basketball player back." Bola put his hand on his heart. "And you did not pay any ransom."

Judd ran through all the inevitable questions he would face from Landon Parker.

"You don't know anything else," Bola said. "Because I'm not telling you."

"That's right," Isabella said. "If we will get Babatunde back tomorrow, you can tell the truth," she shrugged. "You don't know how."

"Don't you think it's suspicious that we arrive in Lagos, meet with a judge, and *voilà*, Babatunde is free?" Judd asked. "Is anyone in Washington possibly going to believe that's the whole story—that you can resolve a kidnapping with a simple phone call?"

Isabella shrugged again.

"Are you even certain it was a kidnapping, my friend?" Bola asked softly.

"Yes!" Judd insisted. "He was taken from his car on the bridge by gunmen. You know this."

"I know that sometimes things are not what they seem. Is this problem a kidnapping or a misunderstanding?"

"What?" Judd winced.

"If there is no kidnapping, then there can be no ransom. Am I not correct?"

"I don't understand, Bola."

"Nigeria, my friend," Bola said, planting a fatherly hand

on Judd's shoulder. "Nothing here is what it appears. You Americans come with your satellites and your drones, but you don't know the people. That's my job. To clean up Nigeria, I need to know the people, their relationships, their history, especially their obligations."

"Obligations? I don't understand."

"Precisely, my friend. That's why you have come here. That's why I can pick up the phone and solve your problem. That's why you need me. And when I come to America and don't understand your system, then I will need you."

"I still don't get it."

"Once we get Tunde Babatunde back tomorrow, you can go back home. Quickly and victorious."

"I like the sound of that," Isabella said.

Judd's mind was racing with questions that he knew were better not to ask. Questions where the answers would only make things . . . more complicated.

"So now we wait," Bola said. "What would you like to do today?"

A new idea flashed in his head. "What about advance fee fraud?" Judd asked. "Can you solve a problem with the 419ers?"

"Ahhh, the Yahooze Boys. What do you want to know?" Bola asked.

"Judd, what are you doing?" Isabella looked nervous.

"Another case. A missing American. We think he disappeared in London after getting entangled with a 419 ring. While we wait for Babatunde to be released, can you help me?"

"I don't think we want to ask the kind judge for another favor, Judd," Isabella said.

"Who is he?" Bola asked.

"A young bond trader named Jason Saunders. I don't know if he was a random victim or if he was . . . on the shadow list."

"Judd, please!" Isabella barked. "Don't waste the judge's time with rumors."

"I can connect you to the Yahooze Boys," Bola said nonchalantly.

"I really don't think that's necessary," Isabella insisted, gripping Judd's arm. "We need to get back to Washington ASAP."

"Bola can fix problems with a phone call," Judd replied, shaking off Isabella's grip. "As long as we got a free day."

"It's very okay, my friend," Bola said, standing between them and taking each of their hands in his. "Special Agent Espinosa, I will do this, too. For a friend. I will connect you to the Yahooze Boys who run the 419. Yes. I will introduce you to the Coyote."

33

Motherfucker, Jessica thought. The Deputy Director of the CIA was really messing with her this time.

She sat at a musty café on a dank side street off Nevsky Prospekt drinking bitter watery coffee and reading the morning *Izvestia* newspaper. The coffee was supposed to help wake her up after the sleepless last leg of her trip. A little caffeine to keep her sharp after the long flights and identity changes at stopovers in Paris and Dubai and Istanbul. But this coffee was dishwater.

She lifted the cup to force down another gulp, casting her eyes toward the alley and the back door to the nightclub. The

Kitty Kat Klub was closed at this hour, but there were three beefy men in cheap suits standing stiffly at the door, trying to stay out of a light rain. She noted multiple security cameras monitoring the door and at the entrance to the dead-end alley. *Motherfucker.*

Her mission was to convince the Bear that she was Queen Sheba—a superefficient contract assassin who was a creation of U.S. intelligence—and receive her next target. She had flown all this way, gone through all this effort, in order to discover the Bear's next move. Was his network expanding into lethal new businesses? Were they merely a criminal enterprise or was he connected into the FSB, the Russian security service? Into the Kremlin? *What was the Bear's game?*

Jessica was under strict orders not to kill the Bear. But first she had to find him.

A few hours earlier Jessica had landed at the St. Petersburg airport under cover as a United Nations official. Jessica had to admit that was a nice touch from the CIA station in Turkey. The UN passport ensured that a young black woman could enter Russia without too much hassle. She had already ditched that identity, along with any potential tails from Russian intelligence, by changing taxis and sneaking out through the back of the city's early-morning meat market. Now she was casing the nightclub, downstairs from where the CIA believed the Bear ran his operation. She just needed to get inside and upstairs.

This wasn't how Jessica normally operated. For a sensitive mission like this, she would have insisted on her own team constructing everything from scratch. Purple Cell should have originated the backstory, created her persona, run surveillance on the targets, determined her infiltration routes, mapped the risk contingencies, and simulated the exfiltration plans. It should have been her operation from start to finish.

Instead the Deputy Director had forced her into some half-baked story about a Russian-speaking Somali contract killer. The whole plan rested on the Bear believing Jessica's identity that she barely believed herself. Her proof would be her demeanor, her confidence, and one special little gift. It was anything but a normal operation. *Motherfucker.*

A shiny jet-black Land Rover pulled up to the club and one of the guards opened the back door. A pale bald man in a snug dark suit got out and quickly disappeared inside. She downed the coffee, threw a hundred-ruble note on the table, and strode across the street.

"Pardon me, is this the way to the Church on Spilled Blood?" she asked in flawless Russian to the tallest of the security men at the back door to the Kitty Kat Klub.

"Spilled Blood? Why would a pretty girl like you want to go to a place like that?" he asked, looking her up and down.

"It is beautiful, no?"

"The church is beautiful, but why would a girl like you go there when there are so many more"—he paused—"exciting things to do in Saint Petersburg?"

"Like what?" Jessica straightened her shoulders and playfully tilted her head to the side. "Where can I find some real fun?" she said innocently, taking another step toward them.

"You are in the wrong part of the city," another said brusquely. "You are lost."

"Lost?" she asked, moving closer.

The third, shorter man flanked to one side, the three goons now surrounding her in a tight circle.

"How did we ever find an African princess who speaks beautiful Russian?" the first one said. "Are you a student in Moscow?"

"Not a student," she said.

"A dancer?"

Jessica was close enough she could smell cigarettes on his breath. "Not a dancer." She held out her palms. "Can't you tell what I am from these?"

The thug winced in confusion. "A girl . . ."

Jessica slowly closed her hands into two tight fists.

One, she thought, looking out of the corner of her eye at the security camera trained on them. She counted *two,* using her peripheral vision to space the three men and judge the exact location and height of each. She sucked in a deep breath . . . *three.*

Her right fist collided with a bone-cracking snap on the chin of the tall man in front. As she drew back her right hand, she twirled and unleashed a sharp left, crushing the soft trachea of the second thug. As he grabbed his throat in agony and doubled over, Jessica released a back kick to the groin of the third man. A fierce uppercut to his nose sent the short one sprawling flat on his back. She spun and swept the leg of goon number two, then knocked him out cold with a quick snap punch to head.

She squared herself and faced the tallest goon, who was still dazed and trying to regain his balance. She snatched his wrist and violently twisted, spinning him around and dislocating his shoulder with a *pop*. Jessica grabbed the back of his head and held it up to the camera. A drip of blood oozed from his nostril.

A few seconds later the door buzzed and clicked open.

She released the man and surveyed the damage. Three down. Time to go to work.

"Not a girl. Not a princess," Jessica told them. "I'm the queen."

And then she stepped inside.

34

The sign out front was a nice touch. *Innocent Chop House.*

Kayode had come up with the name himself. Mama Oyafemi always made the most delicious home-cooked goat pepper soup and fried the sweetest plantains. It was only natural that her restaurant would provide the perfect front for his growing operation. The Innocent Chop House would deliver a secret cover *and a tasty lunch.*

Right now, however, it was nearly 6:00 a.m. and Kayode was thinking about . . . dinner. He had just finished a long overnight shift and he was famished.

Kayode loosened the belt around his jeans and walked into the main café. "Mama, I wan chop," he said to the woman sitting on a stool in the corner, huddling over a steaming cup of tea.

"Why do you still talk like that?" Mama Oyafemi scolded.

"I'm sorry. It's been a long night. What are you serving, Mama?"

"*Ewa* and *agege* is the special. It's almost ready."

"Beans and bread? I don't want breakfast," he pretended to whine. "What do you have for your five-to-nines?"

Kayode was right. Many enterprising Nigerians had a day job plus another side business, something to supplement their income by selling, hustling, scrapping—anything to get by during the off-hours: the *five-to-nines*.

"It's almost six o'clock, eh?" she countered. "You are too late."

"Please, Mama. I am working extra now. I need fuel."

The two of them bantered playfully back and forth in their usual way until she agreed to reheat a bowl of *edikaikong*, a hearty crayfish-and-meat soup, left over from the previous night's shift.

"Thank you, Mama," he said.

"Come back in ten minutes," she commanded.

Kayode returned through the back door into the hub of his operation, which he called Wall Street. His inspiration was the climax scene from his favorite movie, Eddie Murphy's *Trading Places*. Kayode had watched the film years ago on a TV powered by a car battery at a friend's house in Ikeja and he remembered howling with laughter at Murphy's cunning Billy Ray Valentine, a homeless black man who turns the tables on two greedy old rich white men, out-tricking the tricksters. He swapped the stolen intelligence with a false plant about orange juice futures! Ha! He had roared in laughter as they fell into the trap! And then, the big climax, Billy Ray took the old men for everything they had! It was one of the moments that led Kayode to become a Yahooze Boy in the first place.

In reality, Kayode's Wall Street was two forty-foot shipping containers connected end to end. He'd procured them, with a sizable discount, through one of the neighborhood boys who worked security at the Lagos port. Kayode had customized the inside into an efficient workspace, each long wall lined with computer terminals. This allowed Kayode to pace the center aisle and keep a close eye on his troops. A station at the far end of the container held the latest laser printer for special projects. Electric cables were tacked along the ceiling, connected both to the local grid and to a giant diesel generator chained to the exterior and guarded 24/7 by a rotation of Kayode's cousins. Lately the generator had been running nearly full-time.

At this early hour, each of the two dozen computer stations was occupied by young men and women, mainly teens plus a few veterans in their early twenties.

Kayode spied Femi, his youngest recruit at just fourteen, who was already showing great promise. He wandered over and read over Femi's shoulder.

Dearest Charles,

Your last letter was beautiful. I cannot wait for us to finally be together in Paris. For us to walk along the Seine, finally holding hands, feeling your warmth, finally seeing your face with my own two eyes! I was in Paris once as a young girl. Did I ever tell you that? I hardly remember anything. But I'm sooooo excited to discover it all over again. With you, my love.

:-{} xoxoxo

I'm so grateful for the money you sent, my savior Charlie! Thank you! thank you! Fortunately, the doctor accepted cash this time. But the bill was higher than expected. I hate to ask :(((but can you possibly send another $5,000? I promise this will be the last time I ask :))). I'm sooooo sorry to ask you again, but I won't be able to fly to France to meet you until I get the all clear from the hospital. Soooooo many tests! Dr. Menendez swears this is the last round.

Can't wait to see u. Je t'aime Charlie <3 <3 <3

With sincerest love,

Penelope xoxoxoxo

PS—I still owe you a nude picture. I'm working up the courage to take it. Next time! xoxo

Kayode had gotten his own start ten years earlier when he, like Femi, had been given an unimaginable offer he couldn't resist. A schoolmate had shown him how to use a computer to trick gullible foreigners out of a few dollars and invited him to join her crew. Kayode's English wasn't very good and his spelling was awful, but he quickly learned that these didn't matter. In fact, typos and mistakes could be an asset, an easy way of filtering out only the most susceptible. He learned that the key to success in this business, one of the lessons that he now passed to Femi and the others, was to find just the right target. Errors and inconsistencies were simple ways to finding the most vulnerable mark at just the moment of maximum weakness. Finding that sweet spot was essential to any con.

Of course, Kayode was torn about his career as a Yahooze Boy. Convincing weak foreigners to send you money in exchange for false promises was hardly the honorable life his parents had imagined for him. They wanted him to go to school, to become an accountant, but he had always loved computers. His profession was technically illegal, as per Section 419 of the Nigerian Criminal Code. The police regularly raided the Internet cafés and underground centers, rounding up the teenagers and holding them until a bribe was paid for their release.

So who was the more corrupt, the Yahooze Boys or the police? The big men who took the largest cut from any 419 earnings or the *bigger men* who lived in mansions on Victoria Island paid for with the stolen proceeds from Nigeria's oil?

On the streets of Lagos, the opportunities were few, and working at a computer, making real money, was infinitely better than hawking fruit or gum at bus depots. It was mind-numbingly frustrating to spill your blood and sweat to make a few naira, only to have most of it disappear into the pockets of a neighborhood boss man.

Being a Yahooze Boy was a creative outlet, using your wits and guile to make a living. It was a natural, even inevitable reaction to the lack of other options, the incessant power cuts, the lack of jobs, the crushing corruption that was keeping so many down.

Fortunately, Kayode learned quickly and was soon earning plenty of money to support his whole family. Eventually he had saved enough to launch his own crew and build Wall Street.

Now, at twenty-four years, Kayode was the eldest of his team and the boss. Or at least he *was* the boss until one fateful day when he received another offer he couldn't refuse.

Now Kayode and his team worked for the secret big boss, the Oga.

Kayode watched Femi finish his letter and hit SEND.

"Well done, eh," he said. The boy opened a new window and kept typing.

Dearest Andrew,

I miss u too! . . .

With the new Oga came new territory, new responsibilities, new opportunities for Kayode. And a slightly new name, better suited to his new role: *the Coyote*.

35

Jessica climbed the narrow stairwell to find a reinforced steel door at the top. A tiny black bubble camera in the upper corner told her whoever was inside knew she was there. *No turning back now.*

With both hands, she shoved hard on the door, which to her surprise gave way and swung wide open. *They're expecting me.*

Jessica burst into the lair to find a broad-shouldered man in a heavy wool coat sitting at a chunky wooden table. He was holding a fork in one hand and a large steak knife in the other, a steaming plate of brown flesh in front of him. The man, wearing wraparound sunglasses with his long hair slicked straight back, looked up without alarm and leered directly at Jessica. *The Bear.*

She said nothing and glared back.

The door behind her suddenly slammed shut, revealing the bald man in the suit she recognized as the one who had recently arrived in a Range Rover.

"Ooh da fuck do you fink you is?" he snarled in a thick accent from London's East End.

Jessica turned her back on the bald man and faced the Bear with a cold stare.

A few seconds of silence that felt like forever were eventually broken by a familiar metallic *click-clack.* Jessica felt the cold butt of a handgun against the back of her neck.

"Do you know who you're messin' wif? Let me off this bitch right now, boss."

Jessica didn't flinch and her eyes never moved.

The Bear set down the knife and fork. Jessica's heart stopped. She braced for her next move. She counted down: *three, two . . .*

The Bear's shoulders shook. Jessica stopped counting. The Bear's rumble grew from a hollow chuckle into a crescendo of full-bellied laughter.

"You saw what this daft cow did to me boys!" the bald man whined.

The Bear snorted again with glee, then stopped abruptly. "Did *you* see it, Mikey? Put the gun away. For your own safety."

Mikey hesitated for a moment, then shoved the pistol inside his jacket. "Who da fuck are you?" he hissed.

Jessica ignored the question.

"Would you like breakfast, my beauty?" asked the Bear, nodding toward the plate where blood pooled around a slab of overdone beef and boiled potatoes.

"I'm not your beauty."

"That was quite an entrance," said the Bear.

Jessica shifted her weight. "You asked me to come here," she said.

"I asked you?" he shrugged. "Who are you?"

"You know who I am," she said.

"I don't believe we've ever met. If you won't eat, my beauty, how about a drink?" he said, unscrewing a bottle of high-end Yamskaya vodka and pouring two generous glasses. He held up one glass and slid the other across the desk.

Jessica caught the glass and cupped it. "*Nostrovia,*" she said and downed the vodka in one motion.

"*Nostrovia,*" he laughed, and did the same. The Bear wiped his mouth with his sleeve, then announced, "Enough games."

"You called for the Queen Sheba," Jessica said. "I am here."

He sat back and studied her face, stroking his beard. "How do I know you are the queen?"

Jessica nodded toward the security monitor on the wall showing his three goons out on the street, still recovering from her ass-kicking.

"Impressive."

"I didn't come here to impress you."

The Bear jabbed his fork into the meat and watched the juices flow. "When you cut Valderrama's throat in Bogotá"— he took a bite—"did he scream?"

Jessica glared at the Bear for moment. "Valderrama didn't make a sound."

"That's disappointing." The Bear chewed aggressively as he looked Jessica up and down. "He deserved to suffer."

"It wasn't a knife and it wasn't Bogotá. Valderrama was Barcelona. Two shots to the back of the head. You know that."

"What about Goldstein?"

"Johannesburg. Car accident," Jessica said. "That's what's in the police report."

"And Zhang-tao?"

"Poison in his martini. Manila. Body dismembered and dumped at the port."

"She's takin' the piss." Mikey shook his head. "Zhang-tao is well enough alive. Evgeny just seen him on Monday."

The Bear cut another large piece of meat and forced it into his mouth.

Jessica plucked a small blue velvet ring box from her pocket and set it on the table.

"She givin' you a ring?" Mikey sneered.

The Bear swallowed hard, set down his utensils, and pried open the box. Then he met Jessica's gaze.

"Wot is it, boss?"

"Yes, my beauty," he said, spinning around the open clam-shell, showing the severed human finger inside. "What is this?"

"Zhang-tao," she said.

"Zhang-tao?" Mikey erupted. "That's bollocks."

"Check the fingerprint," she said, gesturing toward the finger. "And then you tell me who it is." *A good question,* Jessica thought to herself, not wanting to know whose digit she'd carried in her pocket and hoping that the CIA's new synthetic fingerprint overlay technology would prove good enough for the Russian.

"Zhang-tao," the Bear muttered.

"That's all that's left of him," she said. "The rest is in small pieces at the bottom of Manila Bay."

"Zhang-tao," he said again to himself.

"Enough. Why am I here?" Jessica demanded, trying to turn the tables. "Did you call me here because of one dead Chinese?"

The Bear didn't answer.

"I've delivered proof of death. Now pay the bounty and give me my next assignment," she insisted. "Or I'll walk out of here and you'll never see me again."

The Bear met her gaze.

"I don't care why you want to kill Chinese businessmen," she lied. "Just give me my money and my next target."

Jessica knew the next few seconds were crucial. Either the Bear would accept her and expose his strategy, and she'd gain critical intelligence to bring back to Langley, or he was going to give her nothing. If she walked away empty-handed, she realized, then she'd be burning Queen Sheba's deep cover forever, losing her chance to ever get the Bear. *Time to find out,* she decided.

"You have ten seconds," she said, clearing her throat. "And then I'm gone."

If I reach ten and the Bear doesn't blink, she thought, then I will have no choice but to kill him and his idiot Cockney sidekick. *Right here, right now.*

She counted in her head, *ten, nine* . . . the bald asshole has a sidearm and is closer . . . *eight, seven* . . . I'll grab the steak knife with my left and take him first, then . . . *six, five* . . . I just have to convince the Bear I am Queen Sheba . . . *four, three* . . . that I don't have a tell that gives me away . . . *two* . . . that the Bear can't read my tell . . . *one* . . . like Judd did.

36

U.S. STATE DEPARTMENT HEADQUARTERS, WASHINGTON, D.C.
THURSDAY, 1:02 A.M. EST

D r. Judd Ryker is on it." Landon Parker spoke confidently into the phone, hiding his irritation at yet another call from Capitol Hill. "I don't have an update from Ryker for you yet, but he's only just landed in-country. It's early tomorrow morning over there. . . . No, Congressman, don't mention it. It's no trouble at all. The State Department is open 24/7. . . . Yes, of course I'm still in the office."

Parker glanced at the clock on his wall, just above the photo of him posing with the Secretary of State and Bruce Springsteen.

"Yes, I'll keep you informed," Parker said. "Yes, I know we only have until Friday morning. . . . I'll send someone over to brief you first thing tomorrow. . . . No need to thank me, Shepard. That's my job. . . . I told you already that Ryker is my crisis specialist. He's the firefighter of Foggy Bottom. Our best man for the job. I told you that these kidnappings are always high-risk. Things go wrong all the time. We can't make any promises when it comes to these situations. But if anyone can bring Tunde Babatunde home safe, it's Ryker."

Parker set the phone down and his assistant's head immediately appeared in the doorway.

"Would you like me to reach Dr. Ryker?"

Parker stared at her as he tried to organize his thoughts. Truman seemed convinced that State was doing everything possible to find Babatunde. That was success right there. Ryker was on the ground doing . . . whatever he did. It didn't really matter. If Ryker saved Babatunde, great. Parker would get credit with Truman and pocket a major favor for later. If Ryker failed, then Truman would believe that Parker had done everything possible. The chief of staff had just told the Congressman he'd sent our *best man for the job.* What more could Truman ask? If it ever came to the worst possible outcome, a congressional inquiry, Parker could simply tell the truth. A Washington win-win.

Parker smiled at his assistant. "Not necessary."

"Should I call Embassy Abuja, Mr. Parker? Maybe our ambassador in Nigeria will have some information?"

"No," he said, taking off his wire-rimmed glasses and rubbing his eyes.

"How about I call the motor pool and have a car take you home, sir? You look like you need some sleep."

Parker shook his head. He had spent enough time on Shepard Truman and his kidnappings. He had real work to do.

"It's already after lunch in eastern China. Their foreign minister should have landed back in the capital by now," he announced, without having to check his watch. "I've got a long list of follow-ups from his visit. Get me Embassy Beijing."

37

Jessica felt the adrenaline surge from her toes up through her thighs, hips, chest, biceps, and out to her fingertips. Time slowed as she prepared to launch a lethal attack on the mafia boss and his henchman.

Then the Bear blinked. "It's not one dead Chinese," he said.

"What?" Jessica's body froze.

"It's not just one," he said. "We're going to eliminate them all. The whole list. Everyone standing in our way."

Jessica didn't move or say a word. She was trying to maintain peak fight intensity, but she felt the tension in her muscles retreating.

"You are central to our business plan," the Bear continued. "Queen Sheba, our entire expansion depends on you."

"I don't want to be part of any plan," she insisted. "Just give me my target."

"Transfer the money for delivering Zhang-tao," the Bear ordered to his sidekick, Mikey. "And give her the judge."

"That target's a cock-up, boss," Mikey said. "Remember, the Yanks."

"Not a problem," the Bear said. "Queen Sheba, you don't have a problem killing Americans, do you?"

Americans? They want me to kill an American judge? Maybe this is why the Deputy Director was so anxious. She shook her head. "I've done it before."

"Of course you have, my beauty."

"But the price is higher."

"Of course it is," said the Bear.

"Twice my normal fee," she said.

The Bear nodded without hesitation.

"Who's the target?" Jessica asked.

"The new war is over oil, my beauty," he said. "And we are in a fight to the death."

Oil? she thought. *Since when are Russian mobsters in the oil business?*

"The battleground has shifted. It used to be the Persian Gulf, Saudi Arabia, Iraq. That is now past history. The new battlefront, where the new money is going to be found, is in the corners of the western Pacific, of central Asia, in the waters off West Africa. That is where we know how to operate. That is where we have friends. That is our turf. And that is where we are building our new oil empire."

Where is this going? Jessica kept a poker face.

"Standing in the way," the Bear said, "is China."

China? That's why he's been targeting Chinese oil executives?

"There's a judge that has been making trouble for one of our business partners. That judge is your next target. He must be eliminated."

Jessica nodded.

"No quiet disappearance this time. It has to be public. It has to be spectacular. We need to send a message."

Jessica nodded again.

"And it has to be done . . . tomorrow."

"That's not much time."

"If you can't do it—"

"I can do it," Jessica snapped. "The target is a Chinese judge. You want it in all the papers. I can be in Beijing tomorrow. Or Hong Kong or Shanghai. Not a problem. But you just said"—Jessica narrowed her eyes—"Americans."

"The judge is working closely with the Americans. They are his unwitting accomplices. Helping the Chinese. Like fools!"

The United States is assisting the Chinese?

"The Americans will need to be eliminated, too," he said. "It's unavoidable. Call it collateral damage."

She nodded.

"But the judge is not in China," the Bear said.

"He's not even a bloody Chinaman," Mikey squawked.

"So, who is my target?" Jessica asked. "And where is he?"

"Nigeria."

38

Y ou wan jollof rice, eh?" Mama Oyafemi said. "*Oyinbo*, they always eat the jollof."

Judd and Isabella looked back at her, confused. They had followed Bola's clear instructions to come here to make contact with the Yahooze Boys, one of the organized criminal rings running online scams. Bola assured them that the Coyote was an up-and-coming player and could provide a window into the inner workings of international fraud. Bola didn't ask Judd why exactly he wanted to peek into the 419 underground. Judd started to explain about the missing Jason Saunders in London, but Isabella cut him off.

And Judd hadn't asked Bola how he could be so close to a

criminal boss like the Coyote. Judd also assumed that Bola was being helpful because Mariana Leibowitz had asked him. Or, Judd wondered, perhaps Judge Bola Akinola knew he'd soon need help of his own. They were both playing a game, trying to assist each other without giving too much away.

But now Judd and Isabella were standing in a tiny café, deep in the heart of Lagos, seeking the ringleader. And a rotund Nigerian grandmother was standing in their way.

"The *oyinbo*, the foreigners, *the white people*, like you, they love jollof rice," Mama Oyafemi added helpfully.

"No," Isabella said. "We aren't hungry."

"Yes we are," Judd corrected. "We are very hungry. We will have two big plates of jollof. And do you have soup today?"

"I have a fresh pot of *egusi* soup. And roasted goat, eh."

"Yes," Judd nodded. "We'll have two plates of jollof rice and two bowls of *egusi* soup. No goat for us today."

"Yes, you must eat," Mama Oyafemi declared, looking pleased as she returned to the kitchen.

Judd patted Isabella's arm lightly, trying to reassure his partner. "We have time to eat," he said with raised eyebrows.

A few moments later Mama Oyafemi appeared with large plates of red rice cooked with peppers, tomatoes, and spices. Then she brought steaming bowls of yellow-and-green soup made with melon seeds, dried fish, and spinach.

As Judd and Isabella dug in, Mama Oyafemi stood over them proudly.

"Delicious," Isabella said.

"This jollof is much better than what they cook in Ghana or Senegal," Judd offered.

"Only Nigerian jollof, eh," Mama Oyafemi vigorously agreed.

"Thank you," Judd said, pushing his plate forward and patting his stomach. "We are looking for someone. We were told to meet him here. At the Innocent Chop House."

Mama Oyafemi's smile disappeared.

"We are looking for the Coyote," Judd said.

"No."

"We were told to find Coyote here."

"No Coyote here," Mama Oyafemi insisted.

"We're not here to make trouble," Judd said, holding up his palms. "We were sent"—he lowered his voice to a whisper—"by Judge Bola Akinola."

Mama Oyafemi looked them both up and down. "You wait, eh," she said, before disappearing back into the kitchen.

A few moments later she returned with a young man wearing skinny jeans and an oversized orange hoodie. The man, who appeared to have been woken up from a nap, checked the alley outside, then faced Judd with angry yellow eyes. "Who is looking for the Coyote?"

Judd suddenly wondered if this was all a big mistake.

"We are. We were sent by—"

"Who are you?" he demanded. "What do you want here?"

"We're from—" Judd began.

"What for?" interrupted the man.

"We are searching for a friend," Judd tried to explain.

"Judge Akinola sent us," Isabella interrupted. "He sent us to meet the Coyote."

"Yes, that's right," Judd added. "The judge said we could find the Coyote here and he would show us the Yahooze Boys. How it all works. To help us find our missing friend," she said.

"You American police, eh?"

"No police," Judd said, holding up his hands. "I work for the State Department. We're not here to cause trouble. Just to find the Coyote. Just to learn."

"And you?" He jabbed a finger toward Isabella.

"I'm with him," she said, nodding toward Judd.

The boy traded glances with the older woman, then relaxed. "Yes, the judge, he called me. The big judge is a great man."

"Yes, he is," Isabella agreed.

"We go," the man said.

They followed him through the kitchen, pushing past hanging laundry, then again through another door, down a smoky hallway, past several boys standing guard.

Judd's pulse accelerated and his stomach ached as the doubts returned. *This is crazy.* They arrived at a steel door and the man flipped open the barricade bar with a loud clang. *Jessica would have a fit if she knew. . . .*

The man gestured for them to pass. *Is this a dungeon? Is it a trap?*

Isabella froze. "Are you sure about this?" she asked, grabbing Judd's arm. "Maybe this isn't a good idea."

Judd was thinking the same thing. *What am I doing, just walking into a dangerous criminal's den? What do I really even know about this Bola Akinola?* He knew Mariana Leibowitz had never let him down before. *Jessica would . . .* he thought about this for a second . . . *Jessica would walk right through that door.*

Judd took a deep breath and Isabella's hand. "Let's go," he said, and pulled them through.

The tension vaporized the moment they were inside. It wasn't a dark cell but a long, brightly lit air-conditioned room filled with computer terminals along both sides. Young, smartly dressed African teens typed away on keyboards.

The man revealed a wide, toothy smile. "I am Kayode. The Coyote." He led Judd and Isabella down the center aisle like a tour guide.

"This is where we work," he said, opening his arms wide like a proud farmer showing off a bumper crop.

Up on the wall, above one of the workstations, a simple sign was tacked up:

Teach a man to fish?
I don't want to fish.
I work in IT.

When they reached the far end of the room, Judd noticed a high-end printer alongside stacks of official letterhead. Judd elbowed Isabella, gesturing toward the stationery bearing the logos of JPMorgan Chase, Barclays, Microsoft, Gazprombank, the Bank of England, and the Central Bank of Nigeria.

The Coyote beamed, "Welcome to Wall Street."

"Wall Street?" Judd winced. "I don't understand."

"You are American, eh," the Coyote smiled. "You must know Billy Ray Valentine?"

39

Sunday couldn't sleep. So he'd surrendered to his insomnia, showered, dressed, and trudged back into the office. He'd always had difficulty sleeping through the night. He wanted to count sheep, but his mind had other ideas, churning over whatever problem he was trying to solve. It had been this way as a child in southern California, as a graduate student in Wisconsin, and especially as an analyst for the Central Intelligence Agency. The trouble of work consuming all his mental space had only worsened after he joined Purple Cell.

Jessica Ryker was now somewhere in Russia. She'd been off-line and unreachable for the past—he checked the time—

forty-five hours. That wasn't unusual. That was part of their business. Part of the deal. The MO for Purple Cell was usually the same: accept an impossible puzzle, dig deep until you solved it, and . . . then wait.

Sunday didn't know when Jessica would resurface. Maybe it was the lack of sleep or the stress or the nagging knowledge that it could all end without warning. But he couldn't help but wonder, sitting alone in a dark cubicle on the third floor of the old CIA headquarters building, if this was precisely how Purple Cell might end. Would Jessica Ryker just . . . not come back one day? Would everything she'd done, everything they'd done together, just finish . . . with a long silence?

Just do your part. His mind returned to digging. Not the statistical analysis of attacks on oil facilities that he was doing for Purple Cell. He'd hit a dead end with that. He'd found a correlation in the data but no story, no evidence, to back it up. A statistical anomaly, he decided. Too small a sample size. Or just bad luck. So instead Sunday had concentrated on another project at the request of Jessica's husband, to comb through intelligence on Judge Bola Akinola.

It wasn't the first time Sunday had pulled an all-nighter working on a problem for Judd Ryker. Jessica had never said so explicitly, but Sunday knew she would have wanted him to help Judd. And this time Sunday felt a strong desire to get it right. Because he wanted to help Judd Ryker. Because it was Nigeria, the land of his parents. Because of his cousins back in Kano and Zamfara. Working on Nigeria was, he admitted, a *guilty pleasure.*

But investigating Bola Akinola also made him queasy. The judge was a hero in many ways. A brave hunter trying to kill the beasts of corruption in a country where beasts were everywhere. At great personal risk, Bola Akinola had taken on some of the most crooked politicians, the most notorious criminals in the country. He was staring into the eyes of the monsters and not blinking.

But now Sunday had doubts. There were always accusations against prominent people, of secret bank accounts, of petty vices, of the eventual victory of hidden weaknesses that exist deep in the souls of all men and women. Sunday had thought Akinola was an exception, that he could resist the urges of normal men. But there it was, in the British press in black-and-white: *Judge Bola Akinola, chairman of the Nigerian Crime and Corruption Task Force, had failed to accurately account on his asset disclosures for luxury properties held in Monaco, London's posh Mayfair neighborhood, and a villa in the Cayman Islands.*

Sunday hoped the story was a false plant. Mere propaganda that slipped through the usual journalism filter. The British papers, keen to scoop their competitors and prone to believe the worst about subjects from one of their former colonies, were especially loose with such accusations. And once one paper had the story, surely more would come.

Had Judge Bola Akinola become dirty? Sunday wanted to know the truth. For Judd Ryker. And for himself.

Sunday finished reading through all the open-source reporting on Akinola. Diplomatic cables from Abuja and Lagos hadn't provided any new insights, either. He was about to pull up top secret signals intelligence to seek out any potential clues, when his office phone rang.

Sunday glanced at the clock. *Four thirty-eight a.m.? Who's calling me at this hour?* The incoming ID was a jumble of numbers he didn't recognize.

"Aaay?" he said hesitantly.

"There you are," Jessica said with a huff. "I've been trying to get you on your cell."

"My phone's in the glove box of my car in the parking lot."

"Couldn't sleep again?" she asked, softening her tone.

"No, ma'am," he said. "Are you safe?"

"I'm fine. I can't say where. I'm on a burner phone that I'll flush right after I hang up."

"Yes, ma'am."

"I need your help. I've got something urgent."

Sunday looked at his computer screen listing news articles about Bola Akinola with a slight pang of guilt. Was he being dutiful by surreptitiously helping her husband? *Or disloyal?*

"Go," he said, wondering how he had wound up, again, stuck in the middle of the two Rykers.

"Target acquired," Jessica said. "I need everything you can find on him."

"Roger that. What's the name, ma'am?"

"It's a judge in Nigeria supposedly working with someone in the U.S. government," she said. "We've got to find out what we can about the judge and a way to warn the Americans without blowing my cover."

Sunday's stomach jumped into his throat. "No," he blurted.

"No what?"

"Don't tell me the target is Bola Akinola."

"How do you know?"

"Ma'am"—Sunday paused to swallow—"I'm already investigating him. That's why I'm in the office."

"How's that possible? How do you know my target?"

Sunday closed his eyes. "I was helping a friend. On another problem."

"What friend?" Jessica snapped.

"On what *I thought* was another problem."

"Who is it, Sunday? Who's been asking you about Bola Akinola? *Tell me right fucking now.*"

40

LAGOS, NIGERIA

THURSDAY, 10:05 A.M. WEST AFRICA TIME (5:05 A.M. EST)

The driver from the U.S. Consulate Lagos weaved the Nissan Patrol expertly through the chaos of the city's traffic.

In the backseat, Judd and Isabella sat in silence watching the bustle go by. Swarms of yellow minibuses honked and belched gray smoke. The roadside was packed tight with makeshift shops, the brightly dressed women selling everything from chili peppers to flat-screen high-definition televisions. Rickety pushcarts were piled impossibly high with bottled water, greasy diesel fuel jugs, and mounds of rotting trash. And the crowds, a buzzing river of people just making their way through Africa's biggest metropolis.

But Judd wasn't really seeing the life of the city. His mind was churning with questions about what he had just witnessed. The Coyote had shown them his operation. He'd explained how they worked, how the advance fee scams had evolved from crude letters into sophisticated online campaigns using the latest in technology and marketing. The bait—the pleas, the promises, even the typos—were all deliberately designed to lure just the right targets among all those masses. The art of the scam in the age of free email, the Coyote had explained, was shaping the pitch to catch your perfect marks. The most gullible, the most susceptible, the most corrupt, who would take the bait and run. That's when the scammers knew the hook was set.

There was no shortage of people falling for it, he'd told them. A response rate of 0.01 percent provided plenty of opportunities. The Coyote even tracked hit rates by each of his team members and ran sophisticated data analytics giving him real-time feedback on the productivity of all his operations.

And, despite a crackdown by Nigerian investigators, by the FBI, by British police, by Interpol, the Coyote's team was getting better every day. Better at targeting, better at deceiving, better at avoiding the authorities. Criminal creativity was, as it has always been through the history of civilization, at least one step ahead of law enforcement.

Judd was surprised by how unguarded the Coyote had been about his business secrets. He hadn't seemed the least hesitant to share the inner workings of his operation with

American government officials. Judd guessed it was Bola's introduction that had made such candor possible. But that, too, raised new uncomfortable questions.

The Coyote was cagey about one question: Who did he work for?

"Wall Street is mine. I built it," he said.

"You don't have a boss, a big boss?" Judd asked.

"Of course I work for the Oga, the big Oga," he replied.

But when Judd pressed and the Coyote seemed suddenly nervous, Isabella waved him off.

Sitting in the back of the SUV, thinking through everything he had seen that morning, Judd was, he had to admit, more than a little impressed. The Coyote's operation was run like a real business: inventive, resourceful, efficient. *Unsettlingly professional.*

Yet it was all exactly as Isabella had told him back in Washington three days earlier. So what had he really learned?

Isabella was the first to break the silence. "What are you thinking, partner?"

"Why would the Coyote share so much about his operation? Why would he let us in?" Judd asked.

"Judge Akinola carries a lot of weight. Even among criminals," she said.

"It's awfully suspicious, don't you think? Doesn't that make you nervous about Bola, too?"

"This is Nigeria," Isabella said. "Bola's the man. Everything is connected. Isn't that what Mariana told you?"

"More or less."

"Then what did you expect, Judd?"

"I don't know."

"The world is full of surprises."

"That Coyote is running quite a little business," Judd said. She shrugged and gave him a look of friendly annoyance.

"I know," Judd admitted. "It's just like you told me."

"Imagine if these guys applied their talents to something honest. Something more productive. Imagine what the Coyote and his team could do in the real New York. Or in Silicon Valley."

"Wall Street." Judd flashed his teeth. "They've got a sense of humor, too. You have to give them that."

"*Trading Places.*" She smiled back. "I haven't thought of that movie in years."

"What bothers me is that we didn't get anywhere. We're still no closer to finding Jason Saunders."

"What did you expect, Judd? That seeing how one scam operation works in Nigeria would give you a magical clue to your missing person in London?"

"Maybe the Coyote knew more than he was saying," Judd offered.

"That would be one hell of a coincidence, Judd."

"What if his big boss knows something? It's not impossible. Maybe we should have pressed him harder on this Oga character?"

"Judd, I know criminal investigation isn't your expertise—"

"But he had the letterhead," Judd said. "The Bank of England letterhead. The very same stationery from the letter sent to Jason Saunders before he disappeared."

"So?"

"Isn't that enough to—oh, I don't know, Isabella . . . ask more questions?"

"I think he made it pretty clear he wasn't going to tell us anything about his boss. And he seems smart enough not to incriminate himself. I didn't want you scaring him off."

"So let's raid his office. Come back with an FBI tactical team or one of Bola's task force units and kick some doors in. Squeeze him. Threaten him. Maybe you can use the letter-head connection as leverage. Maybe he knows something and would bargain. Maybe you can get him to give up the Oga."

"You're watching too many cop shows on TV, Judd," she said, turning her face to the window again.

Judd lowered his voice. "Why are you so hesitant, Isabella? That's not like you."

"I don't know what you're talking about," she replied.

"Come on, Special Agent Espinosa. Where is the fighter I know? Where is the pit bull criminal hunter I brought with me to Nigeria?"

She spun and looked him straight in the eyes. "I didn't want to come to Nigeria."

"I know, I know," he said. "But you're here now. You just called me partner. We're in this together. So what's the prob-lem?"

"What do you want me to do, Judd?" she hissed.

"We've just been inside an underground criminal operation. We know it goes higher. We have some evidence. Okay, it's not much, but the letterhead is something, linking their activities to a missing American. An American citizen that I'm trying to find. And you don't want to do anything? Doesn't add up."

Isabella's face gave nothing away.

"What aren't you telling me?" Judd demanded.

She didn't reply. But Judd could see the wheels turning in her head.

As the Nissan swerved away from a heavy fuel truck and up onto a bridge overpass, Judd narrowed his eyes. "Isabella, what is going on?"

"Stop the car," Isabella ordered.

"Not here, ma'am," the driver apologized.

She scanned the highway ahead. "At the end of the bridge, stop on the side of the road. Do it!"

The vehicle came to a halt and Isabella threw open her door. "Come on," she said.

"What?"

"Move it, Judd!" Isabella grabbed his hand and pulled him out of the car. She led him down a gulley to a spot underneath the bridge.

"What are we doing?"

"We don't have much time." She checked over both shoulders. "You want to know what's going on?"

"Yes. But here?"

"I can't take the risk in an embassy vehicle. Not with a driver."

"Can't take what risk?"

"Shut up and listen."

A crowd of onlookers noticed the huddled foreigners.

"We can't hunt for the Oga," she whispered.

"Why not? That could be the key to finding Saunders."

"We can't hunt for the Oga," she explained. "Because the Oga . . . is me."

"What?"

Isabella blinked.

"What?"

"I'm the Coyote's boss," Isabella said.

"What are you talking about?"

"The Coyote is mine," she said.

"What do you mean 'yours'?"

"He's my guy. He doesn't know it, but his team is my team. I've been working with Bola Akinola on a highly classified operation for months."

"*Your* team? Months? *What* operation? What are you talking about?"

The crowd was gathering, people chattering and pointing at the two odd Americans arguing under the bridge.

"You're right about the shadow list. You were right about the letterhead. The letter to Jason Saunders came from the Coyote. It's no scam. It's part of a major international sting operation. The operation that you pulled me off to bring me here. To Nigeria."

"You kidnapped Jason Saunders?"

"Saunders is fine. He was never kidnapped. He's at an undisclosed location in England. He's being held there for his own safety. Until he can testify in court."

"Testify? Against who?"

"I've already told you too much. You can see why I was so pissed off you dragged me here."

"Wait a minute." Judd's head was spinning. "If you're running a scam team as part of a classified sting, your mark has to be a pretty big fish."

"I just said it was a major international operation."

"Then who's your target?"

"We have to go," she said, taking his hand again and pulling him back up the slope, away from the swelling crowd.

"A Nigerian politician?"

Isabella placed a finger over her lips and shook her head.

"Was Saunders' firm laundering money for a Nigerian politician? The President?"

"I can't say. But that's why I've got to get back to Washington as soon as possible."

"Washington? Is it an ambassador? Is that why you can't tell the State Department?"

"I'm not saying another word, Judd."

"An international mob boss? Is that it?"

"I've said all I'm going to tell you, Judd. For your own safety, stop asking questions."

"My own safety? Isabella, I'm *dead in the middle of this*."

41

Big Sammie sat on point. From the very front of the boat's bow, he scouted the shoreline for police, the waterways for military patrols, the sky for surveillance drones. The boat's pilot, who insisted on the nom de guerre Captain Wayne Rooney, banked sharply to the west. Sammie gripped the gunwale with one hand and his AK-47 with the other. The engine roared and the boat raced down one of the endless creeks that formed the impenetrable maze of the Niger Delta.

Big Sammie had small aspirations. He was a tiny boy, a runt among seven brothers and sisters, who originally just wanted to be a fisherman like his father and his grandfather. He dreamed of growing up to have a wife, maybe two wives if he was lucky, surrounded by big pots of food and lots of children. Sammie wanted to live the life he was born into, in the village along the creek, surrounded by family and the comfortable fate of his ancestors. Every weekday Sammie attended the Precious Child Primary School, learning how to read and write, to add and subtract, studying the basics of tropical agriculture.

On Sundays, Sammie liked to show off his education, reading aloud from the Bible, praying with his grandmother at the local branch of the Holy Church of Eternal Prosperity. One beautiful Sunday the week before Easter, a large box arrived from a church in Texas filled with stuffed animals. Sammie was given the honor of distributing the toys to the village children, keeping only a single small pink rabbit for himself.

The village's house of worship was a basic structure of concrete walls and an asbestos roof, built with donations from some faraway place that Sammie didn't know. The centerpiece of the church, a life-sized Jesus on a cross, was a gift from Eternal Prosperity's world headquarters in Lagos. Sammie had seen on television pictures of the glass-and-steel structure that could seat two thousand parishioners. Maybe one day he would be able to visit church headquarters and read aloud on the big stage. Perhaps one day he'd even be on television.

At that time Sammie was focused on a more near-term

goal. He read his prayers, he sang enthusiastically alongside his grandmother and his siblings, all to get ready for the day when the church leader, Pastor Emmanuel, the founder of the Holy Church of Eternal Prosperity, would come to visit his village. Sammie practiced and sang. His grandmother donated a few spare naira into the church collection plate every Sunday, for improvements to the church and to pay for preparations for the big visit. The anticipation of Pastor Emmanuel's arrival, all the way from the big city of Lagos—an ambassador for Jesus Christ himself, from the heavens, coming to bless Sammie's little village—was exhilarating. Sammie hoped and prayed that Pastor Emmanuel would bless him, too.

Until Sammie's entire world came crashing down. It began with an explosion at an oil pipeline, not far upriver. The sky turned black and blocked out the sun. Within hours the fishing grounds were flooded with thick, oily poison. Sammie and his grandmother rushed to the church to alert the authorities of the disaster, to ask for food, to seek help. But the church was locked.

It would be days before the news trickled back to Sammie's village that Pastor Emmanuel had been arrested, his private airplane and antique Rolls-Royce collection confiscated, his bank accounts in Geneva and London frozen, his luxury villas in Lagos, Abuja, and Monaco seized by the authorities. The Holy Church of Eternal Prosperity, it turned out, had been built on thousands, perhaps millions, of people handing over a few naira to support a lavish lifestyle of one man.

Angry men in the village wanted to launch a protest against the church and the oil company. But the elders decided on a more cautious approach. A delegation from the village traveled by bus to the state capital at Asaba to plead for help. After waiting patiently for three days in the capital, they finally met with the assistant to the governor, whom they begged to approach the foreign oil company operating in the area. Their demands: Clean up the spill, pay restitution to those who lost their livelihoods, hire more local men for security, and make improvements to the church. The list of demands was politely accepted and the delegation returned to the village.

That's when the answer arrived. The army swept into Sammie's village, kicking in doors, searching for "troublemakers," rounding up any able-bodied male. The Holy Church of Eternal Prosperity was burned to the ground. The only item Sammie had left from the church was his pink rabbit.

Sammie was thirteen. That's when, for the first time, he saw the world for what it was. And that's when he met a new friend who helped him to become big.

Now fifteen and many more years wiser, Big Sammie sat in the open bow of Captain Wayne Rooney's boat, feeling the roar of the outboard engines in his bones, the wind rippling through his mask, the cold steel of the automatic rifle in his hands. On a lanyard around his neck, he hung the pink stuffed rabbit. It may have looked out of place on a heavily armed rebel fighter, but the toy had become part of Big Sammie's persona.

The boat hugged another sharp corner and came upon a waiting Nigerian navy vessel. The twenty-five-foot American Defender Class response boat looked like an oversized Zodiac, with NNS *Abiku* stenciled in white on the gray foam collar.

Big Sammie heart jumped. He raised his AK and aimed, just as he had been trained, directly at the tallest skull in the boat's wheelhouse. He was never told the nature of their mission that day; he didn't know if this was a real Nigerian naval boat or a counterfeit. He learned to never assume who was friend and who was enemy.

Big Sammie fingered the trigger, narrowed his aim, and tried to slow his breathing.

Captain Wayne Rooney didn't appear surprised. He slowed the engine to a crawl and circled the naval vessel. A man in civilian clothes, jeans, and a crisp white button-down oxford held up his hands and waved to them. The captain gestured to Big Sammie to throw a line to the man and lash the two boats together.

"Twelve o'clock. Right on time. High noon," said the mysterious man.

The captain accepted a suitcase from the man with a grunt. The man flipped open a cell phone, spoke a few words, then nodded. Captain Wayne Rooney released the line, the engines thundered, and Big Sammie with his pink rabbit sped away, back into the creeks.

42

Jessica checked into the Emirates first-class departure lounge, accepted a tall flute of French champagne, and found her way to the private shower room. Once inside, she locked the door and turned the cold water on full blast. She opened the box of a cell phone she'd bought with cash at the Beeline airport kiosk, clicked a prepaid SIM card into place, and fired it up.

She didn't want to make this call, but she knew she had no choice. She had done her job, dropped everything to take the crazy bullshit operation in Russia. She'd accepted the assignment to play the Deputy Director's super-assassin Queen Sheba. She'd found the Bear. She'd gotten his next target.

How could she have foreseen the target being a Nigerian judge? How could she have known the mission would cross paths with her husband, Judd? *What were the chances?*

The only escape now was to pass the target to the Deputy Director and bow out without jeopardizing the operation against the Bear. There was no other option. Most of all, she'd have to find a discreet way to warn Judd that Bola Akinola was in danger. That *he was in danger.* Dammit, this was becoming everything she had been trying to avoid. What had she done? *What had Judd gotten himself into?*

"Pan Western Logistics. How may I direct your call?" asked the nasal woman's voice on the line.

"I've got a special order," Jessica said. "Three hundred and six pounds. Overnight. San Diego to Anchorage."

"Is that via Reno?"

"Las Vegas."

"Please hold."

Click, click, bleep, then "What the fuck phone is this?" barked the CIA's Deputy Director.

"Burner," she said.

"Christ," he hissed. "No names on an open line. You have two minutes. Sounds like you're inside a waterfall. Where the hell are you?"

"Airport. Plane leaves in twenty."

"You see your man?"

"Affirmative."

"You get your target?"

"We've got a problem."

"Did. You. Get. Your. Target?" he repeated.

"Target acquired."

"So, what's the problem?"

"It's a judge," she said.

"So?"

"A well-known foreign judge."

"Where?"

"Nigeria."

"Not a problem," he said quickly. "Send the name and any details via text to the other system as soon as we hang up. Then get back here ASAP. Good work."

"I . . ." Jessica hesitated.

"Spit it out."

"I need out."

"Out of what?" he snapped.

"The operation."

"This operation? No. You aren't out. Just the opposite. I'm bringing you in."

"I don't think so, sir."

"We'll discuss it face-to-face. I'll want you to help run it from HQ. We've got lots of work left to do."

"There's no time for that," she said.

"We've got time. You send the name and I'll have surveillance on the judge by end of the day. We'll have a team in-country within forty-eight hours. Execution and exfiltration will be ready to roll by late next week. Nigeria's a tricky environment, but we've done it before. It'll be quick. You'll see."

"Sorry, sir. It's got to happen tomorrow."

"Tomorrow? What are you talking about?"

"Your man insisted it happen tomorrow. And that it has to be public."

"Why the fuck would you agree to that?" the Deputy Director fumed. "We can't pull off a credible decoy kill in one day."

"You wanted him convinced I was the Queen. I did that. You wanted the target. I got it. But that's the price. It has to happen tomorrow."

The Deputy Director paused on the other end. Jessica could hear him breathing, could feel the wheels turning. "Fine. Tomorrow. I'll make sure of it. Now get on a plane and get back here."

"If there's no time for a decoy kill, sir, what's the play?"

"I'll improvise."

"You said there's no time for a decoy kill."

"That's correct."

"Sir, are you saying—"

"The world is messy and dangerous," he said without emotion.

That's exactly what I told Judd, Jessica thought. She felt sick to her stomach. "But, sir—"

"You're a big girl. Put on your big-girl pants. We're too close to go soft now. This is too important. I shouldn't have to explain this to you."

Jessica listened to the shower run as she thought through the implications of what she was hearing. Was the Deputy Director planning an assassination to protect his operation against the Bear? Of a foreign judge? A judge she now knew was working closely with her husband? Jessica's neck ached.

"He's got a family, sir."

"If one crooked Nigerian judge has to—"

"I didn't say he was crooked," she interrupted.

"A judge in Nigeria?" the Deputy Director scoffed. "That's somehow found his way onto your man's target list? Get real."

"He's surrounded by civilians. You don't want to do this."

"You don't have the big picture."

"It's going to be impossible to keep it clean. There could be collateral damage."

"There's too much at stake. I don't need kosher. I just need this to happen. I'm hanging up now."

"Sir, don't do it." *Motherfucker,* she thought.

"Not your call. You are the one who agreed to the deadline. This is actually on you. It's going to happen tomorrow, one way or the other."

Jessica rolled her head from side to side and felt the vertebrae in her neck crack back into place. *Motherfucker.*

Then she heard herself say, "I'll do it."

43

Fifteen hours, Sunday thought. *I've been at this desk for fifteen long hours.*

He'd given up finding anything more from his data collection on oil facility attacks. Then he'd swept every last corner of the intelligence vault to find anything and everything that the U.S. government had on Judge Bola Akinola. There he'd found circular reporting of rumors, but nothing incriminating. And nothing clearly exonerating.

Sunday was no closer to having solid answers. For Judd Ryker, he still had nothing. For Jessica Ryker, he still had . . . nothing.

Several times over the past few hours, Sunday had logged

off, shut both his computers down . . . and then had one more idea. One more rock to turn over before calling it a day. He tried looking into patterns of security contractors for the oil companies. He searched a database of oil licenses to analyze the structure of the joint ventures. He tracked the principal shareholders for each of the oil companies that had been targeted with violence and come up with long lists of pension and hedge funds but nothing obviously suspicious. No apparent links to terror groups. No obvious connections to international criminal syndicates. No clear national security implications that would need to be sent upstairs or to the DNI. Nothing to set off alarm bells at the White House. Sunday found . . . *nothing.*

Now Sunday was out of ideas. His eyes were bleary. His head ached. He wanted to sleep.

"Hey, S-Man, Lucy and the boys are heading down to the Blarney Stone," his colleague Glen said as he pulled on an overcoat. "I know you're probably too busy or have to walk your cat—"

"I'm in," Sunday said.

"What's that?" Glen stuck out his chin.

"I'm in for the pub. For a drink."

"Well, ain't that a hippo in the Sahara," Glen smirked.

"It's been a long, frustrating day. I could use a distraction," Sunday said, turning off his monitor.

"It's about goddamn time."

"A pint of Guinness is just what I need," Sunday said.

262

"It's Thursday, S-Man. Thursday at the Blarney Stone is Coors light and buffalo wings," Glen said, arching his eyebrows.

"We're going to an Irish pub for light beer and chicken wings?"

"This is northern Virginia, not Dublin. It's not even really Irish."

"The Blarney Stone isn't Irish?"

"Yeah. The manager told me that it's owned by some company based in Amsterdam that's really owned by a hedge fund in Hong Kong or Singapore or somewhere over there." Glen fluttered his hands. "Anything Irish about the Blarney Stone is just a cover to trick the customers."

Sunday plucked his jacket off the hanger on a hook he'd installed on his cubicle wall and zipped up. "A convenient fig leaf of misplaced nationalism?"

"Whatever," Glen said.

"It's clever," Sunday said.

"The Blarney Stone's brilliant. You'll love the buffalo wings."

A convenient fig leaf of misplaced nationalism, Sunday thought.

"I'm . . ." Sunday unzipped his jacket. "I'm going to have to meet you there."

"What?" Glen blurted out.

"I just have one more thing to do," Sunday said, pushing the power button on his monitor.

"Oh, for goodness' sake," Glen huffed in disgust. "I was so close."

"I'll meet you at the pub," Sunday said, waving him away.

But Sunday's evening plans had already drained from his mind. He shuffled his chair in close to his desk and reopened his list of oil company shareholders. Then he logged in to a classified U.S. Treasury database, uploaded his list, and ran an automated query to identify the ownership of each of the shareholding hedge funds.

As he waited for the computer results, Sunday took off his jacket and carefully rehung it on the hanger. He pulled an aerosol can out of a desk drawer and blew the dust out of his keyboard. Just as he finished, his screen flashed.

Results: 26,674 items

It was a long list of every significant international oil company, their principal shareholding firms, and the secondary owners of those funds, along with locations where each was registered. He typed "Russia" into the sort field.

Results: 1,040 items

Still too many to search manually. He typed "Russia + US" for any company that had some ownership shared by both nationalities.

Results: 56 items

As he scanned down the list, he found mostly American pension funds invested in the big Russian oil majors or Russian banks invested in American oil companies. Nothing out of the ordinary here. Until one item caught his eye.

Wildcat Oil LLC, 14664 Energy Corridor Park,
Houston, Texas → Principal: Holden Harriman
Quinn, 419 Park Avenue, New York, NY →
Principal: Bolshaya Neva Fund, Nevsky Prospekt,
St. Petersburg, Russia

DAY FIVE

FRIDAY

44

The hot pink sun had peeked over the horizon only twenty minutes earlier, but it was already heating up the humid West African air. The waves rolled in, crashing onto the beach at steady six-second intervals, like a slow-motion time-keeper. Judd Ryker stood stiffly in the sand, Isabella Espinosa on one side of him and Judge Bola Akinola on the other. The three had their eyes focused on the empty approach road to the east. That was the deal.

"They're late," Judd said, checking his watch again.

"Relax, my friend," Bola said.

The beach was mostly deserted at this early hour. It was a rare open space in the thick density of urban Lagos. A safe neutral place for just such a special delivery. A few homeless early risers had scurried away when the entourage from the U.S. consulate had rolled in before dawn. Judd, Isabella, and Bola had arrived with a small team of armed officers from Diplomatic Security, along with the embassy doctor. Bola had received a phone call earlier that morning with instructions to go to this exact spot at Elegushi Beach, exit their vehicles, and wait for the drop at 7:00 a.m. sharp.

An unexpected twist was the arrival of a fleet of Nigerian federal police military-style trucks, which unloaded a platoon of heavily armed and helmeted officers. They fanned out in a menacing arc formation behind the Americans.

"Maybe the police scared them away?" Judd offered.

"Don't worry, my friend. This"—Bola swept his arm toward the police line—"is just for show. It's not for the militants. *It's for you.*"

"Me?"

"The government wants to show its American friends that they are using the counterterrorism equipment you sent us. That we are taking this business seriously. The militants, they know the deal, too. They aren't afraid. This won't scare them off."

"Wasn't this supposed to be a secret? How did the police even know about the handover?"

"There are few secrets in Nigeria," Bola said.

"Who could have told them?"

Bola didn't say a word.

"The entire deal could be compromised. They could kill

him," Judd said, imagining the newspaper headlines. And the phone call with Landon Parker.

"Don't worry, my friend."

"Isabella, help me out here," Judd pleaded. "Does this seem right to you?"

Isabella didn't answer, either. Instead she scanned the approach road with binoculars.

"Well, how long do we wait?"

Bola took Judd's hand in silence and interlocked his fingers. Judd fought the urge to withdraw his hand, knowing that in some West African cultures men holding hands was a normal gesture, a sign of friendship. Bola was trying to calm Judd's nerves. "They will come," Bola said confidently.

Sure enough, several moments later a battered yellow minivan emerged from the side street about two hundred meters away.

"Here we go," Isabella announced, holding the binoculars with one hand and with the other pulling a gun from a concealed holster at her lower back.

"You're armed?" Judd was surprised.

"You think I'm coming to a hostage drop without my Glock?" she said. "I see the driver plus three—no, four—males inside."

"What are they doing? Can you see Babatunde?" Judd asked.

"Here they come," she said, tightening her grip on the handgun. The taxi's side door opened with a rusty creak. Like a giant crane, an enormous man unfolded himself from the van and stood at attention. His head was covered in a hood, his hands bound behind his back.

"Is that him?" Judd demanded.

"I can't tell," Isabella said, her binoculars fixed on the target.

"It's him," Bola said calmly.

"I'm going to get him." Judd started to move, but Isabella swung her arm in front of him.

"Not yet," she said.

A few seconds later the van's engine roared and the vehicle peeled away.

"Go!" Isabella tucked the gun back into the holster in the small of her back.

Judd Ryker, followed by the embassy security team, raced forward and surrounded the big man. Tunde Babatunde was exhausted from his ordeal but otherwise in fine shape. He seemed embarrassed by all the attention.

Judd explained that they'd take him back to the consulate, do a full medical exam, give him a hot meal, and debrief him. He promised that, unless something unexpected happened, he'd be on Harvey Holden's plane back to New York before lunchtime.

Judd snapped a quick photo of Babatunde with his phone and then excused himself to make a call.

"Got him," Judd said excitedly into the phone.

"What?" Landon Parker sounded confused.

"Sir, sorry to wake you," he whispered. "But I wanted you

to know right away that we got him. Tunde Babatunde is safe and in U.S. custody."

"You didn't wake me."

"We're taking him back to the consulate and then we'll have him wheels-up in a few hours. I'm sending through a photo now, sir."

"That's the problem, Ryker."

"Problem? No, no. We've got him. That's why I'm calling you. So you can let Congressman Truman know it's all okay."

"The photo is the problem," Parker said.

"I don't understand."

"Ryker, I'm looking at another photo of Tunde Babatunde right now. He's surrounded by militants."

Judd's heart sank. "I still don't understand, sir."

"There wasn't supposed to be any exchange of money. The United States doesn't pay ransom for hostages. I told you that's our policy."

"I didn't pay any ransom."

"That's not the story that's going to appear in the press tomorrow. The photo I'm looking at right goddamn now is what the militants say they're selling to the newspapers. They're auctioning it off. This was supposed to be quiet. No press. No money. That's why I sent you, dammit."

"I . . ." Judd paused, unsure what to say.

"Ryker, how did you let this happen?"

45

The Emirates Boeing 777 landed smoothly and taxied to the far end of the runway. *Okay, I'm in Nigeria,* Jessica thought. *Judd's here, somewhere.*

On such short notice, Jessica Ryker hadn't put her team into play in the usual way. This would be a high-risk mission cobbled together, with a high probability of something going very wrong. She ran through her plan: clear the airport, access the safe house, contact Sunday, locate Judd. There'd be no time for a surveillance detection route. That was a risk, she decided, worth taking, not that she had much choice. The bigger challenge was figuring out what exactly to tell Judd.

How to explain her sudden appearance in Lagos? What for? And . . . when?

"Ladies and gentlemen, welcome to Lagos," the pilot announced on the loudspeaker. "Thank you for flying Emirates. The local time is nine forty-five in the morning. Please have your passport ready for inspection by the authorities. . . ."

Outside the plane window, Jessica spied a long line of intimidating federal police vehicles. Armed officers patrolled the airport fence line and surrounded the main terminal building at Nigeria's busiest airport. It wasn't too many years ago that a brash criminal gang blocked one of these runways with oil barrels and robbed the airline passengers. Like a train heist in the Old West. The airport manager and local police chief were all fired after that incident. Now a heavy security presence was a permanent show of force to deter potential troublemakers. That and a presidential blanket order to shoot any tarmac trespassers on sight.

The Lagos airport had also been notorious for chaos, with throngs of people running a gauntlet of bribe seekers, only to then be plunged into a feeding frenzy of taxi drivers, hawkers, and scam artists. In the 1990s the FAA posted warning signs at all American airports alerting travelers that the Murtala Muhammed International Airport in Lagos was a global standout in failing to meet minimum security standards.

But that was not what Jessica discovered on this trip. After deplaning, she walked down a brand-new air-conditioned jetway and was led into the international arrivals hall. It was busy but well-lit and clean. No one would mistake Lagos for Dubai, but to Jessica this felt like a shopping mall you might find in Milwaukee or Sacramento.

"How long do you plan to be in Nigeria, Mrs. Menelik?" the immigration officer asked.

"Only a few days," Jessica replied. "I have to be back in Geneva by Monday."

"What is the purpose of your visit?"

"UN business," she said, tapping her baby-blue United Nations diplomatic passport, another one she had acquired only eight hours earlier from a friendly fixer in the Dubai airport.

"Ahhh, yes." The officer smiled widely. "You are most welcome."

As her passport was aggressively stamped and she was waved through, Jessica's mind returned to her task list. Safe house, communicate with Purple Cell, find Judd . . . but what to tell him exactly? The dilemma nagged like a throbbing toothache, making it hard to concentrate. She had just landed in a new place, with a new identity, on a last-minute mission for which she was barely prepared. She needed to focus, not be distracted.

Jessica weaved through the crowd outside the airport. After a few moments she was relieved to spot her contact in a black designer shirt, holding a handwritten sign for Mrs. Menelik, UN Special Projects Consultation.

What Jessica didn't see was a well-built man, Caucasian, his bald head covered by a woolen flat cap, his eyes hidden behind mirrored aviator sunglasses. He'd sat at the far back of the plane to Dubai, and then several rows behind her on the connection to Lagos. The man had followed her at a safe distance through the airport, met his own contact by the curb, and then trailed Jessica's car as it slipped into the death crawl of Lagos traffic.

46

Congressman, I hope I didn't wake you," Landon Parker lied. He knew Shepard Truman was a night owl. He even had it on good authority that the legislator had been out late the previous night, huddled in the back room of yet another D.C. steak house, meeting with donors and plotting for his run in the U.S. Senate. It was one of those Washington open secrets. Parker knew it was petty and childish to deliberately roust the Congressman rather than wait for a civilized hour. But Parker also knew he'd enjoy it.

"Of course not," a groggy Truman lied back. "You have news?"

"We've got Tunde Babatunde."

"Oh, thank goodness."

"He's now safely in U.S. hands. Judd Ryker is taking Baba-tunde to the airport for a plane back to the States as we speak."

"Did they hurt him? I mean, what's his condition?"

"Babatunde is fine. He'll be ready to play basketball again. I wanted you to be the first to know."

"I appreciate that. Well done, Parker," Truman said. "Please pass my gratitude to Dr. Ryker."

"I'll do that," Parker said. "I've got some less good news, too, Congressman."

"What is it?"

"We've got a complication."

"Spit it out."

"The kidnapping story's likely going to hit the press."

"You told me no media," Truman squealed.

"I know. It was out of our control."

"Out of control is darn right. You told me this Ryker would do it quietly. You assured me that you had your *best man for the job*. That's what you said."

"Judd Ryker is our best man. He got Babatunde back safely. We believe the kidnappers may have sold a photo to the newspapers."

"There're *pictures*?" Truman shouted.

"I need to ask you, Congressman, did Harvey Holden ar-range a payoff?"

"Heck, no. Did you?"

"The United States doesn't pay ransom."

"Well, he didn't pay, either. Our deal was that Holden

wouldn't do anything if I gave you forty-eight hours. So, what happened?"

"I don't have all the facts yet."

"What kind of rogue operation are you running over there at the State Department? How did your man even get Babatunde back? Maybe he paid someone off. Do you know how this Judd Ryker contacted the kidnappers?"

"On cases like this, we work with well-connected local authorities. I can't share any further details, Congressman."

"Who was it?"

"I'm not at liberty to say. I'm sorry."

"Well, it sounds like you got railroaded by one of your own people. Or maybe hoodwinked by the locals."

"I'm looking into it," Parker said.

"Maybe Ryker's connection to the hostage-takers was *too connected*? He sounds like a cowboy to me. Did you ever think of that?"

"I'm looking into it, sir." Parker glanced down at the British newspaper on his desk that his assistant had flagged.

Nigerian Judge to Face Corruption Charges

ABUJA—*Nigeria's attorney general today announced a formal inquiry into the business dealings of a former supreme court judge charged with leading anti-corruption investigations. The surprise move was sparked by allegations in the local press that Judge Bola Akinola . . .*

"Maybe we shouldn't be surprised. We're talking about Nigeria, after all," Truman said. "They're all corrupt over there, you know."

"I assure you that I'll get to the bottom of what happened and, if necessary, we'll cut people loose. Heads will roll."

"I don't want to tell the State Department how to do its business," Truman said.

"Of course not, Congressman," Parker said through gritted teeth.

"But maybe this Judd Ryker isn't what you think, either?"

47

W hat's with the traffic?" Jessica huffed.

"Welcome to Lagos," her contact said from the driver's seat, waving at the parking lot of cars. Out the windshield, they could see an endless caravan of vehicles stretched ahead of them.

"How do you ever run SDRs here?" she asked, looking out the back window to find another long line of cars and trucks. "How can you even move?"

"We have our own ways to run surveillance detection routes, ma'am. Would you like me to take the next exit and double back?"

"Negative. No time." Jessica slumped back in her seat and fidgeted with her phone. "How much longer to the safe house?"

"I couldn't say, ma'am. Hopefully not more than another hour," he said.

That's too long, she thought. She still had too much to do, too many pieces to put in place. *Just sitting here* wasn't an option. She had to improvise.

"Do you have all the materials I requested?"

"Yes, ma'am. They're in the trunk."

"Pull over."

"Ma'am?"

"Pull over!" she ordered. The driver veered the car to the side of the road.

"Now get out," she said, stepping from the car and opening the driver's door. "You find a taxi. I'm taking the car."

"Ma'am, are you sure this is a good idea? Lagos is not the kind of place—"

"Give me your shirt," she demanded.

"Ma'am?"

"Your shirt. Give it to me now."

The driver, now thoroughly confused, unbuttoned his shirt and sheepishly held it out. Jessica grabbed it, slipped behind the wheel, and slammed the door shut. She lurched the car into the sea of pedestrian traffic and leaned on the horn. Once she was on her way and the driver far behind in the rearview mirror, she punched a number into her phone.

"Aaay," Sunday answered.

"Drop everything," Jessica said over the sound of her honking. "I've got a new plan and I need your help."

Six minutes later, in another part of the city, Judd Ryker was sitting on the floor in the back of a cramped windowless van when his phone rang.

"Sunday, I don't have time to talk," he said, his body bobbing from side to side as the van rumbled around potholes.

"Dr. Ryker, are you on your way to the airport?"

"Yes," Judd said, shrugging toward Isabella, who was crouched next to him. "How do you know that?"

"That's why I'm calling," Sunday said. "Are you taking Babatunde to Murtala Airport?"

"Maybe," he said, stealing a glance at the huge basketball star sitting cross-legged across from him. "Why are you asking?"

"Are you with Judge Akinola?"

Judd made eye contact with Bola. "What's . . . going on, Sunday? How do you know all of this?"

"Do you have security with you?"

"Yes, yes." Judd was getting nervous with all the questioning. "We're in an undercover vehicle heading to the airport and we have diplomatic security with us. What's the problem?"

"You have to change routes," Sunday insisted.

"What?"

"We have real-time intel chatter that Bola Akinola is the target of an assassination plot. Right now. You're driving straight into an ambush."

"What chatter?"

"You know I can't say. You need to listen to me, Dr. Ryker."

"How could anyone know our vehicle? How would anyone even know that the judge is with us?"

"I knew," Sunday said. "That's why I need you to listen and follow my instructions. I'm tracking your location right now."

"How?"

"Don't take the Third Mainland Bridge. Get off the expressways."

"What?"

"Tell the driver now. Take the next exit to the west."

"If we're walking into danger—"

"What danger?" Isabella interrupted.

"Dr. Ryker, for your own safety," Sunday pleaded. "I've mapped a safer route. I'll talk you through it. Tell the driver to take the next exit. *Right. Now.*"

"Tell me what danger, Judd," Isabella demanded. "*Qué carajos!* What the hell is going on?"

The line buzzed loudly and then went silent. "Sunday? Sunday?" Judd called into the dead phone.

"Who the hell is Sunday?" Isabella snarled.

"We need to change course," Judd barked. "Stop the van."

Isabella was about to unleash a barrage of new questions,

when Judd's phone rang again. *Thank goodness,* he thought. Until he saw the caller ID. *Oh, no.*

"What now?" Isabella asked.

"Please, Judd, tell us what is happening," Bola asked calmly. Tunde Babatunde nodded nervously and his long frame leaned forward.

"I have to take this," Judd said, and pressed the ANSWER button. "This is Ryker."

"Ryker, are we exposed?" Landon Parker demanded.

"Excuse me, sir?"

"Your fuckup with the press. The Babatunde photo that's likely running in the newspapers tomorrow. Are we exposed?"

"I'm sorry, sir, but I don't know. Can I call you back?"

"I need to know who paid off the kidnappers."

"I don't know, sir."

"You don't know? Or are you telling me it's better not to ask?"

"Sir, this is not a good time for—"

"You're taking Babatunde to the airport, right?"

"I'll call you back, sir. I promise. I have to get off the phone now."

"Ryker, while you're playing cloak and dagger, I've got the FBI on the other line. I need to confirm that Babatunde is in safe custody and we're all straight with the Nigerians. The FBI's ready to release the attack dogs against a major international crime target. I'm holding the leash until you confirm that Babatunde is safe and on his way back. Are you telling me I can let the dogs off the leash?"

"Yes, sir," Judd said. He was about to hang up when Parker spoke up.

"One more thing, Ryker. I know I told you before that you could help this Judge Akeema-something-or-other."

"Bola Akinola," Judd said.

"That's *off.*"

"Sir?" Judd said, locking eyes with Bola.

"Cut him loose."

"I don't think that's—"

"He's a liability," Parker snapped. "The Nigerian attorney general has passed new evidence to us through their ambassador here in Washington that looks pretty bad for your judge. Have you seen the press reports? Looks like he's dirty and we need to keep our distance. I just spoke with Ambassador Katsina and she says—"

"Katsina? You can't believe anything she's telling you."

"You don't have the big picture, Ryker. You're going to have to take my word for it that this Akinola is bad news. Katsina is in and Akinola is out. We cannot be associated with him. You got that?"

"Sir—"

"I want you back here, Ryker. Back on the South China Sea."

"Sir, if I may—"

"You heard me, Ryker. That's an order. Cut the judge loose before it gets any worse. You can't get played by someone taking advantage of his contacts in the United States for protection."

"But, sir—"

"Look, Ryker. There's going to be an inquiry about this whole hostage ransom thing. We need to show that we've been prudent here. If it comes to a congressional hearing, I need to be able to swear on the Bible that we immediately cut ties once we learned the judge was corrupt."

"We don't know that's true—"

"They've issued an arrest warrant and the Nigerian federal police are now hunting for him. An Interpol notice will go out within the hour. Every airport on the planet will be on watch. In fact, if this Judge Akinola calls you again, advise him to turn himself in. And if you see him, have diplomatic security detain him. *Just do it*, Ryker."

The line went dead.

"Judd." Isabella was exasperated. "What the hell is going on?"

48

Viper Six, clear on Massachusetts Avenue," the radio blared.

"Roger that, Viper Six. Viper Seven, what's your status?" the Justice Department's Donatella Kim called into her handset.

Special Agent Kim had come up through DOJ with Isabella Espinosa. The two hit it off from the first day of field training, bonding over being the only two minority women in the training class, each surviving an overbearing immigrant mother, and a mutual love of cheesy vintage cop shows like *Charlie's Angels, Hill Street Blues,* and *Magnum, P.I.*

"Viper Seven, we're making a final pass by our target now. We'll be in position in sixty seconds," the radio reported.

"Roger that, Viper Seven," Donatella said. "Viper Eight?"

"Viper Eight, clear on Wisconsin."

"Roger that, Viper Eight. All units, stand by."

The plainclothes officer in the front spun around in his seat. "Just waiting for your go-order, Special Agent Kim."

"Espinosa should be here right now," Donatella said aloud. "It's not right that she's missing this."

"I heard she was sent to Somalia or someplace like that."

"Someplace like that," Donatella said. "This was her investigation. Her operation. She should really be here."

The radio crackled with static.

"Still waiting on your go-order, ma'am."

"Let's run through it once more."

"We're here off Embassy Row," the officer said, pointing to a white flashing light on the computer screen bracketed into the unmarked vehicle's dashboard. "The eight takedown units are deployed in these locations." He pointed to eight flashing red lights, each one a black Chevy Suburban containing a five-man tactical team. "Viper One is here, outside the British embassy. Viper Two is on this block just behind the Russian ambassador's house. Viper Three and Four are flanking the Nigerian embassy, here and here. The other four teams are standing by on these corners. Here, here, here, and here."

The red lights formed a perfect circular perimeter around the target painted with a beacon that appeared as a green circle on the map.

"What about eyes in the sky? Is the helicopter ready?"

"Confirmed. The tactical aviation unit has a Bell Jet Ranger at the Naval Observatory. It's hot and ready to go on your order. Ma'am, I don't know how you got the Navy or the Secret Service to agree to that."

"The residence is the closest helipad to the target. Plus we lucked out that the Vice President is away on an official visit to Cuba. It's all going into my memoirs," Donatella said. "Are we confirmed the target is still in place?"

"Yes, ma'am. Viper Five visualized the target entering the location late last night and no one's come or gone since."

"Good. What's the estimated time from go to target in custody?"

"Three minutes, ma'am."

"Good. We've got a local MPD radio blackout?"

"Confirmed. Local D.C. police are all cleared for a five-block perimeter and we'll jam the police band signal for the duration of the operation. On your order."

"Espinosa should really be here," Donatella said again, shaking her head.

"Just waiting on your green light, Special Agent Kim."

On cue, Donatella's phone buzzed.

Green light.

49

The consulate van had exited the expressway and, on Judd's direction, weaved its way through the side streets of Lagos.

"Take the next left," Judd ordered. He was leaning against the driver's seat, his phone pressed to his ear, taking instructions from Sunday, who had called back and was now watching them on a live satellite feed from his desk 5,400 miles away. "When you come to the Mr. Bigg's burger stand, take that left. It's bright red and yellow. Coming up in . . . thirty seconds."

"You owe us an explanation," Isabella demanded, pulling Judd into the back of the van. "You still haven't told me why we got off the highway. Why we aren't going to the airport? *Quién carajo* is calling you?"

Judd vigorously shook his head.

"Who is this Sunday?" she demanded.

Bola Akinola and Tunde Babatunde both glared at Judd in anticipation.

"If we're in danger," Isabella said, trying to calm down, "we need to know."

Judd met Isabella's gaze, which had evolved from angry to anxious. "In half a kilometer, take the roundabout exit to the north," Judd directed. "At Yoruba Junction."

"After that exit, go straight until I give you the next turn. I'll call you right back," Sunday said quickly, and then he hung up.

Judd dropped his arm and gave Isabella a barely perceptible nod. "We are going to the airport. We're taking an alternative route. A safer route. On the advice of"—he held up the phone—"a friend back in Washington."

"What is the danger?" Isabella asked.

"Bola, your life is under threat," Judd declared, facing the judge. "You know that, right?"

"When is it not, my friend?" Bola replied.

"No, Bola. *This is different.* We have information that there's a specific plot to assassinate you. Right now. That's why we're taking these side roads. That's why I'm trying to navigate a safer route."

"What about Landon Parker?" Isabella asked. "You just had him on the phone. Why didn't you tell him we had Bola—

that we were bringing him in? If we know Bola's life is in danger, the State Department can give him protection. We can grant him asylum."

"No."

"Why the *carajo* not?"

"The Nigerian attorney general got to Parker first. Or maybe it was Ambassador Katsina."

"What does that mean?"

"Officially, Bola is a fugitive. We can't bring him in now." Judd faced the judge. "Your government has issued an arrest warrant for you."

"I know, my friend."

"And the Nigerian federal police are on a nationwide hunt."

"Yes."

"Well, then Bola's coming with us," Isabella insisted.

Tunde Babatunde spoke up. "Why not sneak him onto my plane?"

"That's exactly what we'll do," Isabella said. "You just get back on the phone with your secret friend and get us to the airport safely. Once we're airborne, they can't stop us. We'll be home free."

"What do you think, Bola?" Judd asked.

Before he could answer, Judd's phone buzzed. "This is Ryker," he said.

"Stop the van," Sunday commanded.

"Stop the van!" Judd shouted.

"You're surrounded." Sunday tried to calm his voice and

slow down. "To the immediate west is an abandoned industrial park. Pull the van inside the main gate, cut the engine, and wait."

"There!" Judd pointed at a cluster of disused warehouses, a broken sign for Sahara Sunny Fabrics hanging precariously on the front gate. "Pull in there and kill the engine."

The driver followed Judd's instructions.

"Now what?" Judd asked.

"Wait there. I'll call you right back," Sunday said.

"What?" Judd started to protest, but it was too late. Sunday was gone.

Isabella was about to unleash another round of questioning, when her own phone buzzed with a text:

Your operation is on.

50

W e are a go," Donatella Kim announced, the adrenaline surging through her bloodstream.

"Airborne Buffalo One, you are go," the officer announced into the radio. "All Vipers, we're a go. Repeat, we are a go. Move to assault positions and await final instructions."

Donatella watched the helicopter take off, rising over the tree line about three blocks away and then circling at a low altitude, its spotlight dark for now. Her own vehicle's engine turned over and crawled slowly to the east. The eight SUVs with the FBI tactical teams also moved in unison, converging on the target location.

Donatella's car pulled just within sight line of the target, a white stucco house with grand pillars in the Greek neoclassical style, like a pint-sized replica of the White House. Mercedes and BMWs were parked on both sides of the leafy residential street, one that was only affordable to Old Money Washington or the expense accounts of senior foreign embassy staff.

Donatella couldn't see the strike teams from her vantage point. Instead she watched them close in via the monitor. Once all the teams were in place, Donatella seized the radio microphone again. She cleared her throat, swallowed hard, then double-checked the screen. She could hear the steady beat of the helicopter engine, a noise that would be only too familiar in that neighborhood.

Everything was in place for the takedown. Eight red lights in a tight circle around the green one. Eight SUVs packed with highly trained tactical officers of the Federal Bureau of Investigation. The Bell Jet Ranger helicopter ready with its massive spotlight to turn the night into day and lead a hot pursuit if the target somehow went on the run.

And, most important of all, the single sheet of paper tucked into her inside jacket pocket: the arrest warrant, covertly signed by a federal judge only minutes earlier in a tightly choreographed dance to ensure no leaks. And no time for any political objections to be raised over what was about to happen.

"Viper One, you are the lead team going in through the front," she said into the radio. "Viper Two, you have the back door. All other Vipers, move on my orders. We need this quick and clean, everybody. No time for the target to call backup. No time for any evidence to be destroyed. *Quick and clean.*"

She released the radio mic. "This is for you, Espinosa," she whispered to herself.

Donatella pressed the button on the radio again and heard the familiar crackle. She licked her lips. "Light it up."

51

Judd, Isabella, Bola, and Tunde all sat quietly in the back of the consulate van waiting for the phone to ring.

The silence was broken by the diplomatic security officer, sitting up front with the driver. "Dr. Ryker, I need to call this in. We can't just do nothing."

"Negative," Judd said.

"Sir, we've diverted from our planned route to Murtala and now we're just sitting here. No one knows we're here. I don't even know where we are."

"We're waiting for new instructions. Give me five minutes."

"My orders from the Regional Security Officer are to escort Mr. Babatunde to the airport. I'm already breaking protocol by allowing Judge Akinola to join us. The ambassador's going to have my ass. And now this."

"Your orders are to support me and Special Agent Espinosa. And our orders have changed. No calls."

"Dr. Ryker, if this has become an intelligence operation, then the station chief should have relayed this to the RSO, who would have given me the green light to change course. I don't like it."

"I don't like it, either—" Judd was about to lose his cool when a noise outside stopped him cold.

"What was that?" Isabella held up both hands.

"I'm not sitting here any longer," the officer said, drawing his weapon. "We're checking it out." He and the driver stepped out of the van. "Everyone, stay here."

Come on, Sunday, Judd thought. *Call me back already.*

Judd and the others listened as the officer and the driver circumnavigated the van in opposite directions. Then the sound of their footsteps stopped.

Judd and Isabella looked at each other for a long minute.

"I'm going out there," Isabella whispered, pulling her handgun from behind her lower back.

"No, let me go," Judd said.

"You're not taking my Glock," she said.

"I'm coming with you," Tunde said. "You're all in this mess because of me."

"No—"

The back door of the van was flung open and the four of

them spun around. "It was just a dog," the security officer said, standing there with the driver.

Judd let out a deep breath.

"*Gracias a Dios,*" Isabella said with relief. She reholstered her gun at the small of her back and crossed herself.

"What about your phone friend?" the officer asked. "Where the hell is he?"

Judd fingered his cell, trying to decide whether to call Sunday back or just wait.

"We need to get Mr. Babatunde to the airport and Judge Akinola to a safe location," the security officer said. "The first thing we need to do is—"

A flash of light blinded Judd, followed half a second later by a deafening *ka-boom.* He shut his eyes tight and covered his ears. The next few moments were a blur, a high-speed whirlwind of noise, light, and total confusion. Smoke, shadows, the outlines of a masked man. Judd felt strong arms shove him to the ground. His hands were tied and a hood was slipped over his head. *It's happening again.*

"Isabella!" he shouted. The only reply was the sound of men fighting and muffled yelling. Then three gunshots. *Bang! bang! bang!*

Judd twisted his neck in futility. His mind raced with fear and adrenaline. Who did they shoot? Did the gang come back for Tunde? No, that doesn't make sense. . . . It must be assassins for Bola. . . . Sunday must have been right about the intel. . . . Someone was tracking us. . . . Sunday was trying to help us escape, but . . . he never called back. We almost got

Tunde and Bola to the airport but . . . *we failed.* The killers got Bola. The officer and driver must have been the first shots. . . . That makes three. . . . They will kill Tunde, too. . . . And Isabella. And . . . *This is it,* he thought. *I'm going to die in an abandoned factory in Nigeria.*

Judd's thoughts jumped to his wife, Jessica—amazing, brave Jessica—on a mission somewhere on the other side of the world. Would she ever know what really happened to him? And his beautiful, innocent children, Toby and Noah, home with yet another babysitter while he was off globetrotting, on some half-baked assignment for who-knows-what, far away rather than home with his family. Would the boys understand? How would they remember their father? *Would they remember him?*

Judd felt a surge of guilt and remorse. Why hadn't he spent more time with his children instead of so many long hours in the office? How had he so often allowed work to come before family? How could he not have seen it? It was all so clear now. Judd felt sick. Helplessly facing the end of his life, his death-bed regrets were . . . a Hollywood cliché. *Pathetic.* A pitiful end to an unfinished life, he thought. Full of regrets. No inner bravery. Jessica would not be proud. *Jessica was wrong.*

Judd shut his eyes tight and waited for a bullet in the back of the head, an explosion followed in an instant by darkness, by total silence. But it didn't come. Instead he smelled . . . gasoline.

52

L ight it up," Viper One team leader repeated into his earpiece.

Battering rams simultaneously blew open the front and back doors of the target's house. Flash-bang grenades were tossed inside each entrance, which exploded with harmless pops intended to blind and confuse. Next came a flood of officers in midnight-black assault gear, pouring through the doors and windows like a mudslide swallowing a house.

"Lower floor clear. Moving to the second level," the Viper One team leader announced into his headset. Then "Go, go, go!" directing his team up a grand winding staircase.

Once on the upper floor, the team leader silently pointed

for two men to position themselves at each of the six bedroom doors. Once they were all in place: "Go!"

Six bedroom doors blew open in unison. Five were empty. But in the main master bedroom, officers found the target sitting up in bed, furiously trying to punch numbers on the bedside phone.

"Target acquired," the radio reported.

The officer snatched the phone from the target's hand and set it down gently in the cradle.

"This is an outrage!" the target fumed. "You don't know who you're dealing with! You have no right to be here! I'm calling—"

The assault team silently swallowed the noise with a hood over the head. Hands bound behind the back. Body shuffled quickly downstairs and bundled into a black van with blacked-out windows.

"Target in custody," the Viper One team leader reported. "Quick and clean, ma'am."

"Move the target to location Foxtrot. We'll take over from there."

53

The gasoline fumes burned inside Judd's nostrils. Then he heard a *whoosh* and, a second later, was hit by a blast of searing heat.

The terrorist group Boko Haram was known to lock people in buildings and then burn the whole place to the ground. *No, no,* he told himself, this wasn't Boko Haram. Maybe it was a militia? He knew gangs in South Africa killed their enemies by forcing a fuel-filled rubber tire around a victim's chest and arms before setting it on fire. They called it "necklacing." But he'd never heard of the practice used by Niger Delta militants.

It must be a criminal gang, he decided. They were notorious for pouring diesel fuel on rivals, lighting a match, and then videotaping their victims as they sizzled to death. The attackers must have poured gasoline. They must be torching the van, he thought. Was Bola inside? Tunde? And, he gulped, Isabella? *Was he next?*

As the thought made him nauseated, Judd was yanked to his feet and dragged away from the fire. He tried to resist but was pushed into another vehicle and the door was slammed shut.

Judd felt a guilty rush of relief. Maybe they weren't going to kill him after all. At least, not yet. But the relief was temporary. As the engine started up, a wave of new questions hit him. Where were they taking him? Was he being saved for a grisly video? Would he wind up on the Internet, an embarrassment to the government? A horror for his family?

Judd blocked out these questions. It was all speculation until he knew their intentions. Their motivations. He couldn't possibly know what would happen next until he knew: *Who was taking him?*

54

The black van peeled off from its SUV escorts and veered down a tree-lined residential street. At the end of the block, it took a sharp left into an alley, then another left into an open garage. A plainclothes officer with a coil wire in his ear checked both sides of the alleyway and pulled the garage door shut.

The target kicked and yelled as the van door slid open. The hooded body was gently carried down a hallway and set in a chair in an otherwise empty living room.

"You've made a *huuuuge* mistake," the hooded voice raged. "You have no idea what you've done. You're all going to pay!"

Special Agent Donatella Kim checked that the camera was on, that the video was recording. She plucked the hood off the target's head.

Congressman Shepard Truman blinked a few times, then narrowed his eyes at Donatella. "Who the hell are you?"

55

As the car pulled away, Judd decided on his next move. If they were going to kill him, whoever they were, if they had already murdered all the others, then he was going down fighting. *That's the brave thing to do. That's what* Jessica would do. *Yes, once they take me to their hideout and stop the car, I'm going to—*

The vehicle suddenly skidded to a halt. They hadn't traveled far.

Judd was yanked out of the car and pushed onto the ground. His hands were untied and the hood whisked off his head. Judd recoiled from the light and covered his eyes.

But then slowly things came into focus. He was . . . in

some kind of an abandoned warehouse. . . . Rows of steel pillars soared up high. . . . Bright midday light was pouring in through the holes in a crumbling ceiling. . . . There was an old white car and . . . Bola and Isabella! The two of them, sitting on the ground, also dazed and readjusting to the light. A wave of relief swept over him. He was alive. They were *all alive*.

"Isabella! Are you okay?"

Isabella, rubbing her newly freed wrists, stared back at him but didn't share his relief. Her face was full of fear. And anger.

That's when Judd noticed a single masked man standing over them. He was thin and shorter than Judd expected. A makeshift hood covered his face, with two jagged eyeholes.

"Who are you?" Judd demanded. "Where are the other men?"

"It's me," said a soft, familiar voice.

Judd winced in confusion.

The attacker slipped off the hood and . . . it wasn't a man at all.

"Jessica?"

Isabella was in shock. "I . . . don't understand."

"How are you . . . here? In Nigeria? Why are you kidnapping us? What . . . is going on?"

"I can't explain right now," Jessica said quickly. "We've got to get all of you out of here. Without being seen. We've got to go now."

"Where's Tunde?" Judd asked. "And the security offi-cers?"

"They're back at the fire," Jessica said. "Let's go!"

"What?"

"Someone had to see the van go up in flames. I had to have witnesses. It had to be credible. I needed the assassination to be convincing."

"Whose assassination?" Bola asked.

"Yours," she said.

"*Qué jodienda!*" Isabella was furious. "What is going on here?"

"I—" Judd wasn't sure what to say.

Isabella turned on Jessica. "We're not going anywhere until you explain!"

At that moment a fat bald head stepped out from behind a steel column. "Yes, love, do explain," Mikey said.

56

'm Special Agent Kim, with the Special Investigations Unit of the Department of Justice," she said. "Uncuff the Congressman. He's not going anywhere."

"Where the fuck am I?" Shepard Truman demanded as his hands were released.

"You are at a safe location," Donatella said. "We brought you here first to avoid the television cameras parked outside FBI headquarters."

"Do you have any idea what you've done? I'm a United States congressman!"

"That's why we brought you here first, sir. As a courtesy."

"A fucking courtesy!"

"You're welcome. I think you meant to say thank you."

"I'm going to fry your ass over this. You know I'm on the House Oversight Subcommittee, for fuck's sake!"

"We're well aware of who you are, sir. That's why you're here and not being frog-marched in front of the Hoover Building and CNN cameras."

"Do you have any idea how much trouble you're in?"

"Funny," Donatella said, deadpan. "That's the exact question I was about to ask you, Congressman."

"I want my lawyer." Truman sat up in his chair. "I'm not saying a word without Fred Faulkner."

"We can play it that way, Congressman. But before you make any more rash decisions, why don't you have a look at this?"

Donatella slid a stack of paper in front of him.

"What the hell is this?" he said, looking down at a government form.

"These are the FEC filings for the Friends of Shepard Truman Political Action Committee. Your PAC."

"So what?"

"Turn to the next page. That's the bank records for the PAC. At the bottom you'll see we've marked three transactions from a bank account in the Cayman Islands."

"You'll have to ask Fred Faulkner about those. I don't have anything to do with the PAC. That's the whole point."

"Bear with me, Congressman. I think you'll want to follow this trail," she said, flipping to the next page and pointing to a yellow circle around an address. "*Here.* We've identified the owner of that account as Harvey Holden. Do you know Mr. Holden?"

"Of course. Harvey's an old friend and a longtime constituent of mine. So what?"

"Mr. Holden is the senior partner at Holden Harriman Quinn. He's also a minority owner of the Brooklyn Nets basketball team."

"Everybody knows that!"

"I'm just establishing some facts, Congressman."

"Whatever Harvey's done has nothing to do with me. Nothing at all."

"What do you know about Turkish bonds?"

"Turkish bonds? I don't know what you're talking about."

"What about Indonesian currency swaps? Or Ukrainian debt?"

"I don't know anything."

"Do you know Mr. Holden's business partners?"

"I have no idea who Harvey does business with. How could I?"

"You're welcome to flip through the next few pages, Congressman. But here's what you'll find. Or, rather, here's what we've discovered. HHQ was in financial trouble. Big trouble. Despite the fancy offices and glowing news profiles, HHQ was technically bankrupt after overpaying for distressed assets, such as Wildcat Oil. Then they doubled down on petroleum and got caught over-leveraged in oil price futures."

"This has nothing to do with me."

"Have you ever heard of the Bolshaya Neva Fund?"

"No."

"Bolshaya Neva is based in St. Petersburg. That's Russia," she added, just to annoy him. "The fund rescued Wildcat Oil and HHQ by taking a silent majority stake."

"I still don't see what any of this has to do with me."

"To make Wildcat Oil profitable again, the plan was for Bolshaya to bring the cash. HHQ brought the political connections. *That was you.*"

"Me?"

"Did you call the U.S. ambassador in Manila on behalf of Harvey Holden on January fourth of last year?"

"I don't recall."

"On February twenty-second, did you contact the Commerce Department seeking information on oil contracts in Indonesia?"

"I'm not answering that."

"Did you call the Justice Department the following month to urge them to open investigations into Chinese companies that were in direct competition with Wildcat Oil?"

"I just want a fair playing field for American companies. That's all. I'm ensuring that American business can operate around the world free from the tyranny of corruption."

"Did you make contact with an official of the Nigerian oil ministry to lobby on behalf of Wildcat?"

"Are you serious? The *Nigerians* are the corrupt ones. I'm trying to protect an American investor. Can't you see it? I'm trying to serve *American national interests.*"

"Did you call the Secretary of State's chief of staff just this week to ask for help finding an HHQ employee, a Mr. Jason Saunders, who reportedly went missing in London?"

"What's wrong with that?"

"Nothing's wrong. It's just ironic."

"What's ironic about helping a constituent? That's what members of Congress do."

"Uh-huh," Donatella said. "What I'm seeing here is a pattern of political favors in exchange for financial contributions."

"What?"

"Another word for this is . . . 'corruption.'"

"This is bullshit. You haven't proved anything. You've got nothing."

"We have a witness already. Mr. Saunders is ready to testify in open court how HHQ funneled money from illegal Russian sources into your campaign fund."

"Saunders?" Truman's face contorted with confusion. "You found the missing kid? How is he . . . involved?"

"Involved? He's right in the middle of it. He's our star witness, Congressman. Jason Saunders is going to blow the whole case wide open."

"I'm not saying anything."

"That's fine. We know everything already. How the money was moved, where it came from, where it went." Donatella Kim cracked her knuckles. "How it was covered up."

"I want my lawyer."

"That's not even the worst part, Congressman."

"I'm not saying another fucking word until my lawyer is present."

"Don't you want to know about Harvey Holden's mystery angel investor?"

"No."

"The Bolshaya Neva Fund is into some strange stuff, Congressman."

"I don't know anything about it."

"Bolshaya Neva launders money for Russian organized crime."

"Go fuck yourself."

"You ever heard of the Bear?" Donatella asked.

"No."

"Well, he knows you. The Bear's responsible for the murder of hundreds of people. He's ruined thousands of lives. He traffics everything from narcotics to arms to people. That's guns, drugs, *little girls*." Donatella paused to let that image sink in. "Now the Bear's moving into the oil business. And guess who is his man in Washington, D.C.?"

Shepard Truman looked up blankly at Donatella Kim.

She arched her eyebrows. "You."

Truman dropped his head.

"Here's the picture that a jury's going to see. The Friends of Shepard Truman Political Action Committee is really a front for Holden Harriman Quinn, which is a front for Wildcat Oil, which is actually a front for Bolshaya Neva, which is a front for a psychopathic Russian mob boss."

"That's quite a story, Special Agent Kim."

"That's exactly what a jury's going to see once we get through connecting all the dots. Shepard Truman, Congressman from New York's Tenth District . . . Works for the Bear."

"This is all circumstantial. You don't have anything on me."

"The FBI's counterpart in Nigeria has been doing some homework on your business partners. The Nigerian Crime and Corruption Task Force is ready to unseal its findings." Donatella dropped a thick bound report on the table with a thud. "Here's an advance copy from Judge Akinola's investigation. Would you like to know what it says?"

"No."

"Well, here are the highlights, Congressman. Oil executives dropping dead. Workers disappearing. Pipelines exploding. The platform that was overrun. The *sixty-four dead men*, including an American engineer with a wife and two kids. It's all part of a plan to use local militias to attack the Chinese. So Wildcat Oil can take over their concessions. Judge Akinola's report brings the whole story into focus."

"You can't connect anything back to me."

"With Akinola's dossier, we can now show exactly how the Bear was trying to muscle in. We can show how Holden was working for the Bear. And we can show how you were a key part of it."

"I haven't done anything wrong. You have no proof."

Donatella tapped the microphone on her radio. "Bring it in."

An agent in an FBI windbreaker entered the room carrying a large red picnic cooler, which he set down.

Donatella sat back in her chair and stared at Truman, savoring the moment and again wishing that Isabella Espinosa could be there. Then, slowly and deliberately, she opened the cooler top and grabbed two black cartons of Breyers ice cream, holding them both out in front of her.

"Congressman, vanilla or chocolate?"

57

W ot am I supposed to tell the Bear, love?" Mikey's fat, bald head was dripping with perspiration. With one hand he aimed a handgun straight at Jessica. In the other hand hung a long, shiny machete.

"Now what?" Isabella gasped.

"Queen Sheba, you was supposed to have sorted out this here judge," Mikey sneered. "Now, I'm going to have to finish your job."

"No!" Jessica yelled.

Mikey raised the machete. "All you, down on your knees!" he ordered, waving the gun.

"What is going on?" Judd asked. "Who is this?"

"I'm sorry, Judd," Jessica said. "I didn't have time—"

"Oi!" Mikey shouted. "Shut your gob or I'll have your head off."

Mikey paced behind the four of them, brandishing the gun and the machete as they knelt on the ground, fingers interlocked on the back of their heads. He finally stopped and stood over Jessica. "That's a bloody good idea I've had. I'm going to take your soddin' head back wif me. Show the boss what I've done. That I've finished your job."

He pressed the gun barrel against the back of Jessica's neck.

"I knew sommink wasn't right wif you," he snarled. "I told you that you didn't know who you was messin' wif." Mikey took a deep breath. "Queen Sheba, my arse. What game you playing, love?"

Jessica didn't move.

"You was supposed to do this here judge." He slid the gun to the back of Bola's neck. "The Bear paid you a shitload of dosh to get this done. And now here I am, watching you run around this shithole, pretending you're on the job. You tryin' to mug me off."

He squeezed the gun against Jessica's neck again. "I fink you been fakin' all them hits. I fink you working for them fuckin' muppet Yanks. That's why you're first." Mikey raised the machete high over his head.

"No!" Isabella shouted, standing up but keeping her hands high over her head. "I'm the one you want," she insisted, stepping straight in front of Judd and stretching her arms as tall as she could, exposing her lower back. Judd watched her, unsure of what she was doing. "Look here," Isabella said slowly. "I'm the one you want. *Look at me.*"

A flash of metal was visible at the small of her back.

"Fuck off," Mikey sneered, turning back to Jessica.

Bang! A gunshot echoed through the hollow warehouse. Time stood still for a moment before a thick ooze ran from a hole in Mikey's forehead. The big man dropped to his knees, the machete and handgun clanged on the ground, and he slumped over, his face hitting the concrete with a dull thud.

All eyes faced the shooter.

Judd Ryker held the smoking Glock tightly with both hands.

DAY SIX

SATURDAY

58

When "Breaking News" flashed across her television screen, Mariana Leibowitz hit the PAUSE button on her treadmill and turned up the volume.

Mariana had been up late the previous evening working her contacts in the national media to make sure they got the story just right. She knew there were too many rumors swirling around, too much misinformation out there, and she saw it as her job to fight back against the tide of lies. She wanted the truth to come out. *Well,* she thought, *mostly the truth.*

"This is CNN and I'm Vijaya Subramanian. We've got breaking news this morning right here in Washington, D.C.," the newscaster announced, excitement gleaming in her eye.

Mariana recognized the look on the reporter's face, like a hungry lion in the savannah that's come across an injured gazelle. A flash of hesitation—imperceptible to most, but Mariana knew what she was witnessing—to savor the moment before the pounce of certain delicious victory. The newscaster ever so slightly licked her lips before sharing the red meat.

"CNN has just learned that the FBI has taken Congressman Shepard Truman into federal custody after a raid on his home early yesterday morning. The FBI isn't yet saying the exact charges they expect to bring against the three-term Congressman from the Tenth District of New York. But they have confirmed that he is now being held by the authorities and his arrest followed a months-long sting operation by a special investigative unit within the Department of Justice."

The screen cut to a wobbly shot of the Congressman in a gray sweatshirt being led out of a van by a pretty Asian woman in a business suit and with a government badge swinging around her neck. Truman held up his handcuffed palms in a futile attempt to block his face from the television cameras.

Mariana winced in sympathy, knowing that, whatever the facts of the case, whatever the outcome of the trial, this was the lasting image that would run on all the news shows for days if not years. *The money shot.*

"For more on this breaking news, let's turn to our legal correspondent, Teri Goldberg, who's outside FBI headquarters. Teri, what more do we know?"

"Thanks, Vijaya. The FBI isn't saying much officially. But CNN has learned that the investigation into Congressman Truman is related to illegal campaign financing and possible links between his campaign, an unnamed New York hedge fund, a foreign oil company, and Russian organized crime. Our sources report that the investigation into Shepard Truman has been ongoing for many months and involved not only the U.S. Department of Justice but extensive cooperation with law enforcement authorities in foreign countries in both Europe and Africa. This was a highly complex and well-coordinated global investigation of a prominent American legislator."

The screen cut back to the newscaster. "If true, that's quite a bombshell, Teri. A U.S. congressman with links to the Russian mafia? Is there any precedent for this?"

"We'll have to see what facts emerge in coming days, but if these initial reports are true, it would indeed be unprecedented. It would also be quite a comedown for the Congressman. Shepard Truman is a handsome, well-liked member of Congress thought to have a bright political future. It was widely known he was planning to run for the vacant New York seat in the U.S. Senate and was tipped to be the primary challenger to District Attorney Arturo Osceola. Truman was best known for serving his constituents and his hard stand against international corruption. Sources on Capitol Hill confirmed to me today that he was planning to introduce the new Truman Zero Tolerance Amendment, which would have imposed new sanctions and fines on corrupt activities and restricted political contributions. That's obviously now dead, Vijaya."

"Thank you, Teri Goldberg, reporting from FBI headquarters in Washington, D.C. Shepard Truman has not made any public statements, but his lawyer Fred Faulkner had this to say. . . ."

"The allegations against Congressman Truman are patently false," declared a dour man in a pin-striped suit, bow tie, and oversized tortoiseshell glasses. "We look forward to a thorough investigation and we are confident that, when all the facts come to light, Congressman Truman will be cleared of all wrongdoing. We will also be asking the attorney general to launch a special independent inquiry into FBI overreach and gross constitutional violations that impinge on the separation of powers that our Founding Fathers held to be sacrosanct."

Mariana admired the lawyer for immediately going on the offense. That's what she would have advised, had she not known exactly what was coming next.

"Let's now turn to Nancy Birdman, who is in upper northwest Washington, D.C., outside the home of Congressman Truman. Nancy, what do you see?"

"Right now, police have cordoned off the entire block around the home of Congressman Truman. They aren't letting anyone in or out, and neither the D.C. Metropolitan Police nor the FBI are saying anything except to confirm that law enforcement activity is under way at this location. However, an unnamed source who we can only describe as well-informed about the details of the operation has shared with CNN that the FBI has discovered a large amount of cash in a freezer in the basement of the Congressman's home."

"You're saying the Congressman was hiding cash in his freezer, Nancy?"

"I don't think we can say that just yet. Only that we have a report that one hundred and fifty thousand dollars in unmarked bills was found inside ice cream tubs in the freezer in the Congressman's basement. We're still seeking public confirmation of this from the FBI."

Ouch, Mariana thought. *This can only get worse.*

"Thank you, Nancy. Let's now go to Anderson Adeola in New York. Anderson, what can you add to this story?'

"I'm here at Park Avenue and Fifty-fifth Street in New York, where the authorities have raided the offices of prominent investment firm Holden Harriman Quinn. HHQ's senior partner Harvey Holden is, we understand, being held for questioning by the FBI. No one is yet saying whether this action is directly related to the Shepard Truman investigation, but the timing suggests that it may be. Harvey Holden is a prominent philanthropist and the principal owner of the Brooklyn Nets basketball team, so he's well known in New York financial and social circles. FEC filings show that Holden has been an active political contributor, including to Shepard Truman, but we still don't yet know if there's any connection to Truman's arrest or what exactly law enforcement was looking for in the raid."

"Thank you. That's Anderson Adeola in New York. We'll keep on this remarkable breaking story of the arrest of Congressman Shepard Truman as it unfolds," the newscaster announced. "In other news, an attack on a U.S. diplomatic convoy in the Nigerian city of Lagos has resulted in the death of one man."

A still shot of a burned-out van was shown on the screen.

"According to a State Department spokesman, this was a routine convoy transporting diplomats to the airport in the early hours of yesterday morning. The cause of the explosion remains under investigation by local authorities, but we understand that one of the embassy vehicles either caught fire or struck an IED. Lagos, a city of some twenty million people, has suffered from a wave of kidnappings in recent months, but no Americans have been targeted so far. Neither the terrorist group Boko Haram nor Niger Delta militants have claimed responsibility. We don't know if this attack is related to a similar incident in Islamabad, Pakistan, last week, where a U.S. embassy vehicle came under heavy gunfire by unknown assailants. The American embassy in Nigeria has confirmed that there were no American casualties from yesterday's incident and that all U.S. personnel are safe and now back home in the United States. One man, being reported on Nigerian television as an innocent bystander, died in the explosion. . . ."

Nothing about Bola Akinola, nothing about Judd Ryker. Relieved and satisfied with what she was hearing, Mariana clicked over to ESPN.

"What a week for Brooklyn Nets star center Tunde Babatunde!" an over-caffeinated broadcaster cried. "Babatunde is back in New York, fresh from a harrowing visit to his homeland in West Africa. Babatunde made a three-day humanitarian trip to Nigeria to open a children's hospital in his name." The television screen cut to video of Babatunde at the hospital ceremony, surrounded by throngs of young children.

"According to initial news reports, he disappeared on Wednesday and team officials could not reach him for forty-eight hours. The Nets front office reportedly contacted the State Department, fearing that Babatunde may have been kidnapped, igniting a frantic search that included American and local authorities. But this crazy story has a happy ending, folks: Yesterday, Babatunde was found unharmed and NBA officials have told ESPN that the incident was just a misunderstanding and there was in fact no kidnapping."

On the screen flashed a still shot of Babatunde sitting in a small boat, holding his knees, surrounded by awkward young men with serious faces. Mariana narrowed her eyes. She thought she could see that one of the boys had a tiny stuffed animal around his neck. *A pink rabbit?*

The shot cut back to the studio. "What a story! The Nets coach insists Babatunde is in top shape and will be ready for the first game of the season. . . ."

Click. Mariana changed over to the Discovery Channel and restarted the treadmill. As the pounding of her feet accelerated, she decided, yes . . . she was very satisfied.

59

Still no word from Mikey?'

"No, boss," said the Greek. The former Olympic boxer had not made it through the first round in the 2004 Athens Games, but he still knew how to throw a punch. "Nothing from Mikey."

"He's dead," said the Bear. He was sitting in his desk chair, grooming his beard with a gold-plated comb.

"No one ever found a body," said the Greek, who was sitting on the white leather couch and fiddling with a thick gold chain around his neck. "We'll keep searching, boss. Maybe he'll turn up."

"No. Michael is gone." The Bear checked his face in a

compact mirror and slid the comb into a desk drawer. "You're promoted, Nico."

The Greek sat forward and dug his elbows into his knees. "You want me to find the bitch?"

The Bear considered his next move.

"You want me to hunt down this Queen Sheba?" the gangster asked, spinning a chunky ring on one hand. "Boss, you want her head in a box? Delivered right here? Just say the word."

"What about New York?"

"Holden was arrested by the FBI. Harvey is done. Finished. But don't worry, boss. We've got another man in New York ready to take his place. The business won't even notice he's gone. The only question is what you want me to do about Holden. Say the word, and the minute he steps inside Rikers Island . . ." The Greek drew a finger across his throat.

The Bear slumped back into his chair. "What's our business, Nico?"

"Money."

The Bear shook his head.

"Power?"

The Bear stared at the Greek with disappointment.

"Blood?"

"Mother Russia," said the Bear. "We serve the motherland. That's our business."

"Yes, boss. If you say so."

The Bear walked to the picture window. "The water of the Neva River, can you see it? It flows from where I drank my mother's milk, through our glorious city, to the world. Everyone drinks from Mother Russia, but no one is aware. The Neva flows silently from me to everyone. I am everywhere, Nico."

"Yes, boss."

"Harvey Holden can't tell them anything," the Bear shook his head. "He doesn't know anything. The American government doesn't know anything."

"Letting Holden live makes us look weak, boss. Let me deal with him. He'll be leaving jail feet first. Or without a head."

The Bear exhaled and then gave a subtle nod.

"And the bitch?"

"You'll never find Queen Sheba," the Bear laughed.

"She killed Mikey. You going to let her get away with that?"

"You'll never find her, Nico." He shook his head. "And if you did, you'd be lucky to get out alive."

"I can do it, boss. I will get Queen Sheba for Mikey. I'll get her for you. I want to do it."

"I need you to deal with our Chinese problem. We can't leave Moscow waiting any longer. Control your emotions. This is about business, not revenge."

"Yes, boss. Whatever you say."

"You deal with the Chinese," he said with a wave.

"I will. Right away." The Greek stood up.

The Bear watched his new lieutenant depart with a restored sense of order. Mikey had vanished, but now he had the Greek.

His New York connection was gone, but that, too, was easily replaceable. There was no shortage of corruptible bankers in New York and London. The Chinese problem would go away once they found a new assassin. Moscow would be happy. The empire would expand. Mother Russia would be served. The Americans wouldn't be any wiser. He would become even more powerful.

Then the Bear made one more decision. The Greek was right about one thing. *He had to hunt down Queen Sheba.*

60

"Where is Jessica Ryker?" the Deputy Director of the CIA roared. The veins in his forehead were pulsating. His secretary knew this was a terrible sign.

"Still trying to track her down," she said.

"Keep trying, dammit!"

"Yes, sir."

"Call the FAA. Have them check every inbound flight over the past twelve hours."

"I already did that. They're reporting no one named Ryker on any inbound commercial flights."

"Well, tell them to check again!" he roared. "And have the CBP check the private plane arrival logs, too."

"Yes, sir."

"And get me the goddamn Crime and Narcotics Center on the line. Right now!"

What the hell happened yesterday in Nigeria? The question spun in his head like a windmill in a typhoon. His last direct contact with Jessica Ryker was their agreement that she would take out the judge, then report back to Langley so they could plot their next move against the Bear. His last update from assets in the field reported that Jessica had arrived safely in Lagos but ditched her Agency fixer soon afterward. She'd thrown him right out of the car and took off by herself. *What the fuck, Jessica?*

The next thing the Deputy Director learned was that there had been an incident just off the airport highway involving a vehicle from the U.S. consulate. SIGINT monitoring of the police and local intelligence communications had reported a fire, multiple gunshots, and eventually a body discovered at the site. The photos from the scene were useless, as the corpse was charred beyond recognition. And he was still waiting for the DNA analysis of the sample an asset had swiped at the morgue. *What the hell happened in Nigeria?*

Then Jessica disappeared. No communication, no electronic footprint. She must have fled the country. *But how?*

"I have CNC on secure line four, sir."

The Deputy Director snatched the phone out of the cradle. "What do you know about the Bear?"

"Chatter spiked yesterday, indicating some disturbance in their network. Someone important in the Bear's inner circle seems to have gone missing."

"Who?"

"We don't know, sir. But the chatter has since dissipated."

"Which means what?"

"We don't know that, either. Not yet. But the channels we had been using to ghost-plant Queen Sheba are dead. Everyone in the chain has gone underground."

"Dead?"

"Yes, sir. Looks like we lost him. Whatever happened in Lagos yesterday spooked the Bear. We're back to square one."

"Sweet Jesus, do you have any idea where Queen Sheba is now?" he demanded, trying to contain his temper.

"No, sir."

"Do you have any new leads on the Bear's links into the FSB or the army or the Politburo?"

"I'm sorry. Nothing new."

"So we still don't know if the Bear is a criminal or working for higher-ups in the Russian government? We don't really know why he's targeting Chinese oil executives?"

"That's correct, sir."

"And now that Queen Sheba is burned, we've lost our best chance to find out?"

"Yes, I believe so, sir."

"Assemble the team at eight o'clock," he demanded. "We need to figure out what the fuck happened. What we need to clean up. And what the fuck we're going to do next. Got it?"

The Deputy Director slammed the phone down before he heard an answer. He was too busy trying to decide what to do with Jessica Ryker. How many times can she go rogue without consequences? *How many times can I let Jessica Ryker off the hook?* To get back on the Bear's trail, *I'm going to need my very best operative. I'm going to need—*

"Got her!" came a shout from outside his office.

The door flew open. "CBP has a 'J. Ryker' on a private plane that touched down at Dulles just after midnight this morning," his secretary announced. "Two J. Rykers, actually."

"She's back in Washington? Are you telling me she's been back for seven hours and hasn't come back online?"

"Looks that way, sir."

"So, where the hell is she?"

"I don't know. She's not picking up any of her phones. They're all going straight to voice mail."

"Keep trying. If she doesn't turn up within the next sixty minutes, send a security team to her house in Georgetown to kick in the fucking door."

How many times can I let Jessica Ryker off the hook?

61

Landon Parker walked straight into the private dining room on the State Department's seventh floor. Inside, the Secretary of State sat alone at an antique Victorian table having her usual early-morning poached egg and half a grapefruit with freshly roasted Ethiopian coffee.

"Good morning, Landon," she said with a smile. "Breakfast?"

"No, ma'am. I'm just here to brief you—"

"Nothing at all?" she interrupted. "At least have coffee. I so hate to eat alone."

"Thank you, ma'am. I won't be here very long. Packed agenda today."

"When isn't it packed, Landon?"

"Yes, ma'am. I want to go over your talking points for your calls today with the Brazilian foreign minister, the President of Latvia, and the Prime Minister of Bangladesh. The World Bank president is paying a courtesy call at nine and then you have a drop-in from Senator McCall at nine-fifteen."

"What does Bryce McCall want this time?"

"I will find out before he gets here. Then we've got back-to-backs with D, P, and G. The new head of the DEA is here at eleven, and then you've agreed to make remarks at the opening of the new panda habitat at the National Zoo."

"Pandas." She smiled. "Make sure Public Affairs alerts the *New York Times*."

"Of course, ma'am," he said. "I want your sign-off for a new high-level oil security initiative I'm launching. It's called the Three Gulfs Oil Security Partnership."

"Okay," she said. "What is it?"

"As you know, ma'am, China is expanding its control of energy resources, grabbing petroleum blocks in every corner of the globe. I want to build a coalition of allies who will work together to ensure that oil continues to flow no matter what the Chinese do."

"This is your South China Sea obsession, isn't it, Landon?"

"No, ma'am. This is the opposite. We need to prepare for every contingency in the South China Sea. But I want an insurance policy if we fail. I want us to lock down other crucial oil-producing regions: the Persian Gulf, the Gulf of Mexico, and the Gulf of Guinea."

"The Three Gulfs."

"That's it, ma'am. I've recruited Qatar to represent the Persian Gulf and the Mexicans are on board. The final piece is the Gulf of Guinea. I've been working quietly with the Nigerians on this, with their envoy here. I've been meeting regularly with Ambassador Katsina for weeks and she's now ready to take it to her President. Once we get their official support, you can announce the Three Gulfs. Maybe ahead of the next NATO summit. This could be one of your biggest legacies."

"Fine," the Secretary said as she sipped her coffee.

"Ma'am, I want your approval for the Three Gulfs before I share any details with the regional bureaus."

"You haven't told any of the regionals?"

"No, ma'am."

"I wouldn't worry about Western Hemisphere or Near Eastern Affairs. They'll go along. Africa might be trickier. You really haven't brought Bill Rogerson into the loop?"

Parker raised his eyebrows at the Secretary of State, a sign he often used with his boss when she already knew the answer.

"Rogerson's touchy. He's is going to bitch and moan that you came to me with another end run," she said. "I can see his face already."

Parker nodded. "So I have your endorsement for the Three Gulfs, Madam Secretary?"

"Do it." She scooped her grapefruit. "But what's the plan for China?"

"Have you had your morning intel briefing yet?"

"The DNI was here already. You just missed him."

"So you're aware of the latest Chinese naval movements in the South China Sea?" Parker asked.

"Yes, that was in the briefing. And these new islands they're building."

"We're going to add sea-lane security and sovereignty issues to the next round of the Pacific trade talks. It'll be the first item on the agenda for your bilateral meeting with the Japanese foreign minister when he's here on Monday. We're also dispatching Tony on a Pacific tour to Manila, Canberra, and Bangkok to make sure we're all on the same page."

"Are we on the same page here *in Washington*?" The Secretary frowned at Parker.

"South China Sea is priority one at the NSC this morning. I've got Wendy camped outside the Situation Room to make sure your equities are defended. If they take any new strategy to POTUS, I'll be sure you're in the Oval when it happens. We won't let the Pentagon jam us again. I've arranged for you to have an early dinner tonight with the SecDef. It'll help smooth things over."

"What about the Joint Chiefs?"

"Not yet, ma'am. When you go to Jakarta next week, we'll add a stopover in Hawaii so you can get the full dog and pony show at PACOM."

"But what's *our plan*, Landon? We can't have the Pentagon driving events in the Pacific without strategic guidance from State. The South China Sea is not just a military problem. Beyond your Three Gulfs idea, what's our *diplomatic plan?*"

"East Asian and Pacific Affairs is assembling road map options for us to consider before we go to the interagency."

"So, where are they?"

"EAP's ideas are all fine, but you haven't seen them yet because they're not quite ready for prime time."

"What's the problem, Landon?"

"They're too conventional, ma'am. We need more creative thinking. If it comes to blows between us and China, we're going to need new ideas."

"So, who's working on *that?*"

"Judd Ryker."

"Okay, so, where is he? Get him in here right now. Let's see what he's got. Let's see what S/CRU can do."

"Ryker's finishing up another project."

"Well, this is a priority, Landon. You just said so yourself. Whatever he's doing now can wait."

"Yes, ma'am," Parker said.

"What exactly *has* Judd Ryker been doing?"

"Do you remember Tunde Babatunde? You hosted the groundbreaking ceremony for his hospital last Tuesday."

"Of course I remember Tunde. What a lovely man. So tall."

"Well, soon after he arrived in Nigeria, Babatunde was kidnapped—"

"What?" the Secretary interrupted, her face flush with horror. "Why wasn't I briefed?"

"—and Judd Ryker has been helping me to get him back."

"And?"

"Success," Parker said, his face deadpan.

"Oh, thank goodness," she said, her face overcome with relief. "That's huge, Landon. Just huge. The State Department rescued an NBA player who was home opening a children's hospital. A superstar and a humanitarian. We couldn't write better copy. Get Public Affairs on this right away. We should bring Tunde back here to the Department for a hero's welcome."

"I don't advise that, ma'am. I think we should be cautious promoting any State Department role in his recovery. At least until I get the full debrief from Ryker."

"What aren't you telling me, Landon?"

"Babatunde is back safely, but it was"—he shrugged—"complicated, ma'am. I assume you've been reading about Shepard Truman?"

"Of course. It's all over the press. It's A1 in the *Washington Post* this morning. What was that lunatic thinking? Taking campaign contributions from the Russian mafia. I mean, really, Shepard."

"Well, one of Truman's constituents is the owner of the Brooklyn Nets, which is Babatunde's team. I'm not going to say any more. You don't *know* any more, Madam Secretary."

"That's correct, I don't," she insisted.

"I'm going to keep it that way, ma'am. You should have full confidence that we didn't do anything wrong. I've made sure of that. There's also no email or memo trail between Truman's office and State on this issue. The phone logs will show I've spoken with the Congressman on numerous occasions in recent weeks, but this is nothing out of the ordinary. The records reflect just the usual legislative affairs with a member of Congress."

"You're sure, Landon?"

"Yes, ma'am. But that's why we're better playing it low-key on the Babatunde incident."

"Fine. Good."

"And Ryker knows to keep quiet, too," Parker said.

The Secretary of State narrowed her eyes. "Where is Judd Ryker?"

"I'm tracking him down now."

62

Judd opened one eye, unsure exactly where he was. Warm cotton sheets hugged his skin. A beam of soft, angelic light peeked through a gap in the bedroom curtains. His nostrils detected a mellow feminine, vaguely vanilla aroma. *Home.*

He rolled over to confirm it was all true, that he really was back home, that the nightmare of the past twenty-four hours was over. And there she was. Jessica lying motionless next to him, sound asleep. Her eyes fluttered gently, her lips barely open, a picture of peaceful serenity. The precise opposite of yesterday's hurricane of violence.

Judd and Jessica had landed in Washington just after midnight and quickly cleared immigration and customs at the private terminal adjacent to Dulles Airport. Then they had all gone their separate ways. Tunde Babatunde got back on the plane to New York, Isabella Espinosa drove herself home to her condo in Arlington, while the Rykers took a taxi home to Georgetown.

Judd and Jessica let themselves into the house, checked on their sleeping children, woke and paid the babysitter, and then crawled straight into bed without a word. The only acknowledgment of what had just happened, and what might be coming next, was their cell phones. Judd turned his off and set it on his nightstand. Jessica removed the battery from hers and slid the separate pieces underneath their bed. They were both sound asleep within seconds.

So what would happen today? Judd genuinely didn't know. *What did he want to happen?*

Jessica opened both eyes.

"Morning, sweets," he whispered.

She blinked in reply.

"You all right?" he asked.

She nodded slightly and wet her lips.

"You sleep?"

She shrugged. "What time is it?"

"Almost eight."

"I'm sorry," she said.

"Sorry? About what?"

"Everything. The lies. The half-truths. The danger. It's all my fault. I brought it all on us, on you, on our family."

"You saved my life again," Judd said.

"No, I didn't. *You saved me.* I'm the one who nearly got you killed yesterday. That would have been on me. I allowed that animal to follow me. I made the mistake. I brought him to you."

"That's not your fault, Jess."

"Of course it is. I was trying to keep us apart, and I failed. I was trying to do my job, and I failed. I was trying to protect you. And I failed."

"How could you know, Jess?"

"I could have taken him out when I had the chance. I could have ended it all before he followed me to Nigeria. But I failed at that, too."

"I don't understand."

"He must have seen my tell. I must have given something away. Judd, remember you saw it earlier in the week. You could *read me.* You knew I was going to Russia. That I was working on organized crime. They must have read me, too."

"You don't know that, Jess."

"I was right about one thing. Your inner bravery. That your courage would show up when we needed it. That you wouldn't hesitate. I told you, Judd." She squeezed his arm. "When your family was in danger, I told you that you'd do what you'd have to. That, to protect me, you'd even *kill.*"

"I did," he said, still not quite believing it himself.

"You killed that monster before he could kill us all. *You did that*, Judd."

"I did," he whispered confidently.

"But no one will ever know," she insisted. "I took care of that. You don't need to worry."

"I'd rather not have seen that," he said.

"Forget about what I did. No one will ever identify his body. No one who matters will ever know he was even there. That he even existed. I've made sure of that."

"What about his bosses back in Russia? They must know he's missing. They must know where he was going. That he was chasing you. Won't they come after you now?"

"I'll handle it. The world is messy—"

"And dangerous. I know that. But what will you do, Jess?"

"I said I'll handle it. A diversion. Maybe a decoy. Have some confidence in me, Judd."

"Confidence," he repeated. "Is everything about confidence? Is everything a con?"

"Not everything."

"The scam I was chasing was really Isabella's operation. A sting against Congressman Truman. The Coyote's business. The shadow list. The whole thing was one big con. I just didn't know the mark."

"Things are rarely what they seem, Judd."

"Like Bola Akinola," he said. "I thought we were helping him fight corruption in his country. I thought we were helping him defend Nigeria's democracy. But it was the other way around. He was helping to defend ours."

"Rarely what they seem," she repeated.

"After everything they threw at Bola, all the false charges, all those stories planted in the press. Mariana was right that it was coming. And that it was all bull."

"Bola Akinola will be fine," Jessica said. "He knows what he's doing."

"He got Tunde free with a single phone call. I still don't know how he pulled that off."

"Sometimes the best cops have to treat the criminals like brothers," she said. "Sometimes you have to go deep into his den to fight the devil."

"So where did the ransom come from? If we didn't pay, then who did?"

Jessica just gently shook her head.

"Bola's playing such a dangerous game," Judd said, exhaling loudly. "I don't think I could do it."

"You couldn't. I couldn't. That's what makes Bola so special."

"I still can't believe he didn't get on the plane," Judd exclaimed. "That he refused asylum. That he chose to stay in Nigeria to clear his name. After everything that's happened."

"When you fight corruption, corruption fights back."

"That's exactly what Isabella said."

"I like that woman." Jessica smiled. "She's got a bright future."

"Yes, she does." Judd sat up. "So . . . what about us?"

"What *about* us?"

"What's our future, Jess? When I walk back into the State Department today, I have no idea if Landon Parker is going to congratulate me for rescuing Babatunde. Or if I'm going to be fired. I don't know what he believes. I don't know if what happened was a confidence game or if it was real. I don't know if S/CRU is the hero or if it's going to be shut down. And the funny thing is"—Judd scrunched his face—"I'm not sure which outcome I really want."

"You have to decide, Judd." She placed both hands on his shoulders. "Are you in or are you out?"

"I should ask you the same question, Jess."

She let go of him and brushed her hair behind one ear.

"Jessica Ryker, are you in or are you out?" he asked. "Are we going to keep playing this game? Are we going to keep testing the Ryker rules of engagement?"

"Avoid, assist, admit . . . or abandon?"

"What do you want to do, Jess?"

"What do *you* want to do, Judd?"

"Whatever we decide, we have to do it together," he said.

Jessica nodded. "Let's see what we're dealing with."

She reached underneath the bed, clicked the battery back into her phone, and powered up. Judd cradled his BlackBerry and watched it light up, too. After a few moments the two phones each bonged and bleeped to life with dozens of missed calls and messages.

Both phones suddenly rang. Jessica held hers up to show Judd a 703 area code but a blank phone number. A scrambled call from northern Virginia. Judd showed his, 202, and nothing more for Washington, D.C.

"Your boss is calling," she said.

"So's yours," Judd said.

Jessica nodded. "Are you ready?"

"Let's do it," he said.

They both tapped their phones and pressed them to their ears. Then, in unison, "This is Ryker."

ACKNOWLEDGMENTS

Inspiration for *The Shadow List* is owed in large part to my friend, the true-life hero and corruption hunter Nuhu Ribadu. I highly recommend *Show Me the Money*, his insider account of building the Nigerian Economic and Financial Crimes Commission. I'm also grateful to unwitting inspiration from Riva Levinson and her *Choosing the Hero*, Dayo Olopade for *The Bright Continent*, Adeola Fayehun for her hilarious news show *Keeping It Real*, and the antics of Congressman William Jefferson. Thanks to Priscilla Agyapong, Maria Barragan-Santana, Kenneth Christian, Judd Devermont, Antony Goldman, Charles Kenny, and Max Moss for edits and suggestions. Thanks to the amazing Putnam team of Neil Nyren, Ashley Hewlett, and Alexis Sattler. Special appreciation to rock star Josh Getzler and no-nonsense Mary Diamond Stirewalt. Most of all, love and gratitude to my best friend and partner in everything, Donna.